THE AM[...]
F[...]

Here is a shocking but realistic picture of America in the distant future—a wild chaotic America, but in many ways a very possible *America.* An America where people pay for protection instead of paying taxes—where games like polo are played in jeeps with 50-caliber machine guns. An America full of the wonders of tomorrow, driven by primitive passions that are ageless...

There have been a thousand tales of future Utopias and possible civilizations, but this is surely a tale of the future you will remember for a long, long time. Join beloved sci-fi author C. M. Kornbluth as he takes you into a future where America is ruled by the Mob.

FOR A COMPLETE SECOND NOVEL, TURN TO PAGE 143

CAST OF CHARACTERS

CHARLES ORSINO
He was family member of the Mob hierarchy, and he was given a dangerous mission that could determine the future of the Syndic.

LEE FALCARO
Another member of the Mob hierarchy. Her expertise was in a totally discredited area of mental science—psychology!

MARTHA
She was a child of ten from the wilds of Ireland. What strange powers did this young tribal girl really possess?

COMMANDER GRINNEL
Ruthless and more than willing to take a life when needed, he was a lot more than just a tough submarine commander.

F. W. TAYLOR
He was known as "Uncle Frank" to Orsino, but he was one of the top men in a mob organization that ruled over much of America.

KEN OLIVER
He was afraid he was dying, so why should he worry about helping two wanted "killers" escape from the mob?

THE SYNDIC

By
C. M. KORNBLUTH

ARMCHAIR FICTION
PO Box 4369, Medford, Oregon 97501-0168

For more information about Armchair Books and products, visit our website at…

www.armchairfiction.com

Or email us at…

armchairfiction@yahoo.com

PROLOGUE

"It was not until February 14th that the Government declared a state of unlimited emergency. The precipitating incident was the aerial bombardment and destruction of B Company, 27th Armored Regiment, on Fort George Hill in New York City. Local Syndic leaders had occupied and fortified George Washington High School, with the enthusiastic cooperation of students, faculty and neighborhood. Chief among them was Thomas 'Numbers' Cleveland, displaying the same coolness and organizational genius that had brought him to pre-eminence in the metropolitan policy-wheel organization by his thirty-fifth year.

"At 5:15 A.M. the first battalion of the 27th Armored took up positions in the area as follows: A Company at 190th Street and St. Nicholas Avenue, with the mission of preventing reinforcement of the school from the I.R.T. subway station there; Companies B, C, and D hill down from the school on the slope of Fort George Hill poised for an attack. At 5:25 the sixteen Patton tanks of B Company revved up and moved on the school, C and D Companies remaining in reserve. The plan was for the tanks of B Company to surround the school on three sides—the fourth is a precipice—and open fire if a telephone parley with Cleveland did not result in an unconditional surrender. There was no surrender and the tanks attacked.

"Cleveland's observation post was in the tower room of the school. Seeing the radio mast of the lead tank top the rise of the hill, he snapped out a telephone order to contact pilots waiting for the word at a Syndic field, floating outside the seven mile limit. The pilots, trained to split second precision in their years of public service, were airborne by 5:26, but this time their cargo was not liquor, cigarettes or luggage. In three minutes, they were whipping, rocket bombs into the tanks of Company B; Cleveland's runners charged the company command post; the trial by fire had begun.

"Before it ended North America was to see deeds as gallant and strategy as inspired as any in the history of war. Cleveland's historic announcement—'It's a great day for the race!'—his death at the head of his runners in a charge on the Fort Totten garrison, the firm hand of Amadeo Falcaro taking up the scattered reins of leadership, parley, peace, betrayal and execution of hostages, the Treaty of Las Vegas and a united Mob-Syndic front against Government, O'Toole's betrayal of the Continental Press wire room and the bloody battle to recapture that crucial nerve center, the decisive march on Baltimore..."

B. Arrowsmith Hynde. The *Syndic—a Short History*.

"No accurate history of the future has ever been written—a fact that I think disposes of history's claim to rank as a science. Astronomers quail at the three-body problem and throw up their hands in surrender before the four-body problem. Any given moment in history is a problem of at least several billion bodies. Attempts at orderly abstraction of manipulable symbols from the realities of history seem to be doomed from the start. I can juggle mean rainfalls, car-loading curves, birth-rates and patent applications, but I cannot for the life of me fit the recurring facial carbuncles of Karl Marx into my manipulations—not even, though we know, well after the fact, that agonizing staphylococcus aureus infections behind that famous beard helped shape twentieth-century totalitarianism. In pathology alone the list could be prolonged indefinitely: Julius Caesar's epilepsy, Napoleon's gastritis, Wilson's paralysis, Grant's alcoholism, Wilhelm II's withered arm, Catherine's nymphomania, George III's paresis, Edison's deafness, Euler's blindness, Burke's stammer, and so on. Is there anybody silly enough to maintain that the world today would be what it is if Marx, Caesar, Napoleon, Wilson, Grant, Wilhelm, Catherine, George, Edison, Euler and Burke—to take only these eleven—were anything but what they were? Yet that is the assumption behind theories of history which exclude the carbuncles of Marx from their referents—that is to say, every theory of history with which I am familiar.

"Am I then saying that history, past and future, is unknowable; that we must blunder ahead in the dark without planning because no plan can possibly be accurate in prediction and useful in application? I am not. I am expressing my distaste for holders of extreme positions, for possessors of eternal truths, for keepers of the flame. Keepers of the flame have no trouble with the questions of ends and means that plague the rest of us. They are quite certain that their ends are good and that therefore choice of means is a trivial matter. The rest of us, far from certain that we have a general solution of the several-billion body problem that is history, are much more likely to ponder on our means…"

F. W. Taylor, *Organization, Symbolism and Morale.*

CHAPTER ONE

Charles Orsino was learning the business from the ground up—even though "up" would never be very high. He had in his veins only a drop or two of Falcaro blood—enough so that room had to be made for him; not enough for it to be a great dearth of room. Counting heavily on the good will of F. W. Taylor, who had taken a fancy to him when he lost his parents in the Brookhaven Reactor explosion of '83, he might rise to a rather responsible position in Alky, Horsewire, Call Girl, Recruitment and Retirement, or whatever line he showed an aptitude for. But at 22 one spring day, he was merely serving a tour of duty as bagman attached to the 101st New York Police Precinct. A junior member of the Syndic customarily handled that job; you couldn't trust the cops not to squeeze their customers and pocket the difference.

He walked absently through the not-unpleasant routine of the shakedown. His mind was on his early-morning practice session of polo, in which he had almost disgraced himself.

"Good afternoon, Mr. Orsino; a pleasure to see you again. Would you like a cold glass of beer while I get the loot!"

"No, but thanks very much, Mr. Lefko—I'm in training, you know. Wish I could take you up on it. Seven phones, isn't it, at ten dollars a phone?"

"That's right, Mr. Orsino, and I'll be with you as soon as I lay off the seventh at Hialeah; all the ladies went for a plater named Hearth-Mouse because they thought the name was cute and left me with a dutch book, I won't be a minute."

Lefko scuttled to a phone and dickered with another bookie somewhere while Charles absently studied the crowd of chattering, laughing horse-players. ("Mister Orsino, did you come out to make a monkey of yourself and waste my time? Confound it, sir, you have just fifty rounds to a chukker and you must make them count!" He grinned unhappily. Old Gilby, the pro, could be abrasive when a bonehead play disfigured the game he loved. Charles had been sure Benny Grashkin's jeep would conk out in a minute—it had been sputtering badly enough—and that he would have had a dirt-cheap scoring shot while Benny changed mounts. But Gilby blew the whistle and wasn't interested in your fine-spun logic. "Confound it, sir, when will you young rufflers learn that you must crawl before you walk? Now let me see a team rush for the goal—and I mean *team*, Mr. Orsino!")

the **SYNDIC**

BY C. M. KORNBLUTH

"*Here* we are, Mr. Orsino, and just in time. There goes the seventh."

Charles shook hands and left amid screams of "Hearth-Mouse! Hearth-Mouse!" from the lady bettors watching the screen.

High up in the Syndic Building, F. W. Taylor—Uncle Frank to Charles—was giving a terrific tongue-lashing to a big, stooped old man. Thornberry, president of the Chase National Bank, had pulled a butch and F. W. Taylor was blazing mad about it.

He snarled, "One more like this, Thornberry, and you are out on your padded can. When a respectable member of the Syndic chooses to come to you for a line of credit, you will in the future give it without any tomfool quibbling about security. You bankers seem to think this is the middle ages and that your bits of paper still have their old black magic.

"Disabuse yourself of the notion. Nobody except you believes in it. The Inexorable Laws of Economics are as dead as Dagon and Ishtar, and for the same reason. No more worshippers. You bankers can't shove anybody around any more. You're just a convenience, like the non-playing banker in a card game.

"What's real now is the Syndic. What's real about the Syndic is its own morale and the public's faith in it. Is that *clear?*"

Thornberry brokenly mumbled something about supply and demand.

Taylor sneered, "Supply and demand, Urim and Thummim. Show me a supply, Thornberry. Show me a—oh, hell, I haven't time to waste re-educating you. Remember what I told you and don't, argue. Unlimited credit to Syndic members. If they overdo it, *we'll* rectify the situation. Now, get out." And Thornberry did, with senile tears in his eyes.

At Mother Maginnis' Ould Sod Pub, Mother Maginnis pulled a long face when Charles Orsino came in. "It's always a pleasure to see you, Mr. Orsino, but I'm afraid this week it'll be no pleasure for you to see me."

She was always roundabout, "Why; what do you mean, Mrs. M.? I'm always happy to say hello to a customer."

"It's the business, Mr. Orsino. It's the business. You'll pardon me if I say that I can't see how to spare twenty-five dollars from the till, not if my life depended on it. I can go to fifteen, but so help me—"

Charles looked grave—graver than he felt. It happened every day. "You realize, Mrs. Maginnis, that you're letting the Syndic down. What would the people in Syndic Territory do for protection if everybody took your attitude?"

She looked sly. "I was thinking, Mr. Orsino, that a young man like you must have a way with the girls—" By a mighty unsubtle maneuver, Mrs. Maginnis' daughter emerged from the back room at that point and began demurely mopping the bar. "And," she continued, "sure, any young lady would consider it an honor to spend the evening with a young gentleman from the Syndic—"

"Perhaps," Charles said, rapidly thinking it over. He would infinitely rather spend the evening with a girl than at a Shakespeare revival as he had planned, but there were drawbacks. In the first place, it would be bribery. In the second place, he might fall for the girl and wake up with Mrs. Maginnis for his mother-in-law—a fate too nauseating to contemplate for more than a moment. In the third place, he had already bought the tickets for himself and bodyguard.

"About the shakedown," he said decisively. "Call it fifteen this week. If you're still doing badly next week, I'll have to ask for a look at your books—to see whether a regular reduction is in order."

She got the hint, and colored. Putting down fifteen dollars, she said, "Sure, that won't be necessary. I'm expecting business to take a turn for the better. It's sure to pick up."

"Good, then." To show there were no hard feelings, he stayed for a moment to ask, "How are your husbands?"

"So-so. Alfie's on the road this week and Dinnie's got the rheumatism again but he can tend bar late, when it's slow."

"Tell him to drop around to the Medical Center and mention my name, Mrs. Maginnis. Maybe they can do something for him."

She glowed with thanks and he left.

It was pleasant to be able to do things for nice people; it was pleasant to stroll along the sunny street acknowledging tipped hats and friendly words. (That team rush for the goal had been a sorry mess, but not his fault—quite. Vladek had loosed a premature burst from his fifty caliber at the ball, and sent it hurling off to the right; they had braked and backed with much grinding of gears to form V again behind it, when Gilby blew the whistle again.)

A nervous youngster in the National Press Service, New York Drop was facing his first crisis on the job. Trouble lights had flashed simultaneously on the Kansas City-New York, Hialeah-New York and Boston-New York trunks. He stood, paralyzed.

His supervisor took it in instantly and banged open the circuit to Service. To the genial face that appeared on the screen, he snapped, "Trace Hialeah, Boston and Kansas City—in that order, Micky."

Micky said, "Okay, pal," and vanished.

The supervisor turned to the youngster. "Didn't know what to do?" he asked genially. "Don't let it worry you. Next time you'll know. You noticed the order of priority?"

"Yes," the boy gulped.

"It wasn't an accident that I gave it to him that way. First, Hialeah because it was the most important. We get the bulk of our revenue from serving the horse-rooms—in fact, I understand we started as a horse-wire exclusively. Naturally the horse-room customers pay for it in the long run, but they pay without pain. Nobody's forcing them to improve the breed, right?

"Second, Boston-New York trunk. That's common carrier while the Fair Grounds isn't running up there. We don't make any profit on common carrier service, the rates are too low, but we owe it to the public that supports us.

"Third, Kansas City-New York. That's common carrier too, but with one terminal in Mob Territory. No reason why we should knock ourselves out for Regan and his boys, but after the other two are traced and closed, we'll get around to them. Think you got it straight now?"

"Yes," the youngster said.

"Good. Just take it easy."

The supervisor moved away to do a job of billing that didn't need immediate doing; he wanted to avoid the very appearance of nagging the boy. He wondered too, if he'd really put it over, and decided he hadn't. Who could, after all. It took years on the wires to get the feel. Slowly your motivation changed. You started by wanting to make a place for yourself and earn some dough. After years you realized, not with a blinding flash, but gradually, that you were working for quite another reason. Nice gang here that treats you right. Don't let the Syndic down. The customers pay for their fun and by heavens, you see that they get it or bust a gut trying.

On his way to the 101st Precinct station house, the ears of Charles Orsino burned as he thought of the withering lecture that had followed the blast on Gilby's whistle. "*Mister* Orsino, is it or is it not your responsibility as team captain to demand that a dangerous ball be taken out of play? And did or did not that last burst from Mister Vladek beat the ball out of round, thus giving rise to a distinct possibility of dangerous ricochets?" The old man was right of course, but it had been a pocked and battered practice ball to start with; in practice sessions, you couldn't afford to be fussy—not with regulation 18-inch armor steel balls selling for thirty dollars each at the pro shop.

He walked between the two green lamps of the precinct station and dumped his bag on the sergeant's desk. Immediately the sergeant started a tale of woe, "Mr. Orsino, I don't like to bother you with the men's personal troubles, but I wonder if you could come through with a hundred-dollar present for a very deserving young fellow here. It's Patrolman Gibney, seven years in the old 101st and not a black mark against him. One citation for shooting it out with a burglar and another for nabbing a past-post crook at Lefko's horse room. Gibney's been married for five years and has two of the cutest kids you ever saw, and you know that takes money. Now he wants to get married again, he's crazy in love with the girl and his first wife don't mind, she says she can use a helping hand around the house, and he wants to do it right with a big wedding."

"If he can do it on a hundred, he's welcome to it," Charles said, grinning. "Give him my best wishes." He divided the pile of bills into two orderly stacks, transferred a hundred dollars to one and pocketed the other.

He dropped it off at the Syndic Building, had an uninteresting dinner in one of its cafeterias and went to his furnished room downtown. He read a chapter in F. W. Taylor's—Uncle Frank's—latest book, *Organization; Symbolism and Morale*, couldn't understand a word he read, bathed and got out his evening clothes.

CHAPTER TWO

A thin and attractive girl entered a preposterously furnished room in the Syndic Building, arguing bitterly with a white-bearded, hawk-nosed old man.

"My dear ancestor," she began, with exaggerated patience.

"Damn it, Lee, don't call me an ancestor! Makes me feel as if I was dead already."

"You might as well be for all the sense you're talking."

"All right, Lee." He looked wounded and brave.

"Oh I didn't mean to hurt your feelings, Edward—" She studied his face with suddenly narrowed eyes and her tone changed. "Listen, you old devil, you're not fooling me for a minute. I couldn't hurt your feelings with the blunt edge of an axe. You're not talking me into anything. It'd just be sending somebody to his death. Besides, they were both accidents." She turned and began to fiddle with a semi-circular screen whose focus was a large and complicated chair. Three synchronized projectors bore on the screen.

The old man said very softly, "And what if they weren't? Tom McGurn and Bob were good men. None better. If the damn Government's knocking us off one by one, something ought to be done. And you seem to be the only person in a position to do it."

"Start a war," she said bitterly, "Sweep them from the seas. Wasn't Dick Reiner chanting that when I was in diapers?"

"Yes," the old man brooded. "And he's still chanting it now that you're in—whatever young ladies wear nowadays. Promise me something, Lee. If there's another try, will you help us out?"

"I am so sure there won't be," she said, "that I'll promise. And lord help you, Edward, if you try to fake one. I've told you before and I tell you now that it's almost certain death."

Charles Orsino studied himself in a three-way mirror.

The evening suit was new; he wished the gun belt was. The holster rode awkwardly on his hip; he hadn't got a new outfit since his eighteenth birthday and his chest had filled out to the last hole of the cross-strap's buckle since then. Well, it would have to wait; the evening would cost him enough as it was. Five bodyguards! He winced at the thought. But you had to be seen at these things and you had to do it right or it didn't count.

He fell into a brief reverie of meeting a beautiful, *beautiful* girl at the theater, a girl who would think he was interesting and handsome and a wonderful polo player, a girl who would happily turn out to be in the direct Falcaro line with all sorts of powerful relations to speak up for him...

Someone said on his room annunciator, "The limousine is here, Mr. Orsino. I'm Halloran, your chief bodyguard."

"Very well, Halloran," he said casually, just as he'd practiced it in the bathroom that morning and rode down.

The limousine was a beauty and the guards were faultlessly turned out. One was democratic with one's chief guard and a little less so with the others. As Halloran drove, Charles chatted with him about the play, which was Julius Caesar in modern dress. Halloran said he'd heard it was very good.

Their arrival in the lobby of the Costello created no sensation. Five bodyguards wasn't a lot of bodyguards, even though there seemed to be no other Syndic people there. So much for the beautiful Falcaro girl. Charles chatted with a television director he knew slightly. The director explained to him that the theater was sick, very sick, that Harry Tremaine—he played Brutus—made a magnificent stage picture but couldn't read lines.

By then Halloran was whispering in his ear that it was time to take their seats. Halloran was sweating like a pig and Charles didn't get around to asking him why. Charles took an aisle seat. Halloran was across the aisle and the others sat to his side, front and rear.

The curtain rose on "New York—A Street."

The first scene, a time-killer designed to let fidgeters subside and coughers finish their coughing, was a 3-D projection of Times Square, with a stylized suggestion of a public relations consultant's office "down in one" on the apron.

When Caesar entered, Orsino started, and there was a gratified murmur around the auditorium. He was made up as French

Letour, one of the Mobsters from the old days—technically a hero, but one who had sailed mighty close to the wind. This promised to be interesting.

"Peace, ho! Caesar speaks."

And so to the apron where the soothsayer—public relations consultant—delivered the warning contemptuously ignored by Letour-Caesar, and the spotlight shifted to Cassius and Brutus for their long, foreboding dialogue, Brutus' back was to the audience when it started; he gradually turned—

"What means this shouting? I do fear the people will choose Caesar for their king!"

And you saw that Brutus was Falcaro—old Amadeo Falcaro himself, with the beard and hawk nose and eyebrows.

Well, let's see now. It must be some kind of tortured analogy with the Treaty of Las Vegas when Letour made a strong bid to unite Mob and Syndic and Falcaro had fought against anything but a short-term, strictly military alliance. Charles felt kind of sore about Falcaro not getting the title role, but he had to admit that Tremaine played Falcaro as the gusty magnifico he had been. When Caesar re-entered, the contrast became clear; Caesar-Letour was a fidgety, fear-ridden man. The rest of the conspirators brought on through Act One turned out to be good fellows all, fresh and hearty; Charles guessed everything was all right and he wished he could grab a nap. But Cassius was saying,

"Him and his worth and our great need of him—"

All very loyal, Charles thought, smothering a yawn. A life for the Syndic and all that, but a highbrow version. Polite and dignified, like a pavanne at Roseland. Sometimes—after say, a near miss on the polo field—he would wonder how polite and dignified the great old days actually had been. Amadeo Falcaro's Third Year Purge must have been an affair of blood and guts. Two thousand shot in three days, the history books said, adding hastily that the purged were unreconstructed, unreconstructable thugs whose usefulness was past, who couldn't realize that the job ahead was construction and organization.

And Halloran was touching Charles on the shoulder. "Inter-mission in a second, sir."

They marched up the aisle as the curtain fell, to applause and the rest of the audience began to rise. Then the impossible happened.

Halloran had gone first; Charles was behind him, with the four other guards hemming him in. As Halloran reached the door to the lobby at the top of the aisle, he turned to face Charles and performed an inexplicable, pantomime. It was quite one second before Charles realized that Halloran was tugging at his gun, stuck in the holster.

The guard to the left of Charles softly said, "Damn!" and threw himself at Halloran as the chief guard's gun came loose. There was a .45 caliber roar, muffled. There was another that crashed, unmuffled, a yard from Charles' right ear. The two figures at the head of the aisle collapsed limply and the audience began to shriek. Somebody with a very loud voice roared, "Keep calm! It's all part of the play! Don't get panicky! It's part of the play!"

The man who was roaring moved up to the aisle door, fell silent, saw and smelled the blood—and fainted.

A woman began to pound the guard on Charles' right with her fists, yelling, "What did you do to my husband? You shot my husband!" She meant the man who had fainted; Charles peeled her off the bodyguard.

Somehow they got into the lobby, followed by most of the audience. The three bodyguards held them at bay. Charles found he was deaf in his right ear and supposed it was temporary. Least of his worries. Halloran had taken a shot at him. The guard named Weltfisch had intercepted it. The guard named Donnel had shot Halloran down.

He said to Donnel, "You know Halloran long?"

Donnel, not taking his eyes from the crowd, said, "Couple of years, sir. He was just a guy in the bodyguard pool."

"Get me out of here," Orsino said. "To the Syndic Building."

In the big black car, he could almost forget the horror; he could hope that time would erase it completely. It wasn't like polo. That shot had been *aimed*.

The limousine purred to a halt before the titanic bulk of the Syndic Building; was checked and rolled on into the Unrestricted Entrance. An elevator silently lifted the car and passengers past floors devoted to Alcohol Clerical, Alcohol Research, and Testing, Transport, Collections Audit and Control, Cleaning and Dying, Female Recruitment and Retirement, up, up, up, past sections and subsections Charles had never entered. Syndic member though he was, to an automatic stop at a floor whose indicator said: *enforcement and public relations.*

It was only 9:45 P.M.; F. W. Taylor would be in and working. Charles said, "Wait here, boys," and muttered the code phrase to the door. It sprang open.

F. W. Taylor was dictating, in machine-gun fashion, to a mike. He looked dog-tired. His face turned up with a frown as Charles entered and then the frown became a beam of pleasure.

"Charles, my boy! Sit down!" He snapped off the machine.

"Uncle—" Charles began.

"It was so kind of you to drop in. I thought you'd be at the theater."

"I was, Uncle, but—"

"I'm working on a revision for the next edition of *Organization, Symbolism, and Morale.* You'd never guess who inspired it…"

"I'm sure I wouldn't, Uncle. Uncle—"

"Old Thornberry, President of the Chase National. He had the infernal gall to refuse a line of credit to young McGurn. Bankers! You won't believe it, but people used to beg them to take over their property, tie up their incomes, virtually enslave them. People demanded it. The same way they demanded inexpensive liquor, tobacco and consumer goods, clean women and a chance to win a fortune; and our ancestors obliged them. Our ancestors were sneered at in their day, you know. They were called criminals when they distributed goods and services at a price people could afford to pay."

"Uncle!"

"Hush, boy, I know what you're going to say. You can't fool the people forever! When they'd had enough hounding and restriction, they rose in their might.

"The people demanded freedom of choice, Falcaro and the rest rose to lead them in the Syndic and the Mob, and they drove the Government into the sea."

"Uncle Frank—"

"From which it still occasionally ventures to annoy our coastal cities," F. W. Taylor commented. He warmed to his subject. "You should have seen the old banker blubber away. The last of the old-time bankers, and they deserved everything they got. They brought it on themselves. They had what they called *laissez-faire,* and it worked for a while until they got to tinkering with it. They demanded things called protective tariffs, tax remissions, subsidies—regulation, regulation, regulation, always of the other fellow. But there were enough bankers on all sides for everybody to be somebody else's other fellow. Coercion snowballed and the Government lost public acceptance. They had a thing called the public debt, which I can't begin to explain to you except to say that it was something written on paper and that it raised the cost of everything tremendously. Well, believe me or not, they didn't just throwaway the piece of paper or scratch out the writing on it. They let it ride until ordinary people couldn't afford the pleasant things in life."

"Uncle—"

A cautious periscope broke the choppy water off Sea Island, Georgia. At the other end of the periscope were Captain Van Dellen of the North American Navy, lean as a hound, and fat little Commander Grinnel.

"You might take her in a little closer, Van," said Grinnel mildly.

"The exercise won't do you any lasting damage," Van Dellen said. Grinnel was very, very, near to a couple of admirals and normally Van Dellen gave him the kid-glove treatment in spite of out-ranking him. But this was his ship and no cloak-and-dagger artist from an O.N.I. desk was telling him how to con it.

Grinnel smiled genially at the little joke. "I could call it a disguise," he said patting his paunch, "but you know me too well."

"You'll have no trouble with a sea like this," Van Dellen said, strictly business. He tried to think of some appropriate phrase to recognize the danger Grinnel was plunging into with no resources except quick wits, a trick ring and a pair of guns. But all that bubbled up to the top of his head was: *Thank heavens I'm getting rid of this bastardly little Sociocrat. He'll kill me some day if he gets a clean shot and the chance of detection is zero. Thankfully I'm a Constitutionist. We don't go in for things like that—or do we? Nobody ever tells me anything. A hack of a pigboat driver. And this little bastard's going to be an admiral some day. But that boy of mine'll be an admiral. He's brainy, like his mother.*

Grinnel smiled and said, "Well, this would be it, wouldn't it?"

"Eh?" Van Dellen asked. "Oh, I see what you mean." He called over to a sailor nearby, "Chuck! Break out the Commander's capsule. Pass the word to stand by for ejection."

The Commander was fitted, puffing, into the capsule. He growled at the storekeeper and said, "You sure this thing was just unsealed? It feels sticky already."

A brash jaygee said, "I saw it unsealed myself three minutes ago, Commander. It'll get stickier if we spend any more time talking. You have"—he glanced at his chronometer—"seventeen minutes now. Let me snap you in."

The Commander huddled down after a searching glance at the jaygee's face, which photographed it forever in his memory. The top snapped down. Some day—some happy day—that squirt would very much regret telling him off. He gave an okay sign to Van Dellen who waved back meagerly and managed a smile. Three crewmen fitted the capsule into its lock.

Foomf!

It was through the batch and bobbing on the surface. Its color matched the water's automatically. Grinnel waggled the lever that aimed it inshore and began to turn the propeller crank. He turned fast; the capsule—rudders, crank, flywheel, shaft and all—would dissolve in approximately fifteen minutes. It was his job to be ashore when that happened.

And ashore he'd be practically a free agent with the loosest sort of roving commission, until January 15. Then his orders became most specific.

CHAPTER THREE

Charles Orsino squirmed in the chair. "Uncle—" he pleaded.

"Yes," F. W. Taylor chuckled, "Old Amadeo and his colleagues were called criminals. They were called bootleggers when they got liquor to people without worrying about the public debt or excise taxes. They were called smugglers when they sold cheap butter in the South and cheap margarine in the North. They were called counterfeiters when they sold cheap cigarettes and transportation tickets. They were called high-jackers when they wrested goods from the normal inflation-ridden chain of middlemen and delivered them at a reasonable price to the consumers.

"They were criminals. Bankers were pillars of society.

"Yet these bankers who dominated society, who were considered the voice of eternal truth when they spoke, who thought it was insanity to challenge their beliefs, started somewhere and perhaps they were the best thing for their day and age that could be worked out…"

Father Ambrosius gnawed at a bit of salt herring, wiped his hands, dug through the litter in his wooden chest and found a goose quill and a page of parchment. He scrubbed vigorously with vinegar-soaked sponge at the writing on the parchment and was pleased to see that it came off nicely, leaving him a clean surface to scribble his sermon notes on. He cut the quill and slit it while waiting for the parchment to dry, wondering idly what he had erased. (It happened to be the last surviving copy of Tacitus' Annals, VII, i-v.)

To work then. The sermon was to be preached on Sexagesima Sunday, a prelude to the solemn season of Lent. Father Ambrosius' mind wandered in search of a text. Lent…salt herring…penitence…the capital sins…avarice…usury…delinquent pew rent…fat-headed young Sir Baldwin in his tumbledown castle on the hill…salt herring now and *per saeculae saeculorum* unless Sir Baldwin paid up his delinquent pew rent.

At that moment, Sir Baldwin came swaggering into the cell.

Father Ambrosius rose courteously and said, with some in-sincerity, *"Pax vobiscum."*

"Eh?" asked Sir Baldwin, his silly blue eyes popping as he looked over his shoulder. "Oh, you meant me, padre. It don't do a bit of good to chatter at me in Latin, you know. The King's Norman is what I speak. I mean to say, if it's good enough for His Majesty Richard, it's good enough for me, what? Now, what can I do for you, padre?"

Father Ambrosius reminded him faintly, "You came to see *me,*

Sir Baldwin."

"Eh? Oh. So I did. I was huntin' stag, padre, and I lost him after chasin' the whole morning, and what I want to know is, who's the right saint chap to ask for help in a pickle like that? I mean to say, I wanted to show the chaps some good sport and we started this beast and he got clean away. Don't misunderstand me, padre, they were good chaps and they didn't rot me about it, but that kind of talk gets about and doesn't do one a bit of good, what? So you tell me like a good fellow who's the right saint chap to put the matter in the best light for me?"

Father Ambrosius repressed an urge to grind his teeth, took thought and said, "St. Hubert, I think, is interested in the stag hunt."

"Righto, padre! St. Hubert it is. Hubert, Hubert. I shan't forget it because I've a cousin named Hubert. Haven't seen him for years, poor old chap. He had the fistula—lived on slops and couldn't sit on his horse for a day's huntin'. Poor old chap. Well, I'm off—no, there's another thing I wanted. Suppose this Sunday you preach a howlin' strong sermon against usury, what? That chap in the village, the goldsmith fellow, has the infernal gall to tell me I've got to give him Fallowfield! Forty acres, and he has the infernal gall to tell me they aren't mine any more. Be a good chap, padre, and sort of glare at him from the pulpit a few times to show him who you mean, what?"

"Usury is a sin," Father Ambrosius said cautiously, "but how does Fallowfield enter into it?"

Sir Baldwin twiddled the drooping ends of his limp, blond mustache with a trace of embarrassment. "Fact is, I told the chap when I borrowed the twenty marks that Fallowfield would stand as security. I ask you, padre, is it my fault that my tenants are a pack of lazy, thieving Saxon swine and I couldn't raise the money?"

The parish priest bristled unnoticeably. He was pure Saxon himself. "I shall do what I can," he said. "And Sir Baldwin, before you go—"

The young man stopped in the doorway and turned. "Before you go, may I ask when we'll see your pew rent, to say nothing of the tithe?"

Sir Baldwin dismissed it with an airish wave of the hand. "I thought I just told you, padre, I haven't a farthing to my name and here's this chap in the village telling me to clear out of Fallowfield that I got from my father and his father before him. So how the devil—excuse me—can I pay rent and tithes and Peters pence and all the other things you priest chaps expect from a man, what?" He held up his gauntleted hand as Father Ambrosius started to speak. "No, padre, not another word about it, I know you'd love to tell me I won't go to heaven if I act this way, I don't doubt you're learned and all that, but I can still tell you a thing or two, what? The fact is, I *will* go to Heaven. You see, padre, God's a gentleman and he wouldn't bar another gentleman over a trifle of money trouble that could happen to any gentleman, now would he?"

The fatuous beam was more than Father Ambrosius could bear; his eyes fell.

"Rightoh," Sir Baldwin chirped, "And that saint chap's name was St. Hubert. I didn't forget, see? Not quite the fool some people think I am." And he was gone, whistling a recheat.

Father Ambrosius sat down again and glared at the parchment. Preach a sermon on usury for that popinjay. Well, usury *was* a sin, Christians were supposed to lend to one another in need and not count the cost or the days. But who had ever heard of Sir Baldwin ever lending anything? Of course, he was lord of the manor and protected you against invasion, but there didn't seem to be any invasions anymore...

Wearily, the parish priest dipped his pen and scratched on the parchment: RON. XIII ii, viii, XV i. "Whosoever resisteth the power resisteth the ordinance of God...owe no man any thing...we that are strong ought to bear the infirmities of the weak..." A triple-plated text, which, reinforced by a brow of thunder from the pulpit should make the village goldsmith think twice before pressing his demand on Sir Baldwin. Usury *was* a sin.

There was a different knock on the doorframe.

The goldsmith, a leather-aproned fellow named John, stood there twisting his cap in his big, burn scarred hands.

"Yes, my son? Come in." But he scowled at the fellow involuntarily. He should know better than to succumb to the capital sin of avarice. "Well...what is it?"

"Father," the fellow said, "I've come to give you this." He passed a soft leather purse to the priest. It clinked.

Father Ambrosius emptied it on his desk and stirred the broad silver coins wonderingly with his finger. Five marks and eleven silver pennies. No more salt herring until Lent! Silver forwarded to his bishop in an amount that would do credit to the parish! A gilding job for the image of the Blessed Virgin! Perhaps glass panes in one or two of the church windows!

And then he stiffened and swept the money back into the purse. "You got this by sin," he said flatly. "The sin of avarice worked in your heart and you practiced the sin of usury on your fellow Christians. Don't give this money to the Church; give it back to your victims."

"Father," the fellow said, nearly blubbering, "excuse me but you don't understand! They come to me and come to me. They say it's all right with them, that they're hiring the money the way you'd hire a horse. Doesn't that make sense? Do you think I *wanted* to become a moneylender? No! I was an honest goldsmith and an honest goldsmith can't help himself. All the money in the village drifts somehow into his hands. One leaves a mark with you for safekeeping and pays you a penny the year to guard it. Another brings you silver coins to make into a basin, and you get to keep whatever coins are left over. And then others come to you and say 'Let me have so-and-so's mark to use for a year and then I'll pay it back and with it another mark'. Father, they beg me! They say they'll be ruined if I don't lend to them, their old parents will die if they can't fee the leech, or their dead will roast forever unless they can pay for masses and what's a man to *do?*"

"Sin no more," the priest answered simply. It was no problem.

The fellow was getting angry. "Very well for you to sit there and say so, father. But what do you think paid for the masses you said for the repose of Goodie Howat's soul? And how did Tom the Thatcher buy his wagon so he could sell his beer in Glastonbury at a better price? And how did Farmer Major hire the men from Wealing to get in his hay before the great storm could ruin it? And a hundred things more. I tell you, this parish would be a worse place without John Goldsmith and he doesn't propose to be pointed at any longer as a black sinner! I didn't want to fall into usury but I did, and when I did, I found out that those who hoist their noses highest at the moneylender when they pass him in the road are the same ones who beg the hardest when they come to his shop for a loan!"

The priest was stunned by the outburst. John seemed honest, the facts were the facts—can good come out of evil? And there were stories that His Holiness the Pope himself had certain dealings with the Longobards—benchers, or bankers or whatever they called themselves...

"I must think on this, my son," he said. "Perhaps I was over hasty. Perhaps in the days of St. Paul, usury was another thing entirely. Perhaps what you practice is not *really* usury but merely something that resembles it. You may leave this silver with me."

When John left, Father Ambrosius squeezed his eyes tight shut and pressed the knuckles of both hands to his forehead. Things *did* change. Under the dispensation of the Old Testament, men had more wives than one. That was sinful now, but surely Abraham, Isaac and Jacob were in heaven? Paul wrote his epistles to little islands of Christians surrounded by seas of pagans. Surely in those days it was necessary for Christians to be bound closely together against the common enemy, whereas in these modern times, the ties could be safely relaxed a trifle? How could sinning have paid for the repose of Goodie Howat's soul, got a better price for brewer Thatcher's ale and saved the village hay crop? The Devil was tricky, but not that tricky, surely. A few more such tricks and the parish would resemble the paradise terrestrial!

Father Ambrosius dashed from his study to the altar of the little stone church and began furiously to turn the pages of the huge metal-bound lectern Bible.

"For the love of money is the root of all evil—"

It burst on Father Ambrosius with a great light that the words of Paul were in reference not to *John Goldsmith's* love of money but to *Sir Baldwin's* love of money.

He dashed back to his study and his pen began to squeak over the parchment, obliterating the last dim trace of Tacitus' Annals, VII i.v. The sermon would be a scorcher, all right, but it wouldn't scorch John Goldsmith. It would scorch Sir Baldwin for ruthlessly and against the laws of God and man refusing to turn Fallowfield over to the moneylender. There would be growls of approval in the church that Sunday, and many black looks directed against Sir

Baldwin for his attempt to bilk the parish's friend and benefactor, the moneylender.

"And that," F. W. Taylor concluded, chuckling, "is how power passes from one pair of hands to another, and how public acceptance of the change follows on its heels. A strange thing—people always think that each exchange of power is the last that will ever take place."

He seemed to be finished.

"Uncle," Orsino said, "somebody tried to kill me."

Taylor stared at him for a long minute, speechless. "What happened?" he finally asked.

"I went formal to the theater, with five bodyguards. The chief guard, name of Halloran, took a shot at me. One of my boys got in the way. He was killed."

Taylor's fingers began to play a tattoo on his annunciator board. Faces leaped into existence on its various screens as he fired orders. "Charles Orsino's chief bodyguard for tonight—Halloran. Trace him. The works. He tried to kill Orsino."

He clicked off the board switches and turned grimly to Orsino. "Now you," he said.

"What have *you* been up to?"

"Just doing my job, uncle," Orsino said uneasily.

"Still bagman at the 101st?"

"Yes."

"Fooling with any women?"

"Nothing special, uncle. Nothing intense."

"Disciplined or downgraded anybody lately?"

"Certainly not. The precinct runs like a watch. I'll match their morale against any outfit east of the Mississippi. Why are you taking this so heavy?"

"Because you're the third. The other two—your cousin, Thomas McGurn and your uncle, Robert Orsino—didn't have guards to get in the way. One other question."

"Yes, uncle."

"My boy, why didn't you tell me about this when you first came in?"

CHAPTER FOUR

A family council was called the next day. Orsino, very much a junior, had never been admitted to one before. He knew why the exception was being made, and didn't like the reason.

Edward Falcaro wagged his formidable white beard at the thirty-odd Syndic chiefs around the table and growled, "I think we'll dispense with reviewing production and so on. I want to talk about this damn gunplay. Dick, bring us up to date."

He lit a vile cigar and leaned back.

Richard W. Reiner rose. "Thomas McGurn," he said, "killed April 15th by a burst of eight machine gun bullets in his private dining room at the Astor. Elsie Warshofsky, his waitress, must be considered the principal suspect, but—"

Edward Falcaro snapped, "Suspect, hell! She killed him, didn't she?"

"*I was about to say,* but the evidence so far is merely cumulative. Mrs. Warshofsky jumped—fell—or was pushed—from the dining room window. The machine gun was found beside the window.

"There are no known witnesses. Mrs. Warshofsky's history presents no unusual features. An acquaintance submitted a statement—based, she frankly admitted, on nothing definite—that Mrs. Warshofsky sometimes talked in a way that led her to wonder if she might not be a member of the secret terrorist organization known as the D.A.R. In this connection, it should be noted that Mrs. Walsohofsky's maiden name was Adams.

"Robert Orsino, killed April 21st by a thermite bomb concealed in his pillow and fuzed with a pressure-sensitive switch. His valet, Edward Blythe, disappeared from view. He was picked up April 23rd by a posse on the beach of Montauk Point, but died before he could be questioned. Examination of his stomach contents showed a lethal quantity of sodium fluoride. It is presumed that the poison was self-administered."

"Presumed!" the old man snorted, and puffed out a lethal quantity of cigar smoke.

"Blythe's history," Reiner went on blandly, "presents no

26

unusual features. It should be noted that a commerce-raider of the so-called United States Government Navy was reported off Montauk Point during the night of April 23rd-24th by local residents.

"Charles Orsino, attacked April 30th by his bodyguard James Halloran in the lobby of the Costello Memorial Theater. Halloran fired one shot, which killed another bodyguard, and was then himself killed. Halloran's history presents no unusual features except that he had a considerable interest in—uh—history. He collected and presumably read obsolete books dealing with pre-Syndic Pre-Mob America. Investigators found by his bedside the first volume of a work published in 1942 called *The Growth of the American Republic* by Morison and Commager. It was opened to "Chapter Ten. The War of Independence.""

Reiner took his seat.

F. W. Taylor said dryly, "Dick, did you forget to mention that Warshofsky, Blythe and Halloran are known officers of the U. S. Navy?"

Reiner said, "You are being facetious. Are you implying that I have omitted pertinent facts?"

"I'm implying that you artistically stacked the deck. With a rumor, a dubious commerce-raider report and a note on a man's hobby, you want us to sweep the bastards from the sea, don't you—just the way you always have?"

"I am not ashamed of my expressed attitude on the question of the so-called United States Government and will defend it, at any proper time and place."

"Shut the hell up, you two," Edward Falcaro growled; "I'm trying to think." He thought for perhaps half a minute and then looked up, baffled. "Has anybody got any ideas?"

Charles Orsino cleared his throat, amazed at his own temerity. The old man's eyebrows shot up, but he grudgingly said, "I guess you can say something, since they thought you were important enough to shoot."

Orsino said, "Maybe it's some outfit over in Europe or Asia?"

Edward Falcaro asked, "Anybody know anything about Europe or Asia? Jimmy, you flew over once, didn't you? To see about Anatolian poppies when the Mob had trouble with Mex labor?"

Jimmy Falcaro said creakily, "Yeah. It was a waste of time. They have these little dirt farmers scratching out just enough food for the family and maybe raising a quarter-acre of poppy. That's *all* there is from the China Sea to the Mediterranean. In England— Frank, you tell 'em. You explained it to me once."

Taylor rose. "The forests have come back to England. When finance there lost its morale and couldn't hack its way out of the paradoxes that was the end. When that happens you've got to have a large, virile criminal class ready to take over and do the work of distribution and production. Maybe some of you know how the English were. The poor beggars had civilized all the illegality out of the stock. They couldn't do anything that wasn't respectable. From sketchy reports, I gather that England is now forest and a few hundred starving people. One fellow says the men still wear derbies and stagger to their offices in the city.

"France is peasants, drunk three-quarters of the time.

"Russia is peasants, drunk *all* the time.

"Germany—well, there the criminal class was *too* big and *too* virile. The place is a cemetery."

He shrugged, "Say it, somebody. The Mob's gunning for us."

Reiner jumped to his feet. "I will *never* support such a hypothesis!" he shrilled. "It is *mischievous* to imply that a century of peace has been ended, that our three-thousand-mile border with our friend to the West—"

Taylor intoned satirically, "*Un*-blemished, my friends, by a *single* for-ti-fi-*ca*-tion—"

Edward Falcaro yelled, "Stop your damn foolishness, Frank Taylor! This is no laughing matter."

Taylor snapped, "Have you been in Mob Territory lately?"

"I have," the old man said. He scowled.

"How'd you like it?"

Edward Falcaro shrugged irritably. "They have their ways, we have ours. The Regan line is running thin, but we're not going to forget that Jimmy Regan stood shoulder to shoulder with Amadeo Falcaro in the old days. There's such a thing as loyalty."

F. W. Taylor said, "There's such a thing as blindness."

He had gone too far. Edward Falcaro rose from his chair and

leaned forward, bracing himself on the table. He said flatly, "This is a statement, gentlemen. I won't pretend I'm happy about the way things are in Mob Territory. I won't pretend I think old man Regan is a balanced, dependable person. I won't pretend I think the Mob clients are enjoying anywhere near the service that Syndic clients enjoy. I'm perfectly aware that on our visits of state to Mob Territory we see pretty much what our hosts want us to see. But I cannot believe that any group which is rooted on the principles of freedom and service can have gone very wrong.

"Maybe I'm mistaken, gentlemen. But I cannot believe that a descendant of Jimmy Regan would order a descendant of Amadeo Falcaro murdered. We will consider every other possibility first. Frank, is that clear?"

"Yes," Taylor said.

"All right," Edward Falcaro grunted. "Now let's go about this thing systematically. Dick, you go right down the line with the charge that the Government's responsible for these atrocities. I hate to think that myself. If they are, we're going to have to spend a lot of time and trouble hunting them down and doing something about it. As long as they stick to a little commerce raiding and a few coastal attacks, I can't say I'm really unhappy about them. They don't do much harm, and they keep us on our toes and— maybe this one is most important—they keep our client's memories of the bad old days that we delivered them from alive. That's a great deal to surrender for the doubtful pleasures of a long, expensive campaign. If assassination's in the picture I suppose we'll have to knock them off—but we've got to be *sure*."

"May I speak?" Reiner asked icily.

The old man nodded and re-lit his cigar.

"I have been called—behind my back, naturally—a fanatic," Reiner said. He pointedly did not look anywhere near F. W. Taylor as he spoke the word. "Perhaps this is correct and perhaps fanaticism is what's needed at a time like this. Let me point out what the so-called Government stands for—brutal taxation, extirpation of gambling, denial of life's simple pleasures to the poor, and severe limitation of them to all but the wealthy, sexual prudery viciously enforced by penal laws of appalling barbarity, endless regulation and coercion governing every waking minute of the day. That was its record during the days of its power and that would be its record if it returned to power. I fail to see how this menace to our liberty can be condoned by certain marginal benefits which are claimed to accrue from its continued existence." He faltered for a moment as his face twisted with an unpleasant memory. In a lower, unhappier voice, he went on, "I—I was alarmed the other day by something I overheard. Two small children were laying bets at the Kiddy Counter of the horse room I frequent, and I stopped on my way to the hundred-dollar window for a moment to hear their childish prattle. They were doping the forms for the sixth at Hialeah, I believe, when one of them digressed to say, 'My Mommy doesn't play the horses. She thinks all the horse rooms should be closed.'

"It wrung my heart, gentlemen, to hear that. I wanted to take that little boy aside and tell him, 'Son, your Mommy doesn't have to play the horses. Nobody has to play the horses unless he wants to. But as long as one single person wants to lay a bet on a horse and another person is willing to take it, nobody has the right to say the horse rooms should be closed.' Naturally I did not take the little boy aside and tell him that. It would have been an impractical approach to the problem. The practical approach is the one I have always advocated and still do. Strike at the heart of the infection! Destroy the remnants of Government and cauterize the wound so that it will never re-infect again. Nor is my language too strong. When I realize that the mind of an innocent child has been corrupted so that he will prattle that the liberties of his brothers must be infringed on, that their harmless pleasures must be curtailed, my blood runs cold and I call it what it is—*treason*."

Orsino had listened raptly to the words and joined in a burst of spontaneous applause that swept around the table. He had never had a brush with Government himself and he hardly believed in the existence of the shadowy, terrorist D.A.R., but Reiner had made it sound so near and menacing!

But Uncle Frank was on his feet. "We seem to have strayed from the point," he said. "For anybody who needs his memory refreshed, I'll state that the point is two assassinations and one near miss. I fail to see the connection, if any, with Dick Reiner's paranoid delusions of persecution. I especially fail to see the relevance of the word 'treason.' Treason to what—us? The Syndic is not a government. It must not become enmeshed in the symbols and folklore of a government or it will be first chained and then strangled by them. The Syndic is an organization of high morale and easygoing, hedonistic personality. The fact that it succeeded the Government occurred because the Government had become an organization of low morale and inflexible, puritanic, sado-masochistic personality. I have no illusions about the Syndic lasting forever, and I hope nobody else here has. Naturally I want it to last our lifetime, my children's lifetime, and as long after that as I can visualize my descendants—but don't think I have any burning affection for my unborn great-great grandchildren. Now, if there is anybody here who doesn't want it to last that long, I suggest to him that the quickest way to demoralize the Syndic is to adopt Dick Reiner's proposal of a holy war for a starter. From there we can proceed to an internal heresy hunt, a census, excise taxes, income taxes and wars of aggression. Now, what about getting back to the assassinations?"

Orsino shook his head, thoroughly confused by now. But the confusion vanished as a girl entered the room, whispered something in the ear of Edward Falcaro and sat down calmly by his side. He wasn't the only one who noticed her. Most of the faces there registered surprise and some indignation. The Syndic had a very strong tradition of masculinity.

Edward Falcaro ignored the surprise and indignation. He said placidly, "That was very interesting, Frank, what I understood of it. But it's always interesting when I go ahead and do something because it's the smart thing to do, and then listen to you explain my reasons—including fifty or sixty that I'm more than positive never crossed by mind."

There was a laugh around the table that Charles Orsino thought was unfair. He knew…Edward Falcaro knew…and everybody knew that Taylor credited Falcaro with sound intuitive judgment rather than analytic power. He supposed the old man—intuitively—had decided a laugh was needed to clear the air of the quarrel and irrelevance.

Falcaro went on, "The way things stand now, gentlemen, we don't know very much, do we?" He bit a fresh cigar and lighted it meditatively. From a cloud of rank smoke he said, "So the thing to do is find out more, isn't it?" In spite of the beard and the cigar, there was something of a sly, teasing child about him. "So what do you say to slipping one of our own people into the Government to find out whether they're dealing in assassination or not?"

Charles Orsino alone was naive enough to speak; the rest knew that the old man had something up his sleeve. Charles said, "You can't do it, sir! They have lie detectors and drugs and all sorts of things—" His voice died down miserably under Falcaro's too-benign smile and the looks of irritation verging on disgust from the rest. The enigmatic girl scowled. *Damn them all!* Charles thought, sinking into his chair and wishing he could sink into the earth.

"The young man," Falcaro said blandly, "speaks the truth—no less true for being somewhat familiar to us all. But what if we have a way to get around the drugs and lie detectors, gentlemen? Which of you bold fellows would march into the jaws of death by joining the Government, spying on them and trying to report back?"

Charles stood up, prudence and timidity washed away by a burning need to make up for his embarrassment with a grandstand play. "I'll go, sir," he said very calmly. *And if I get killed that'll show 'em; then they'll be sorry.*

"Good boy," Edward Falcaro said briskly, with a 'well that's that' air. "The young lady here will take care of you."

Charles steadily walked down the long room to the head of the table, thinking that he must be cutting a rather fine figure. Uncle Frank ruined his exit by catching his sleeve and halting him as he passed his seat. "Good luck, Charles," Uncle Frank whispered. "And for Heaven's sake, keep a better guard up. Can't you see the old devil planned it this way from the beginning?"

"Goodbye, Uncle Frank," Charles said, suddenly feeling quite sick as he walked on. The young lady rose and opened the door for him. She was graceful as a cat, and a conviction overcame Charles Orsino that he was the canary.

CHAPTER FIVE

Max Wyman shoved his way through such a roar of voices and such a crush of bodies as he had never known before. Scratch Sheet Square was bright as day—brighter. Atomic lamps, mounted on hundred-story buildings, hosed and squirted the happy mob with blue-white glare. The Scratch Sheet's moving sign was saying in fiery letters seventy-five feet tall: *"11:58 PM EST...December 31st...Cops say two million jam NYC streets to greet New Year...11:59 PM EST...December 31st...Falcaro jokes on TV 'Never thought we'd make it'...12:00 midnight January 1st...Happy New Year..."*

The roar of voices had become insane. Max Wyman held his head, hating it, hating them all, trying to shut them out. Half a dozen young men against whom he was jammed were tearing the clothes off a girl. They were laughing and she was too, making only a pretense of defending herself. It was one of New York's mild winter nights. Wyman looked at the white skin not knowing that his eyes gloated. He yelled curses at her, and the young men. But nobody heard his whiskey-hoarsened young voice.

Somebody thrust a bottle at him and made mouths, trying to yell, "Happy New Year!" He grabbed feverishly at the bottle and held it to his mouth, letting the liquor gurgle once, twice, three times. Then the bottle was snatched away, not by the man who had passed it to him. A hilarious fat woman plastered herself against Wyman and kissed him clingingly on the mouth, to his horror and disgust. She was torn away from him by a laughing, white-haired man and turned willingly to kissing him instead.

Two strapping girls jockeyed Wyman between them and began to tear *his* clothes off, laughing at their switcheroo on the year's big gag. He clawed out at them hysterically and they stopped, the laughter dying on their lips as they saw his look of terrified rage. A sudden current in the crowd parted Wyman from them; another bottle bobbed on the sea of humanity. He clutched at it and this time did not drink. He stuffed it hurriedly under the waistband of his shorts and kept a hand on it as the eddy of humanity bore him on to the fringes of the roaring mob.

"Syndic leaders hail New Year...Taylor praises Century of Freedom...12:05 AM EST January 1st..."

Wyman was mashed up against a girl who first smiled at his young face invitingly...and then looked again. "Get away from me!" she shrieked, pounding on his chest with her small fists. You could hear individual voices now, but the crowd was still dense. She kept screaming at him and hitting him until suddenly Scratch

Sheet Square Upramp loomed and the crowd fizzed onto it like uncorked champagne, Wyman and the screaming girl carried along the moving plates underfoot. The crowd boiled onto the northbound strip, relieving the crush; the girl vanished, whimpering, into the mob.

Wyman, rubbing his ear mechanically, shuffled with downcast eyes to the eastbound ramp and collapsed onto a bench gliding by at five miles per hour. He looked stupidly at the ten-mile and fifteen-mile strips, but did not dare step onto them. He had been drinking steadily for a month. He would fall and the bottle would break.

He lurched off the five-mile strip at Riverside Downramp. Nobody got off with him. Riverside was a tangle of freightways over, under, and on the surface. He worked there.

Wyman picked his way past throbbing conveyors roofed against pilferage, under gurgling fuel and water and waste pipes, around vast metal warehouses and storage tanks. It was not dark or idle in Riverside. Twenty-four hours was little enough time to bring Manhattan its daily needs and carry off its daily waste and manufactures. Under daylight-atomics, the transport engineers—in their glass perches—read the dials and turned the switches. Breakdown crews scurried out from emergency stations as bells clanged to replace a sagging plate, remag a failing ehrenhafter, unplug a jam of nylon bales at a too-sharp corner.

He found Breakdown Station 26, hitched his jacket over the bottle and swayed in, drunk enough to think he could pretend he was sober. "Hi," he said hoarsely to the shift foreman. "Got jammed up in the celebration."

"We heard it clear over here," the foreman said, looking at him closely. "Are you all right, Max?"

The question enraged him. "'Smatter?" he yelled. "Had a couple, sure. Think 'm drunk? Tha' wha' ya think?"

"Gee," the foreman said wearily. "Look, Max, I can't send you out tonight. You might get killed. I'm trying to be reasonable and I wish you'd do as much for me. What's biting you, boy? Nobody has anything against a few drinks and a few laughs. I went on a bender last month myself. But you get so damned *mean* I can't stand you and neither can anybody else."

Wyman spewed an obscenity at him and tried to swing at him. He was surprised and filled with self-pity when somebody caught his arm and somebody else caught his other arm. It was Dooley and Weintraub, his shift-mates, looking unhappy and concerned.

"Lousy rats!" Wyman choked out. "Leas' a man's buddies c'd do is back'm up…" He began to cry, hating them, and then fell asleep on his feet. Dooley and Weintraub eased him down onto the floor.

The foreman mopped his head and appealed to Dooley. "He always like this?" He had been transferred to Station 26 only two weeks before.

Dooley shrugged. "You might say so. He showed up about three months ago. Said he used to be a breakdown man in Buffalo, on the yards. He knew the work all right. But I never saw such a mean kid. Never a good word for anybody. Never any fun. Booze, booze, booze. This time he really let go."

Weintraub said unexpectedly, "I think he's what they used to call an alcoholic."

"What the hell's that?" the foreman demanded.

"I read about it. It's something they used to have before the Syndic. I read about it. Things were a lot different then. People picking on you all the time, everybody mad all the time. The girls were scared to give it away and the boys were scared to take it— but they did anyway and it was kind of like fighting with yourself *inside* yourself. The fighting wore some people out so much they just couldn't take it any more. Instead of going on benders for a change of pace like sensible people, they boozed *all* the time—and they had a fight inside themselves about *that* so they boozed harder." He looked defensive at their skeptical faces. "I *read* it, he insisted.

"Well," the foreman said inconclusively, "I heard things used to be pretty bad. Did these alcoholers get over it?"

"I don't know," Weintraub admitted. "I didn't read that far."

"Hmm. I think I'd better can him." The foreman was studying their faces covertly, hoping to read a reaction. He did. Both the men looked relieved. "Yeh. I think I'd better can him. He can go to the Syndic for relief if he has to. He doesn't do us much good here. Put some soup on and get it down him when he wakes up."

The foreman, an average kindly man, hoped the soup would help.

But at about three-thirty, after two trouble calls in succession, they noticed that Wyman had left leaving no word.

The fat little man struggled out of the New Year's eve throng; he had been caught by accident, Commander Grinnel did not go in for celebrations. When he realized that January fifteenth was now fifteen days away, he doubted that he would ever celebrate again. It was a two-man job he had to do on the fifteenth, and so far he had not found the other man.

He rode the slidewalk to Columbus Square. He had been supplied with a minimum list of contacts. One had moved, and in the crazily undisciplined Syndic Territory it was impossible to trace anybody. Another had died of too much morphine. Another had beaten her husband almost to death with a chair leg and was in custody awaiting trial. The Commander wondered briefly and querulously: why do we always have such unstable people here? Or does that louse Emory deliberately saddle me with them when I'm on a mission? Wouldn't put it past him.

The final contact on the list was a woman. She'd be worthless for the business of January fifteenth. That called for some physical strength, some technical knowledge, and a residual usefulness to the Government, Professor Speiser had done some good work here on industrial sabotage, but taken away from the scene of possible operations, she'd just be a millstone. He had his record to think of.

Sabotage—

If a giggling threesome hadn't been looking his way from a bench across the slidewalk, he would have ground his teeth. In recent weeks, he had done what he estimated as an easy three million dollars worth of damage to Mob Territory industry. And the stupid fools hadn't *noticed* it! Repair crews had rebuilt the fallen walls, mechanics had tut-tutted over the wrecked engines and replaced them, troubleshooters had troubleshot the scores of severed communications lines and fuel mains.

He had hung around.

"Sam, you see this? Melted through, like with a little thermite bomb. How in the hell did a thing like that happen?"

"I don't know, I wasn't here. Let's get it fixed kid."

"Okay…you think we ought to report this to somebody?"

"If you want to, I'll mention it to Larry. But I don't see what he can do about it. Must've been some kids. You gotta put it down as fair wear and tear. But boys will be boys."

Remembering, he did grind his teeth. But they were at Columbus Square.

Professor Speiser lived in one of the old plastic brick faculty houses. Her horsy face, under a curling net, looked out of the annunciator plate, "Yes? What is it?"

"Professor Speiser, I believe you know my daughter, Miss *Freeman*. She asked me to look you up while I was in New York. Have I come much too late?"

"Oh, dear. Why, no. I suppose not. Come in, Mr.—Mr. Freeman."

In her parlor, she faced him apprehensively. When she spoke she rolled out her sentences like the lecturer she was. "Mr. Freeman—as I suppose you'd prefer me to call you—you asked a moment ago whether you'd come too late. I realize that the question was window-dressing, but my answer is quite serious. You have come too late. I have decided to dissociate myself from—let us say, from your daughter, Miss Freeman."

The Commander asked only, "Is that irrevocable?"

"Quite. It wouldn't be fair of me to ask you to leave without an explanation. I am perfectly willing to give one. I realize now that my friendship with Miss Freeman and the work I did for her stemmed from, let us say a certain vacancy in my life."

He looked at a picture on her desk of a bald, pleasant-faced fellow with a pipe.

She followed his eyes and said with a sort of shy pride, "That is Dr. Mordecai, of the University's Faculty of Dentistry. Like myself, a long-time celibate. We plan to marry."

The Commander said, "Do you feel that Dr. Mordecai might like to meet my daughter?"

"No I do not. We expect to have very little time for outside activities, between our professional careers and our personal lives. Please don't misunderstand, Mr. Freeman. I am still your daughter's friend. I always shall be. But somehow I no longer find in myself an urgency to express the friendship. It seems like a beautiful dream—and a quite futile one. I have come to realize that one can live a full life without Miss Freeman. Now, it's getting quite late—"

He smiled ruefully and rose. "May I wish you every happiness, Professor Speiser?" he said, extending his hand.

She beamed with relief. "I was so afraid you'd—"

Her face went limp and she stood swaying drunkenly as the needle in the ring popped her skin.

The Commander, his face as dead as hers, disconnected his hand and sheathed the needle carefully again. He drew one of his guns, shot her through the heart and walked out of the apartment.

Old fool! She should have known better.

Max Wyman stumbled through the tangle of Riveredge, his head a pot of molten lead and his legs twitching under him as he fled from his shame.

Dimly, as if with new eyes, he saw that he was not alone. Riveredge was technically uninhabited. Then what voices called guardedly to him from the shadows: "Buddy—buddy—wait up a minute, buddy—did you score? Did you score?"

He lurched on and the voices became bolder. The snaking Conveyors and ramps sliced out sectors of space. Storage tanks merged with inflow mains to form sheltered spots where they met. No spot was without its whining, appealing voice. He stood at last, quivering, leaning against a gigantic I-beam that supported a heavy-casting freightway. A scrap sheet of corrugated iron rested against the bay of the I-beam, and the sheet quivered and fell outward. An old man's voice said, "You're beat, son. Come on in."

He staggered a step forward and collapsed on a pallet of rags as somebody carefully leaned the sheet back into place again.

CHAPTER SIX

Max Wyman woke raving with the chuck horrors. There was somebody there to hand him candy bars, sweet lemonade, lump sugar. There was somebody to shove him easily back into the pallet of rags when he tried to stumble forth in a hunt for booze.

On the second day he realized that it was an old man whose face looked gray and paralyzed. His name was T. G. Pendelton, he said.

After a week, he let Max Wyman take little walks about their part of Riverside—but not by night. "We've got some savage people here," he said. "They'd murder you for a pint. The women are worse. If one calls to you, don't go. You'll wind up dumped through a manhole into the Hudson. Poor folk."

"You're *sorry* for them?" Wyman asked, startled. It was a new idea to him. Since Buffalo, he had never been sorry for anybody. Something awful had happened there, some terrible betrayal...he passed his bony hand across his forehead. He didn't want to think about it.

"Would I live here if I weren't?" T. G. asked him. "Sometimes I can help them. There's nobody else to help them. They're old and sick and they don't fit anywhere. That's why they're savage. You're young—the only young man I've ever seen in Riveredge. There's so much outside for the young. But when you get old it sometimes throws you."

"The damned Syndic," Wyman snarled, full of hate.

T. G. shrugged. "Maybe it's too easy for sick old people to get booze. They lose somebody they spent a life with and it throws them. People harden into a pattern. They always had fun, they think they always will. Then half of the pattern's gone and they can't stand it, some of them. You got it early. What was the ringing bell?"

Wyman collapsed into the bay of the I-beam as if he'd been kicked in the stomach. A wave of intolerable memory swept over him. A ringing bell, a wobbling pendulum, a flashing light, the fair face of his betrayer, the hateful one of Hogan, stirred together in a hell brew. "Nothing," he said hoarsely, thinking that he'd give his life for enough booze to black him out. "Nothing."

"You kept talking about it," T. G. said. "Was—it real?"

"It couldn't have been," Wyman muttered. "There aren't such things. No. There was her and that Syndic and that louse Hogan. I don't want to talk about it."

"Suit yourself."

He did talk about it later, curiously clouded though it was. The years in Buffalo. The violent love affair with Inge. The catastrophic scene when he found her with Regan, kingpin mobster. The way he felt turned inside out, the lifetime of faith in the Syndic behind him and the lifetime of a faith in Inge ahead of him, both wrecked, the booze, the flight from Buffalo to Erie, to Pittsburgh, to Tampa, to New York. And somehow, insistently, the ringing bell, the wobbling pendulum and the flashing light that kept intruding between episodes of reality.

T. G. listened patiently, fed him, hid him when infrequent patrols went by. T. G. never told him his own story, but a bloated woman who lived with a yellow-toothed man in an abandoned storage tank did one day, her voice echoing from the curving, windowless walls of corrugated plastic. She said T. G. had been an alky chemist, reasonably prosperous, reasonably happy, reasonably married. His wife was the faithful kind and he was not. With unbelievable slyness she had dulled the pain for years with booze and he had never suspected. They say she had killed herself after one frightful weeklong debauche in Riveredge. T. G. came down to Riveredge for the body and returned after giving it burial and drawing his savings from the bank. He had never left Riveredge since.

"Worsh'p the grun' that man walks on" the bloated woman mumbled. "Nev' gets mad, nev' calls you hard names. Give y'a bottle if y' need' it. Talk to y' if y' blue. Worsh'p that man."

Max Wyman walked from the storage tank, sickened. T. G.'s charity covered that creature and him.

It was the day he told T. G, "I'm getting out of here."

The gray, paralyzed-looking face almost smiled. "See a man first?"

"Friend of yours?"

"Somebody who heard about you. Maybe he can do something for you. He feels the way you do about the Syndic."

Wyman clenched his teeth. The pain still came at the thought. Syndic, Hogan, Inge and betrayal. Oh to be able to hit back at them!

The red ride ebbed. Suddenly he stared at T. G. and demanded, "Why? Why should you put me in touch? What is this?"

T. G. shrugged. "I don't worry about the Syndic. I worry about people. I've been worrying about you. You're a little insane,

Max, like all of us here."

"Damn you!"

"He has…"

Max Wyman paused a long time and said, "Go on, will you?" He realized that anybody else would have apologized, but he couldn't and he knew that T. G. knew he couldn't.

The old man said, "A little insane. Bottled-up hatred. It's better out of you than in. It's better to sock the man you hate and stand a chance of having him sock you back than it is just to hate him and let the hate gnaw you like a grave-worm."

"What've you got against the Syndic?"

"Nothing, Max. Nothing against it and nothing for it. What I'm for is people. The Syndic is people. You're people. Slug 'em if you want and they'll have a chance to slug you back. Maybe you'll pull down the Syndic like Samson in the temple; more likely it'll crush you. But you'll be doing something about it. That's the great thing. That's the thing people have to learn—or they wind up in Riveredge."

"You're crazy."

"I told you I was, or I wouldn't be here."

The man came at sunset. He was short and pudgy, with a halo of wispy hair and the coldest, grimmest eyes that Wyman had ever seen. He shook hands with Wyman, and the young man noted simultaneously a sharp pain in his finger and that the stranger wore an elaborate gold ring. Then the world got hazy and confused. He had a sense that he was being asked questions, that he was answering them that it went on for hours and hours.

When things quite suddenly came into focus again, the pudgy man was saying, "I can introduce myself now. Commander Grinnel, of the North American Navy. My assignment is recruiting. The preliminary examination has satisfied me that you are no plant and would be a desirable citizen of the N. A. Government. I invite you to join us."

"What would I do?" Wyman asked steadily.

"That depends on your aptitudes. What do you think you would like to do?"

Wyman said, "Kill me some Syndics."

The commander stared at him with those cold eyes. He said at last, "It can probably be arranged. Come with me."

They went by train to Cape Cod. At midnight on January 15th, the commander and Wyman left their hotel room and strolled about the streets. The commander taped small packets to the four legs of the microwave relay tower that connected Cape Cod with the Continental Press common carrier circuits and taped other packets to the police station's motor pool gate.

At 1:00 A.M., the tower exploded and the motor pool gate fused into an impassible puddle of blue-hot molten metal. Simultaneously, fifty men in turtleneck sweaters and caps appeared from nowhere on Center Street. Half of them barricaded the street, firing on citizens and cops who came too close. The others systematically looted every store between the barricade and the beach.

Blinking a flashlight in code, the commander approached the deadline unmolested and was let through with Wyman at his heels. The goods, the raiders, the commander and Wyman were aboard a submarine by 2:35 and under way ten minutes later.

After Commander Grinnel had exchanged congratulations with the sub commander, he presented Wyman.

"A recruit. Normally I wouldn't have bothered, but he had a rather special motivation. He could be very useful."

The sub commander studied Wyman impersonally, "If he's not a plant."

"I've used my ring. If you want to get it over with, we can test him and swear him in now."

They strapped him into a device that recorded pulse, perspiration, respiration, muscle-tension and brainwaves. A sweatered specialist came and mildly asked Wyman matter-of-fact questions about his surroundings while he calibrated the polygraph.

Then came the payoff. Wyman did not fail to note that the sub commander loosened his gun in his holster when the questioning began.

"Name, age and origin?"

"Max Wyman. Twenty-two. Buffalo Syndic Territory."

"Do you like the Syndic?"

"I hate them."

"What are your feelings toward the North American Government?"

"If it's against the Syndic, I'm for it."

"Would you rob for the North American Government?"

"I would."

"Would you kill for it?"

"I would."

"Have you any reservations yet unstated in your answers?"

"No."

It went on for an hour. The questions were re-phrased continuously; after each of Wyman's firm answers, the sweatered technician gave a satisfied little nod. At last it ended and he was unstrapped from the device.

Max was tired.

The sub commander seemed a little awed as he got a small book and read from it, "Do you, Max Wyman, solemnly renounce all allegiances previously held by you and pledge your allegiance to the North American Government?"

"I do," the young man said fiercely.

In a remote corner of his mind, for the first time in months, the bell ceased to ring, the pendulum to beat, and the light to flash.

Charles Orsino knew again who he was and what was his mission.

CHAPTER SEVEN

It had begun when the girl led him through the conference room door. Naturally one had misgivings; naturally one didn't speak up. But the vault-like door far downstairs was terrifying when it yawned before you and even more so when it closed behind you.

"What is this place?" he demanded at last. "Who are you?"

She said, "Psychology lab."

It produced on him the same effect that "alchemy section" or "Division of astrology" would have on a well-informed young man in 1950. He repeated flatly, "Psychology lab. If you don't want to tell me, very well. I volunteered without strings." Which should remind her that he was a sort of hero and should be treated with a certain amount of dignity and that she could save her corny jokes.

"I meant it," she said, fiddling busily with the locks of yet another vault-like door. "I'm a psychologist. I'm also by the way, Lee Falcaro—since you asked."

"The old ma—Edward Falcaro's line?" he asked.

"Simon pure. He's my father's brother. Father's down in Miami, handling the tracks and gaming in general."

The second big door opened on a brain-gray room whose air had a curiously dead feel to it. "Sit down," she said, indicating a very unorthodox chair. He did, and found that the chair was the most comfortable piece of furniture he had ever known. Its contact with his body was so complete that it pressed nowhere, it poked nowhere. The girl studied dials in its back nevertheless and muttered something about adjusting it. He protested.

"Nonsense," she said decisively. She sat down herself in an ordinary seat. Charles shifted uneasily in his chair to find that it moved with him. Still no pressure, still no poking.

"You're wondering," she began, "about the word 'psychology'. It has a bad history and people have given it up as a bad job. It's true that there isn't pressure nowadays to study the human mind. People get along. In general what they want they get, without crippling effort. In your Uncle Frank Taylor's language, the Syndic is an appropriately-structured organization of high morale and wide public acceptance. In my language the Syndic is a father-image that does a good job of fathering. In good times, people aren't introspective.

"There is, literally, no reason why my line of the family should have kept up a tradition of experimental psychology. Way, way back, old Amadeo Falcaro often consulted Professor Oscar Sternweiss of the Columbia University psychology faculty—he wasn't as much of a dashing improviser as the history books make him out to be. Eventually one of his daughters married one of Sternweiss' sons and inherited the Sternweiss notebooks and library and apparatus. It became an irrational custom to keep it alive. When each academic school of psychology managed to prove that every other school of psychology was dead wrong and psychology collapsed as a science, the family tradition was unaffected; it stood outside the wrangling.

"Now, you're wondering what this has to do with trying to slip you into the Government."

"I am," Charles said fervently. If she'd been a doll outside the Syndic, he would minutes ago have protested that all this was foolish and walked out. "Since she was not only in the Syndic, but in the Falcaro line, he had no choice except to hear her babble and *then* walk out. It was all rot, psychology, Id, oversoul, mind-vectors, counseling, psychosomatics—rot from sick-minded old men. Everybody knew—

"The Government, we know, uses de-inhibiting drugs as a first screening of its recruits. As an infallible second screening, they use a physiological lie detector based on the fact that telling a lie causes tensions in the liar's body. We shall get around this by slipping you in as a young man who hates the Syndic for some valid reason—"

"Confound it, you were just telling me that they can't be fooled!"

"We won't fool them. You'll *be* a young man who hates the Syndic. We'll tear down your present personality a gray cell at a time. We'll pump you full of Seconal every day for a quarter of a year… "We'll obliterate your personality under a new one. We'll bury Charles Orsino under a mountain of suggestions, compulsions and obsessions shoveled at you sixteen hours a day while you're too groggy to resist. Naturally the supplanting personality will be neurotic, but that works in with the mission."

He struggled with a metaphysical concept for the first time in his life. "But—but—how will I know I'm *me?*"

"We think we can put a trigger on it. When you take the Government oath of allegiance, you should bounce back."

He did not fail to note a little twin groove between her brows that appeared when she said *think* and *should*. He knew that in a sense he was nearer death now than when Halloran's bullet had been intercepted.

"Are you staying with it?" she asked simply.

Various factors entered into it. *A life for the Syndic*, as in the children's history books. That one didn't loom very large. But multiply it by *it sounds like more fun that hot-rod polo*, and that by *this is going to raise my stock sky-high with the family* and you had something. Somehow, under Lee Falcaro's interested gaze, he neglected to divide it by *if it works.*

"I'm staying with it," he said.

She grinned. "It won't be too hard," she said. "In the old days there would have been voting record, social security numbers, military service, addresses they could, check on—hundreds of things. Now about all we have to fit you with is a name and a subjective life."

It began that spring day and went on into late fall.

The ringing bell.

The flashing light.

The wobbling pendulum.

You are Max Wyman of Buffalo Syndic Territory. You are Max Wyman of Buffalo Syndic Territory. You are Max Wyman of Buffalo Syndic…

Mom fried pork sausages in the morning, you loved the smell of pumpernickel from the bakery on Vesey Street.

Mr. Watsisname the English teacher with the mustache wanted you to go to college—

Nay, ye cannot, though ye had Argus eyes,
In abbeyes they haue so many suttyll spyes;
For ones in the yere they have secret vvsytacyons,
And yf ony prynce rejorme…

—but the stockyard job was closer, they needed breakdown men—

You are Max Wyman of Buffalo Syndic Territory. You are—

The ringing bell.

The flashing light.

The wobbling pendulum.

And the pork sausages and the teacher with the mustache and poems you loved and *page, 24, paragraph 3, maximum speed on a live-cattle walk-way is three miles per hour; older walkways hold this speed with reduction gears coupled to a standard 18-inch ehrenhafter unit. Standard practice in new construction calls for holding speed by direct drive from a specially wound ehrenhafter. This places a special obligation in breakdown maintenance men, who must distinguish between the two types, carry two sets of wiring diagrams and a certain number of mutually-uninterchangeable parts, though good design principles hold these to a minimum. The main difference in the winding of a standard 18-incher and a low-speed ehrenhafter rotor—*

Of course things are better now, Max Wyman, you owe a great debt to Jim Hogan, Father of the Buffalo Syndic, who fought for your freedom in the great old days, and to his descendants who are tirelessly working for your freedom and happiness.

And now happiness is a girl named Inge Klohbel now that you're almost a man.

You are Max Wyman of Buffalo Syndic Territory. You are Max Wyman of Buffalo Syndic Territory.

And Inge Klohbel is why you put away the crazy dream of scholarship, for her lips and hair and eyes and legs mean more to you than anything, more than...

Later phonologic changes include palatal mutation; i.e., before ht *and* hs *the diphthongs* eo, io, *which resulted from breaking, became* ie (i, y) *as in* cneoht, chieht, *and* seox (x *equaling* hs), siex, six, syx...

The crazy dream of scholarship, what kind of a way is that to repay the Mob and...

The ringing bell.

The flashing light.

The wobbling pendulum.

Repay the Syndic and young Mike Hogan all over the neighborhood suddenly and Inge says he did stop and say hello but of course he was just being polite.

So you hit the manuals hard and one day you go out on a breakdown call and none of the older men could figure out why the pump was on the blink—a roaring, chewing monster of a pump it was, sitting there like a dead husk and the cattle feed backed up four miles to a storage tank in the suburbs and the steers in the yards bawling with hunger, and you traced the dead wire, you out with the spot-welder, a zip of blue flame and the pump began to chew again and you got the afternoon off.

And there they were.

Lee Falcaro: (Bending over the muttering, twitching carcass) Adrenaline. Brighter picture and louder sound.

Assistant: (Opening a pinchcock in the tube that enters the arm, increasing video contrast, increasing audio): He's weakening.

Lee Falcaro: (In a whisper) I know. I know. But this is IT.

Assistant: (Inaudibly) you cold-blooded witch.

You are Max Wyman. You are Max Wyman, and you don't know what to do about the Syndic that betrayed you, about the girl who betrayed you with the living representative of the Syndic, about the dream of scholarship that lies in ruins, the love that lies in ruins after how many promises and vows, the faith of twenty years that lies in ruins after how many declarations.

The ringing bell.

The flashing light.

The wobbling pendulum.

And a double whiskey with a beer chaser.

Lee Falcaro: The alcohol.

(It drips from a sterile graduate, trickles through the rubber tubing and into the arm of the mumbling, sweating carcass. The molecules mingle with the molecules of serum. In seconds they are washed against the cell walls of the forebrain. The cell walls, lattices of jelly, crawl and rearrange their structure as the alcohol molecules bumble against them; the lattices of jelly that wall in the cytoplasm and nuclear jelly become thinner than they were. Streams of electrons that had coursed in familiar paths through chains of neurons find easier paths through the poison-thinned cell walls. A "Memory" or an "Idea" or a "Hope" or a "Value" that was a configuration of neurons linked by electron streams vanishes When the electron streams find an easier way to flow anew "Memories," "Ideas," "Hopes" and "Values" that are configurations of neurons linked by electron streams are born.)

Love and loyalty die, but not as if they had never been. Their ghosts remain. Max Wyman and you are haunted by them. They hound you from Buffalo to Erie, but there is no oblivion deep enough in the Mex joints, or in Tampa tequila or Pittsburgh zubrovka or New York gin.

You tell incurious people who came to the place on the corner for a shot and some talk that you're the best breakdown man that ever came out of Erie; you tell them women are no damn good, you tell them the Syndic—here you get sly and look around with drunken caution, lowering your voice—you tell them the Syndic's no damned good, and you drunkenly recite poetry until they move away, puzzled and annoyed.

Lee Falcaro: (Passing a weary hand across her forehead) well, he's had it. Disconnect the tubes, give him a 48-hour stretch in bed and then get him on the street pointed towards Riveredge.

Assistant: Does the apparatus go into dead storage?

Lee Falcaro: (Grimacing uncontrollably) No. Unfortunately, no.

Assistant: (Inaudibly, as she plucks needle-tipped tubes from the carcass' elbows) who's the next sucker?

CHAPTER EIGHT

The submarine surfaced at dawn. Orsino had been assigned a bunk and, to his surprise, had fallen asleep almost at once. At eight in the morning, he was shaken awake by one of the men in caps.

"Shift change," the man explained laconically.

Orsino started to say something polite and sleepy. The man grabbed his shoulder and rolled him onto the deck, snarling, "You going to *argue?*"

Orsino's reactions were geared to hot-rod polo—doing the split-second right thing after instinctively evaluating the roll of the ball, the ricochet of bullets, the probable tactics and strategy of the opposing four. They were not geared to a human being who behaved with the blind ferocity of an inanimate object. He just gawked at him from the deck, noting that the man had one hand on a sheath knife.

"All right, buster," the man said contemptuously, apparently deciding that Orsino would stay put. "Just don't mess with the Guard." He rolled into the bunk and gave a good imitation of a man asleep until Orsino worked his way through the crowded compartment and up a ladder to the deck.

There was a heavy, gray overcast. The submarine seemed to be planing the water; salt spray washed the shining deck. A gun crew was forward, drilling with a five-incher. The rasp of a petty-officer singing out the numbers mingled with the hiss and gurgle of the spray. Orsino leaned against the conning tower and tried to comb his thoughts out clean and straight.

It wasn't easy.

He was Charles Orsino, very junior Syndic member, with all memories pertaining thereto.

He was also, more dimly, Max Wyman with *his* memories. Now, able to stand outside of Wyman, he could recall how those memories had been implanted—down to the last stab of the last needle. He thought some very bitter thoughts about Lee Falcaro—and dropped them, snapping to attention as Commander Grinnel pulled himself through the hatch. "Good morning, sir," he said.

The cold eyes drilled him. "Rest," the commander said. "We don't play it that way on a pigboat. I hear you had some trouble about your bunk."

Orsino shrugged uncomfortably.

"Somebody should have told you," the commander said. "The boat's full of Guardsmen. They have a very high opinion of themselves—which is correct. They carried off the raid in good style. You don't mess with Guards."

"What are they?" Orsino asked.

Grinnel shrugged. "The usual elite," he said. "Loman's gang." He noted Orsino's blank look and smiled coldly. "Loman's President of North America," he said.

"On shore," Orsino hazarded, "we used to hear about somebody named Ben Miller."

"Obsolete information. Miller had the Marines behind him. Loman was Secretary of Defense. He beached the Marines and broke them up into guard detachments. Took away their heavy weapons. Meanwhile, he built up the Guard, very quietly—which, with the Secretary of Information behind him, he could do. About two years ago, he struck. The Marines who didn't join the Guard were massacred. Miller had the sense to kill himself. The Veep and the Secretary of State resigned, but it didn't save their necks. Loman assumed the Presidency automatically, of course, and had them shot. They were corrupt as hell anyway. They were owned body and soul by the southern bloc."

Two seamen appeared with a folding cot, followed by the sub commander. He was red-eyed with lack of sleep. "Set it there," he told them, and sat heavily on the sagging canvas, "Morning, Grinnel," he said with an effort. "Believe I'm getting too old for the pigboats. I want sun and air. Think you can use your influence at court to get me a corvette?" He bared his teeth to show it was a joke.

Grinnel said, with a minimum smile, "If I had any influence, would I catch the cloak-and-dagger crap they sling at me?"

The sub commander rolled back onto the cot and was instantly asleep, a muscle twitching the left side of his face every few seconds.

Grinnel drew Orsino to the lee of the conning tower, "We'll let him sleep," he said. "Go tell that gun crew Commander Grinnel says they should lay below."

Orsino did. The petty officer said something exasperated about the gunnery-training bill and Orsino repeated his piece. They secured the gun and went below.

Grinnel said, with apparent irrelevance, "You're a rare bird, Wyman. You're capable—and you're uncommitted. Let's go below. Stick with me."

He followed the fat little commander into the conning tower. Grinnel told an officer of some sort, "I'll take the con, mister. Wyman here will bike the radar watch." He gave Orsino a look that choked off his protests. Presumably, Grinnel knew that he was ignorant of radar.

The officer, looking baffled, said, "Yes, Commander." A seaman pulled his head out of a face-fitting box and told Wyman, "It's all yours, stranger." Wyman cautiously put his face into the box and was confronted by meaningless blobs of green, numerals in the dark, and a couple of arrows to make confusion complete.

He heard Grinnel say to the helmsman, "Get me a mug of joe, sailor, I'll take the wheel."

"I'll pass the word, sir."

"Nuts you'll pass the word, sailor. Go get the coffee—and I want it now and not when some steward's mate decides he's ready to bring it."

"Aye, aye, sir." Orsino heard him clatter down the ladder. Then his arm was gripped and Grinnel's voice muttered in his ear, "When you hear me bitch about the coffee, sing out: 'Aircraft 265, DX 3,000'. Good and loud. No, don't stop looking. Repeat it."

Orsino said, his eyes crossing on double images of the meaningless, luminous blobs, "Aircraft 265, DX 3,000. Good and loud. When you bitch about the coffee."

"Right. Don't forget it."

He heard the feet on the ladder again. "Coffee, sir."

"Thanks, sailor." A long sip and then another. "I always said the pigboats drink the lousiest joe in the Navy."

"Aircraft 265, DX 3,000!" Orsino yelled.

A thunderous alarm began to sound. "Take her down!" yelled Commander Grinnel.

"Take her down, sir!" the helmsman echoed, "But sir, the skipper—"

Orsino remembered him too then, dead asleep in his cot on the deck, the muscle twitching the left side of his face every few seconds.

"Damn it, those were aircraft! *Take her down!*"

The luminous blobs and numbers and arrows swirled before Orsino's eyes as the trim of the ship changed, hatches clanged to and water thundered into the ballast tanks. He staggered and caught himself as the deck angled sharply underfoot.

He knew what Grinnel had meant by saying he was uncommitted, and he knew now that it was no longer true.

He thought for a moment that he might be sick into the face-fitting box, but it passed.

Minutes later, Grinnel was on the mike, his voice sounding metallically through the ship. "To all hands. To all hands. This is Commander Grinnel. We lost the skipper in that emergency dive—but you and I know that that's the way he would have wanted it. As senior line officer, aboard, I'm assuming command for the rest of the voyage. We will remain submerged until dark. Division officers report to the wardroom. That's all."

He tapped Orsino on the shoulder. "Take off," he said. Orsino realized that the green blobs (clouds, were they?) no longer showed, and recalled that radar didn't work through water.

He wasn't in on the wardroom meeting, and wandered rather forlornly through the ship, incredibly jammed as it was with sleeping men, coffee-drinking men, and booty. Half a dozen times he had to turn away close questioning about his radar experience and the appearance of the aircraft on the radarscope. Each time he managed it, with the feeling that one more question would have cooked his goose.

The men weren't sentimental about the skipper they had lost. Mostly they wondered how much of a cut Grinnel would allot them from the booty of Cape Cod.

At last the word passed for "Wyman" to report to the captain's cabin. He did, sweating after a fifteen-minute chat with a radar technician.

Grinnel closed the door of the minute cabin and smirked at him. "You have trouble, Wyman?" he asked.

"Yes."

"You'd have worse trouble if they found out for sure that you don't know radar. I'd be in the clear. I could tell them you claimed to be a qualified radar man. That would make me out to be pretty gullible, but it would make you out to be a murderer. Who's backing you, Wyman? Who told you to get rid of the skipper?"

"Quite right, sir," Orsino said. "You've really got me there."

"Glad you realize it, Wyman. I've got you and I can use you. It was a great bit of luck, the skipper corking off on deck. But I've always had a talent for improvisation. If you're determined to be a leader, Wyman, nothing is more valuable. Do you know I can relax with you? It's a rare feeling. For once I can be certain that the man I'm talking to isn't one of Loman's stooges, or one of Clinch's N.A.B.I. ferrets or anything else but what he says he is—

"But that's beside the point. I have something else to tell you. There are two sides to working for me, Wyman. One of them's punishment if you get off the track. That's been made clear to you. The other is reward if you stay on. I have plans, Wyman, that are large-scale. They simply eclipse the wildest hopes of Loman, Clinch, Baggot and the rest. And yet, they're not wild. How'd you like to be on the inside when the North American Government returns to the mainland?"

Orsino uttered an authentic gasp and Commander Grinnel looked satisfied.

CHAPTER NINE

The submarine docked at an indescribably lovely bay in the south of Ireland. Orsino asked Grinnel whether the Irish didn't object to this, and was met with a blank stare. It developed that the Irish consisted of a few hundred wild men in the woods— maybe a few thousand. The stupid shore-bound personnel couldn't seem to clean them out. Grinnel didn't know anything about them, and he cared less.

Ireland appeared to be the naval base. The government proper was located on Iceland, vernal again after a long, climatic swing. The Canaries and Ascencion were outposts.

Orsino had learned enough on the voyage to recognize the Government for what it was. It had happened before in history; Uncle Frank had pointed it out. Big-time Caribbean piracy had grown from very respectable origins. Gentlemen-skippers had been granted letters of marque and reprisal by warring govern-ments, which made them a sort of contract navy. Periods of peace had found these privateers unwilling to give up their hard-earned complicated profession and their investments in it. When they could no longer hoist the flag of England or France or Spain, they simply hoisted the Jolly Roger and went it alone.

Confusing? Hell, yes! The famous Captain Kidd thought he was a gallant privateer and sailed trustingly into New York. Somewhere he had failed to touch third base; they shipped him to London for trial and hanged him as a pirate. The famous Henry Morgan had never been anything but a pirate and a super-pirate; as admiral of a private fleet he executed a brilliant amphibious operation and sacked the city of Panama. He was knighted, made governor of a fair-sized English island in the West Indies and died loved and respected by all.

Charles Orsino found himself a member of a pirate band that called itself the North American Government.

More difficult to learn were the ins and outs of pirate politics, which were hampered with an archaic, structurally inappropriate nomenclature and body of tradition. Commander Grinnel was a Sociocrat, which meant that he was in the same gang as President Loman. The late sub commander had been a Constitutionist, which meant that he was allied with the currently-out "southern bloc." The southern bloc did not consist of southerners at this stage of the North American Governments history but of a clique that tended to include the engineers and maintenance men of the Government. That had been the reason for the sub commander's erasure. The Constitutionists traditionally commanded pigboats and aircraft while surface vessels and the shore establishments were in the hands of the Sociocrats—the fruit of some long-forgotten compromise.

Commander Grinnel cheerfully explained to Charles that there was a crypto-Sociocrat naval officer primed and waiting to be appointed to the command of the sub. The Constitutionist gang would back him to the hilt and the Sociocrats would growl and finally assent. If, thereafter, the Constitutionists ever counted on the sub in a coup, they would be quickly disillusioned.

There wasn't much voting. Forty years before there had been a bad deadlock following the death by natural causes of President Powell after seventeen years in office. An ad hoc bipartisan conference called a session of the Senate and the Senate elected a new president.

It was little information to be equipped with when you walked out into the brawling streets of New Portsmouth on shore leave.

The town had an improvised look that was strange to Orsino. There was a sanitation reactor every hundred yards or so, but he mistrusted the look of the ground-level mains that led to it from the houses. There were houseflies from which he shied violently. Every other shack on the waterfront was a bar or a notch joint. He sampled the goods at one of the former and was shocked by the quality and price. He rolled out, his ears still ringing from the belt of raw booze, as half a dozen sweatered Guards rolled in, singing some esoteric song about their high morale and even higher venereal rate. A couple of them looked at him appraisingly, as though they wondered what kind of a noise he'd make if they jumped on his stomach real hard, so he hurried away from them.

The other entertainment facilities of the waterfront were flatly ruled out by a quick inspection of the wares. He didn't know what to make of them. Joints back in Syndic Territory if you were a man, made sense. You went to learn the ropes, or because you were afraid of getting mixed up in something intense when you didn't want to, or because you wanted a change, or because you were too busy, lazy, or shy to chase skirts on your own. If you were a woman and not too particular, a couple of years in a joint left you with a considerable amount of money and some interesting memories that you were under no obligation to discuss with your husband or husbands.

But the sloppy beasts, who called to him from the windows of the joints here on the waterfront, left him puzzled and disgusted. He reflected, strolling up Washington Street with eyes straight ahead, that women must be in short supply if they could make a living—or that the male citizens of the Government had no taste.

A whiff from one of those questionable sewer mains sent him reeling. He ducked into another saloon in self-defense and leaned groggily against the bar. A pretty brunette demanded, "What'll you have?"

"Gin, please." He peeled a ten off the roll Grinnel had given him. When the girl poured his gin he looked at her and found her fair. In all innocence, he asked her a question, as he might have asked a barmaid back home. She could have answered, "Yes," "No," "Maybe," or "What's in it for me?"

Instead she called him a lousy bastard, picked up a beer mug and was about to shatter it on his head when a hand caught her and a voice warned, "Hold it, Mabel! This guy's off my ship.

"He's just out of the States; he doesn't know any better. You know what it's like over there." Mabel snarled, "You better wise him up, then, friend. He can't go around talking like that to decent women." She slapped down another glass, poured gin and flounced down the bar.

Charles gulped his gin and turned shakily to his deliverer, a little reactor specialist he had seen on the sub once or twice, "Thanks," he said feeling inadequate. "Maybe you better wise me up. All I said was, 'Darling, do you—' "

The reactor man held up his hand. "That's enough," he said. "You don't talk that way over here unless you want your scalp parted."

Charles, buzzing a little with the gin, protested hotly, "But what's the harm? All she had to say was no; I wasn't going to throw her down on the floor."

It was all very confusing.

A shrug. "I heard about things in the States—Wyman, isn't it? I guess I didn't really believe it. You mean I could go up to any woman and just ask her how's about it?"

"Within, reason, yes."

"And *do* they?"

"Some do, some don't—like here."

"Like hell, like here! Last liberty—" and the reactor man told him a long, confusing story about how he had picked up this pig, how she had dangled it in front of him for one solid week while he managed to spend three hundred and eighty-six dollars on her, and how finally she had bawled that she couldn't, she just hated herself but she couldn't do anything like that and bang went the door in his face, leaving him to finish out the evening in a notch joint.

"Good gosh!" Charles said, appalled. "Was she out of her mind?"

"No," the reactor man said glumly, "but I must have been. I should of got her drunk and raped her the first night."

Charles was fully conscious that values were different here. Choking down something like nausea, he asked carefully, "Is there much rape?"

The little man signaled for another gin and downed it. "I guess so. Once when I was a kid a dame gave me this line about her cousin raped her when she was little so she was frigid. I had more ambition then, so I said, 'Then this won't be anything new to you, baby.' I popped her on the button——"

"I've got to go now," Charles said, walking straight out of the saloon. He was beginning to understand the sloppy beasts in the windows of the notch joint and why men could bring themselves to settle for nothing better. He was also overwhelmed by a great wave of homesickness.

The ugly pattern was beginning to emerge. Prudery, rape, frigidity, intrigue for power—and assassination? Beyond the one hint, Grinnel had said nothing that affected Syndic Territory.

But nothing would be more logical than for this band of brigands to lust after the riches of the continent.

Back of the waterfront were ship fitting shops and living quarters. Work was being done by a puzzling combination of mechanization and muscle-power. In one open shed he saw a lathe-hand turning a gun barrel out of a forging; the lathe was driven by one of those standard 18-inch ehrenhaft rotors Max Wyman knew so well. But a vertical drillpress next to it—Orsino blinked. Two men, sweating and panting, were turning a stubborn vertical drum as tall as they were, and a belt drive from the drum whirled the drill bit as it sank into a hunk of bronze. The men were in rags, dirty rags. And it came to Orsino with a stunning shock when he realized what the dull, clanking things were that swung from their wrists. They were chained to the handles of the wheel.

He walked on, almost dazed, comprehending now some cryptic remarks that had been passed aboard the sub.

"No Frog has staying power. Give a Limey his beef once a day and he'll out-sweat a Frog."

"Yeah, but you can't whip a Limey. They just go bad when you whip a Limey."

"They just get sullen for awhile. But let me tell you, friend, don't ever whip a Spig. You whip a Spig, he'll wait twenty years if he has to but he'll *get* you—right between the ribs."

"If a Spig wants to be boiled, I should worry."

It had been broken up in laughter.

Boiled! Could such things be?

Sixteen ragged, filth-crusted sub-humans were creeping down the road, each straining at a rope. An inch at a time, they were dragging a skid loaded with one huge turbine gear whose tiny herringbone teeth caught the afternoon sun.

The Government had reactors, the Government had vehicles— why this? He slowly realized that the Government's metal and machinery and atomic power went into its warships; that there was none left over for consumers and the uses of peace. The Government had degenerated into a dawn-age monster, specialized all to teeth and claws and muscles to drive them with. The Government was now, whatever it had been, a graceless, humorless incarnate ferocity. Whatever lightness or joy survived was the meaningless vestigal twitching of an obsolete organ.

Somewhere a child began to bawl and Charles was surprised to feel a profound pity welling up in him. Like a sedentary man who, after a workout aches in muscles he never knew he owned, Charles was discovering that he had emotions that had never been poignantly evoked by the bland passage of the hours in Syndic Territory.

Poor little kid, he thought, growing up in this hellhole. I don't know what having slaves to kick around will do to you, but I don't see how you can grow up a human being. I don't know what fear of love will do to you—make you a cheat? Or a graceful rutting animal with a choice only between graceless rutting violence and a stinking scuffle with a flabby and abstracted stranger in a strange unloved room? We have our guns to play with and they're good toys, but I don't know what kind of monster you'll become when they give you a gun to live with and violence for a god.

Reiner was right, he thought unhappily. *We've got to do something about this mess.*

A man and a woman were struggling in an alley as he passed.

Old habit almost made him walk on, but this wasn't the playful business of ripping clothes as practiced during hilarious moments in Mob Territory. It was a grim and silent struggle—

The man wore the sweater of the Guards. Nevertheless, Charles walked into the alley and tore him away from the woman; or rather, he yanked at the man's rock-like arm and the man, in surprise, let go of the woman and spun to face him.

"Beat it," Charles said to the woman, not looking around. He saw from the corner of his eye that she was staying right there.

The man's hand was on his sheath knife. He told Charles, "Get lost. Now. You don't mess with the Guards."

Charles felt his knees quivering, which was good. He knew from many a chukker of polo that it meant that he was strung to the breaking point, ready to explode into action. "Pull that knife," he said, "and the next thing you know you'll be eating it."

The man's face went dead calm and he pulled the knife and came in low, very fast. The knife was supposed to catch Charles in the middle. If Charles stepped inside it, the man would grab him in a bear hug and knife him in the back.

There was only one answer. He caught the thick wrist from above with his left hand as the knife flashed toward his middle and shoved out. He felt the point catch and slice his cuff. The Guardsman tried a furious and ill-advised kick at his crotch; with his grip on the knife-hand, Charles toppled him into the filthy alley as he stood one-legged and off balance. He fell on his back, floundering, and for a black moment, Charles thought his weight was about to tear the wrist loose from his grip. The moment passed, and Charles put his right foot in the socket of the Guardsman's elbow, reinforced his tiring left hand with his right and leaned, doubling the man's forearm over the fulcrum of his boot. The man roared and dropped the knife. It had taken perhaps five seconds.

Charles said, panting, "I don't want to break your arm or kick your head in or anything like that. I just want you to go away and leave the woman alone." He was conscious of her, vaguely hovering in the background. He thought angrily. She *might at least get his knife.*

The Guardsman said thickly, "You give me the boot and I

swear to God I'll find you and cut you to ribbons if it takes me the rest of my life."

Good, Charles thought. *Now he can tell himself he scared me. Good.* He let go of the forearm, straightened and took his foot from the man's elbow, stepping back. The Guardsman got up stiffly, flexing his arm, and stooped to pick up and sheath his knife without taking his eyes off Charles. Then he spat in the dust at Charles' feet. "Yellow crud," he said. "If the damn crow was worth it, I'd cut your heart out." He walked off down the alley and Charles followed him with his eyes until he turned the corner into the street.

Then he turned, irritated that the woman had not spoken.

She was Lee Falcaro.

"Lee!" he said, thunderstruck, "What are you doing here?" It was the same face, feature for feature, and between her brows appeared the same double groove he had seen before. But she didn't know him.

"You know me?" she asked blankly. "Is that why you pulled that ape off me? I ought to thank you. But I can't place you at all. I don't know many people here. I've been ill, you know."

There was a difference apparent now. The voice was a little querulous. And Charles would have staked his life that never could Lee Falcaro have said in that slightly smug, slightly proprietary, slightly 'aren't I Interesting' tone: "I've been ill, you know."

"But what are you *doing* here? Damn it, don't you know me? I'm Charles Orsino!"

He realized then that he had made a horrible mistake.

"Orsino," she said. And then she spat, *"Orsino! Of the Syndic!"* There was black hatred in her eyes.

She turned and raced down the alley. He stood there stupidly, for almost a minute, and then ran after her, as far as the alley's mouth. She was gone. You could run almost anywhere in New Portsmouth in almost a minute.

A weedy little seaman wearing crossed quills on his cap was lounging against a building. He snickered at Charles. "Don't chase that one, sailor," he said. "She is the property of O.N.I."

"You know who she is?"

The yeoman happily spilled his inside dope to the fleet gob,

"Lee Bennet. Smuggled over here couple months ago by D.A.R. The hottest thing that ever hit Naval Intelligence. Very small potato in the Syndic—knows all the families, who does what, who's a figurehead and who's a worker. Terrific, inside stuff! Hates the Syndic. A gang of big-timers did her dirt."

"Thanks," Charles said, and wandered off down the street.

It wasn't surprising. He should have *expected* it.

Noblesse oblige.

Pride of the Falcaro line. She wouldn't send anybody into deadly peril unless she was ready to go herself.

Only somehow the trigger that would have snapped neurotic, synthetic Lee Bennet into Lee Falcaro hadn't worked.

He wandered on aimlessly, wondering whether it would be minutes or hours before he'd be picked up and executed as a spy.

CHAPTER TEN

It took minutes only. He had headed back to the waterfront, afraid to run, with some vague notion of stealing a boat. Before he reached the row of saloons and joints, a smart-looking squad of eight tall men overtook him.

"Hold it, mister," a sergeant said. "Are you Orsino?"

"No," he said hopelessly. "That crazy woman began to yell at me that I was Orsino, but my name's Wyman. What's this about?"

The other men fell in beside and behind him. "We're stepping over to O.N.I.," the sergeant said.

"There's the son of a bitch!" somebody bawled. Suddenly there were a dozen sweatered Guardsmen around them. Their leader was the thug Orsino had beaten in a fair fight. He said silkily to the sergeant, "We want that boy, leatherneck. Blow."

The sergeant went pale. "He's wanted for questioning by the O.N.I.," he said stolidly.

"Get the marine three-striper!" the Guardsman chortled. He stuck his jaw into the sergeant's face. "Tell your squad to blow. You marines ought to know by now that you don't mess with the Guard."

A very junior officer appeared. "What's going on here, you men?" he shrilled. "Atten*shun!*" He was ignored as Guardsmen and marines measured one another with their eyes. "I said *attention!* Dammit, sergeant, *report!*" There was no reaction. The officer yelled, "You men may think you can get away with this but by God, you're wrong!" He strode away, his fists clenched and his face very red.

Orsino saw him stride through a gate into a lot marked *Bupers Motor Pool.* And he felt a sudden wave of communal understanding that there were only seconds to go. The sergeant played for time, saying, "I'll be glad to surrender the prisoner," he started, "if you have anything to show in the way of—"

The Guardsman kicked for the pit of the sergeant's stomach. He was a sucker Orsino thought abstractedly as he saw the sergeant catch his foot, dump him and pivot to block another Guardsman. Then he was fighting for his life himself, against three bellowing Guardsmen.

A ripping, hammering noise filled the air suddenly. Like cold magic, it froze the milling mob where it stood. Fifty-caliber noise.

The jaygee was back, this time in a jeep with a twin fifty. And he was glaring down its barrels into the crowd. People were beginning to stream from the saloons, joints and ship fitting shops.

The jaygee cocked his cap rakishly over one eye. *"Fall in!"* he rasped, and a haunting air of familiarity came over Orsino.

The waiting jeep, almost bucking in its eagerness to be let loose—Orsino on the ground, knees trembling with tension—a perfect change of mount scene in a polo match. He reacted automatically.

There was a surrealist flash of the jaygee's face before he clipped him into the back of the square little truck. There was another flash of spectators scrambling as he roared the jeep down the road.

From then on it was just a question of hanging onto the wheel with one hand, trying to secure the free-traversing twin-fifty with the other, glancing back to see if the jaygee was still out, avoiding yapping dogs and pedestrians, staying on the rutted road, pushing all possible speed out of the jeep, noting landmarks, estimating the possibility of dangerous pursuit. For a two-goal polo player, a dull little practice session.

The road, such as it was, wound five miles inland through scrubby woodland and terminated at a lumber camp where chained men in rags were dragging logs.

Orsino backtracked a quarter-mile from the camp and jolted overland in a kidney-cracking hare and hounds course at fifty per.

The jeep took it for an hour in the fading afternoon light and then bucked to a halt. Orsino turned for an overdue check on the jaygee and found him conscious, but greenly clinging to the sides of the vehicle. But he saw Orsino staring and gamely struggled to his feet, standing in the truck bed. "You're under arrest, sailor," he said. "Striking an officer, abuse of government property, driving a government vehicle without a trip-ticket—" His legs betrayed him and he sat down, hard.

Orsino thought very briefly of letting him have a burst from the twin-fifty, and abandoned the idea.

He seemed to have botched up everything so far, but he was still on a mission. He had a commissioned officer of the Government approximately in his power. He snapped, "Nonsense. *You're* under arrest."

The jaygee seemed to be reviewing rapidly any transgressions he may have committed, and asked at last, cautiously, "By what authority?"

"I represent the Syndic."

It was a blockbuster. The jaygee stammered, "But you can't— but there isn't any way—but how—"

"Never mind how."

"You're crazy. You must be, or you wouldn't stop here. I don't believe you're from the continent and I don't believe the jeep's broken down." He was beginning to sound just a little hysterical. "It can't break down here. We must be more than thirty miles inland."

"What's special about thirty miles inland?"

"The natives, you fool!"

The natives again. "I'm not worried about natives. Not with a pair of fifties."

"You don't understand," the jaygee said, forcing calm into his voice. "This is The Outback. They're in charge here. We can't do a thing with them. They jump people in the dark and skewer them. Now fix this damn jeep and let's get rolling!"

"Into a firing squad? Don't be silly, lieutenant. I presume you won't slug me while I check the engine."

The jaygee was looking around him. "My God, no," he said. "You may be a gangster, but—" He trailed off.

Orsino stiffened. Gangster was semi-dirty talk. "Listen, pirate," he said nastily, "I don't believe—"

"Pirate?" the jaygee roared indignantly, and then shut his mouth with a click, looking apprehensively about. The gesture wasn't faked; it alarmed Orsino.

"Tell me about your wildmen," he said.

"Go to hell," the jaygee said sulkily.

"Look, you called me a gangster first. What about these natives? You were trying to trick me, weren't you?"

"Kiss my royal North American eyeball, gangster."

"Don't be childish," Charles reproved him, feeling adult and superior. (The jaygee looked a couple of years younger than he.) He climbed out of his seat and lifted the hood. The damage was trivial; a shear pin in the transmission had given way. He reported mournfully, "Cracked block. The jeep's through forever. You can get on your way, lieutenant. I won't try to hold you."

The jaygee fumed, "You couldn't hold me if you wanted to, gangster. If you think I'm going to try and hoof back to the base alone in the dark, you're crazy. We're sticking together. Two of us may be able to hold them off for the night. In the morning, we'll see."

Well, maybe the officer did *believe* there were wildmen in the woods. That didn't mean there *were*.

The jaygee got out and looked under the hood uncertainly. It was obvious that in the first place he was no mechanic and in the second place he couldn't conceive of anybody voluntarily risking the woods rather than the naval base. "Uh-huh," he said. "Dismount that gun while I get a fire started."

"Yes, sir," Charles said sardonically, saluting. The jaygee absently returned the salute and began to collect twigs.

Orsino asked, "How do these aborigines of yours operate?"

"Sneak up in the dark. They have spears and a few stolen guns. Usually they don't have cartridges for them but you can't count on that. But they do have...witches."

Orsino snorted. He was getting very hungry indeed. "Do you know any of the local plants we might eat?"

The jaygee said confidently, "I guess we can get by on roots until morning"

Orsino dubiously pulled up a shrub, dabbed clods off its root and tasted it. It tasted exactly like a root. He sighed and changed the subject, "What do we do with the fifties when I get them both off the mount?"

"The jeep mount breaks down some damn way or other into two low-mount tripods. See if you can figure it out while I get the fire going."

The jaygee had a small, smoky fire barely going in twenty minutes. Orsino was still struggling with the jeep gun mount. It came apart, but it couldn't go together again. The jaygee strolled over at last contemptuously to lend a hand. He couldn't make it work either.

Two lost tempers and four split fingernails later it developed the "elevating screw" really held the two front legs on and that you elevated by adjusting the rear tripod leg.

"A hell of an officer you are," Orsino sulked.

It began to rain, putting the fire out with a hiss. They wound up prone under the jeep, not on speaking terms, each tending a gun, each presumably responsible for 180 degrees of perimeter.

Charles was fairly dry, except for a trickle of icy water following a contour that meandered to his left knee. After an hour of eye straining—nothing to be seen—and ear-straining—only the patter of rain—he heard a snore and kicked the jaygee.

The jaygee cursed wearily and said, "I guess we'd better talk to keep awake."

"*I'm* not having any trouble, pirate."

"Oh, knock it off—where do you get that pirate bit, gangster?"

"You're outlaws, aren't you?"

"Like hell we are. *You're* the outlaws. You rebelled against the lawfully constituted North American Government. Just because you won—for the time being—doesn't mean you were right."

"The fact that we won does mean that we were right. The fact that your so-called Government lives by raiding and scavenging off us means you were wrong. The things I've seen since I joined up with you thugs!"

"I'll bet. Respect for the home, sanctity of marriage, sexual morality, law and order—you never saw anything like that back home, did you gangster?" He looked very smug.

Orsino clenched his teeth. "Somebody's been telling you a pack of lies," he said. "There's just as much home and family life and morality and order back in Syndic Territory as there is here. And probably a lot more."

"Bull. I've seen intelligence reports; I know how you people live. Are you telling me you don't have sexual promiscuity? Polygamy? Polyandry? Open gambling? Uncontrolled liquor trade? Corruption and shakedowns?"

Orsino squinted along the barrel of the gun into the rain. "Look," he said, "take me as an average young man from Syndic Territory. I know maybe a hundred people. I know just three women and two men who are what you'd call promiscuous. I know one family with two wives and one husband. I don't really know any people personally who go in for polyandry, but I've met three casually. And the rest are ordinary middle-aged couples."

"Ah-*hah!* Middle-aged! Do you mean to tell me you're just leaving out anybody under middle age when you talk about morality?"

"Naturally," Charles said, baffled. "Wouldn't you?"

The only answer was a snort.

"What are bupers?" Charles asked.

"Bu-Pers," the jaygee said distinctly. "Bureau of Personnel, North American Navy."

"What do you do there?"

"What *would* a personnel bureau do?" the jaygee said patiently. "We recruit, classify, assign, promote and train personnel."

"Paperwork, huh? No wonder you don't know how to shoot or drive."

"If I didn't need you to cover my back, I'd shove this MG down your silly throat. For your information, gangster, all officers do a tour of duty on paperwork before they're assigned to their permanent branch. I'm going into the pigboats."

"Why?"

"Family. My father commands a sub. He's Captain Van Dellen."

Oh, God. Van Dellen. The sub commander that Grinnel—and he—had murdered. The kid hadn't heard yet that his father had been "lost" in an emergency dive.

The rain ceased to fall; the pattering drizzle gave way to irregular, splashing drops from leaves and branches.

"Van Dellen," Charles said. "There's something you ought to know."

"It'll keep," the jaygee answered in a grim whisper. The bolt of his gun clicked. "I hear them out there."

CHAPTER ELEVEN

She felt the power of the goddess working in her, but feebly. Dark...so dark...and so tired...how old was she? More than eight hundred moons had waxed and waned above her head since birth. And she had run at the head of her spearmen to the motor sounds. A motor meant the smithymen from the sea, and you killed smithymen when you could.

She let out a short shrill chuckle in the dark. There was a rustling of branches. One of the spearmen had turned to stare at the sound. She knew his face was worried. "Tend to business, you fool!" she wheezed. "Or by Bridget—" His breath went in with a hiss and she chuckled again. You had to let them know who was the cook and who was the potatoes every now and then. Kill the fool? Not now; not when there were smithymen with guns waiting to be taken.

The power of the goddess worked stronger in her withered breast as her rage grew at their impudence. Coming into her woods with their stinking metal!

There were two of them. A grin slit her face. She had not taken two smithymen together for thirty moons. For all her wrinkles and creaks, what a fine vessel she was for the power, to be sure! Her worthless, slow-to-learn niece could run and jump and she had a certain air, but she'd never be such a vessel. Her sister— the crone spat—these were degenerate days. In the old days, the sister would have been spitted when she refused the ordeal in her youth. The little one now, whatever her name was, she would make a fine vessel for the power when she was gathered to the goddess. If her sister or her niece didn't hold her head under water too long, or have a spear shoved too deep into her gut or hit her on the head with too heavy a rock.

These were degenerate days. She had poisoned her own mother to become the vessel of power.

The spearmen to her right and left shifted uneasily. She heard a faint mumble of the two smithymen talking. Let them talk! Doubtless they were cursing the goddess obscenely; doubtless that was what the smithymen all did when their mouths were not stuffed with food.

She thought of the man called Kennedy who forged spearheads and arrow-points for her people—he was a strange one, touched by the goddess, which proved her infinite power. She could touch and turn the head of even a smithyman. He was a strange one. Well now, to get on with it. She wished the power were working stronger in her; she was tired and could hardly see. But by the grace of the goddess there would be two new heads over her holy hut come dawn. She could hardly see, but the goddess wouldn't fail her…

She quavered like a screech owl, and the spearmen began to slip forward through the brush. She was not allowed to eat honey lest its sweetness clash with the power in her, but the taste of power was sweeter than the taste of honey.

With frightful suddenness there was an ear-splitting shriek and a trampling rush of feet. By sheer reflex, Orsino clamped down on the trigger of his fifty, and his brain rocked at its thunder. Shadowy figures were blotted out by the orange muzzle-flash. You're supposed to fire neat, spaced bursts of eight he told himself. I wonder what old Gilby would say if he could see his star pupil burning out a barrel and swinging his gun like a fire hose?

The gun stopped firing; end of the belt. Twenty, fifty or a hundred rounds? He didn't remember. He clawed for another belt and smoothly, in the dark, loaded again and listened.

"You all right, gangster?" the jaygee said behind him, making him jump.

"Yes," he said. "Will they come back?"

"I don't know."

"You filthy swine," an agonized voice wheezed from the darkness. "Me back is broke, you stinking lice." The voice began to sob.

They listened to it in silence for perhaps a minute. At last he said to the jaygee, "If the rest are gone maybe we can at least make him comfortable."

"Too risky," the jaygee said after a long pause.

The sobbing went on. As the excitement of the attack drained from Orsino, he felt deathly tired, cramped and thirsty. The thirst he could do something about. He scooped water from the muddy puddle by his knee and sucked it from his palms twice. The third time, he thought of the thirst that the sobbing creature out in the dark must be feeling, and his hand wouldn't go to his mouth.

"I'm going to get him," he whispered to the jaygee.

"Stay where you are! That's an order!"

He didn't answer, but began to work his cramped and aching body from under the jeep. The jaygee, a couple of years younger and more lithe than he, slid out first from his own side. Orsino sighed and relaxed as he heard his footsteps cautiously circle the jeep.

"Finish me off!" the wounded man was sobbing. "For the love of the goddess, finish me off, you bitches' bastards! You've broke me back—*ah!*" That was a cry of savage delight.

There was a strangled noise from the jaygee and then only a soft, deadly thrashing noise from the dark. Hell, Orsino thought bitterly. It was my idea. He snaked out from under the jeep and raced through wet brush.

The two of them were a tangled knot of darkness rolling on the ground. A naked back came uppermost; Orsino fell on it and clawed at its head. He felt a huge beard, took two handfuls of it and pulled as hard as he could. There was a wild screech and a flailing of arms. The jaygee broke away and stood up, panting hoarsely. Charles heard a sharp crunch and a snap, and the flailing sweaty figure beneath him lay still.

"Back to the guns," the jaygee choked. He swayed, and Orsino took him by the arm... While they were on the way back to the jeep, they stumbled over something that certainly appeared to be a body.

Orsino's flesh shrank from lying down again in the mud behind his gun, but he did, shivering. He heard the jaygee thud wearily into position, "What did you do to him?" he asked, "Is he dead?"

"Kicked him," the jaygee choked. "His head snapped back and there was that crack. I guess he's dead. I never heard of that broken-wing trick before, I guess he wanted to take one more with him. They have a kind of religion."

The jaygee sounded as though he was teetering on the edge of breakdown. Make him mad, intuition said to Orsino. He might go howling off among the trees unless he snaps out of it.

"It's a hell of way to run an island," he said nastily. "You beggars were chased out of North America because you couldn't run it right and now you can't even control a lousy little island for more than five miles inland." He added with deliberate, superior amusement, "Of course, they've got witches."

"Shut your mouth, gangster *I'm warning you.*" The note of hysteria was still there. And then the jaygee said dully, "I didn't mean that. I'm sorry. You did come out and help me after all."

"Surprised?"

"Yes. Twice. First time when you wanted to go out yourself, I suppose you can't help being born where you were. Maybe if you came over to us all the way, the Government would forgive and forget. But no—I suppose not," He paused, obviously casting about for a change of subject. He still seemed sublimely confident that they'd get back to the naval base with him in charge of the detail. "What ship did you cross in?"

"Atom sub *Taft,*" Orsino said. He could have bitten his tongue out.

'Taft? That's my father's pigboat! Captain Van Dellen. How is he? I was going down to the dock when—"

"He's dead," Orsino said flatly. "He was caught on deck during an emergency dive."

The jaygee said nothing for a while and then uttered an unconvincing laugh of disbelief. "You're lying," he said. "His crew'd never let that happen. They'd let the ship be blown to hell before they took her down without the skipper."

"Grinnel had the con. He ordered the dive and roared down the crew when they wanted to get your father inboard. I'm sorry."

"Grinnel," the jaygee whispered, "Grinnel. Yes, I know Commander Grinnel. He's—he's a good officer. He must have done it because he had to. Tell me about it, please."

It was more than Orsino could bear. "Your father was murdered," he said harshly. "I know because Grinnel put me on radar watch—and I don't know a damned thing about reading a radarscope. He told me to sing out 'enemy planes' and I did because I didn't know what the hell was going on. He used that as an excuse to crash-dive while your father was sleeping on deck. Your good officer murdered him."

He heard the jaygee sobbing hoarsely. At last he asked Orsino in a dry, choked voice, "Politics?"

"Politics," Orsino said.

Orsino jumped wildly as the jaygee's machine gun began to roar a long burst of twenty, but he didn't fire himself. He knew that there was no enemy out there in the dark, and that the bullets were aimed only at an absent phantom.

"We've got to get to Iceland," the jaygee said at last, soberly, "It's our only chance."

"Iceland?"

"This is one for the C.C. of the Constitutionists. The Central Committee. It's a breach of the Freiberg Compromise. It means we call the Sociocrats, and if they don't make full restitution—war."

"What do you mean, we?"

"You and I. You're the source of the story—you're the one who'd be lie-tested."

You've got him, Orsino told himself, but don't be fool enough to count on it. He's been lightheaded from hunger and no sleep and the shock of his father's death. You helped him in a death struggle and there's team spirit working on him. The guy covering my back, how can I fail to trust him, how could I dare not to trust him? But don't be fool enough to count on it after he's slept. Meanwhile, push it for all it's worth.

"What are your plans?" he asked gravely.

"We've got to slip out of Ireland by sub or plane;" the jaygee brooded. "We can't go to the New Portsmouth or Com-Surf organizations; they're Sociocrat, and Grinnel will have passed the word to the Sociocrats that you're out of control."

"What does that mean?"

"Death," the jaygee said.

CHAPTER TWELVE

Commander Grinnel, after reporting formally, had gone straight to a joint. It wasn't until midnight that he got the word, from a friendly O.N.I. lieutenant who had dropped into the house.

"What?" Grinnel roared, "Who is this woman? Where is she? Take me to her at once!"

"Commander!" the lieutenant said aghast. "I just got here!"

"You heard me, mister! At once!"

While Grinnel dressed he demanded particulars. The lieutenant dutifully scoured his memory. "Brought in on some cloak-and-dagger deal, Commander. The kind you usually run. Lieutenant-Commander Jacobi was in Syndic Territory on a recruiting, sabotage and reconnaissance mission and one of the D.A.R. passed the girl on to him. A real Syndic member—priceless. And, as I said, she identified this fellow as Charles Orsino, another Syndic. Why are you so interested, if I may ask?"

The Commander dearly wanted to say to him grimly, "You may not," but he didn't dare. Now was the time to be frank and open. One hint that he had anything to hide or cover up would put his throat to the knife. "The man's my baby, lieutenant," he said. "Either your girl's mistaken or Van Dellen and his polygraph tech and I were taken in by a brand-new technique." *That* was nice work, he congratulated himself. Got in Van Dellen and the tech. Maybe, come to think of it, the tech was crooked? No—there was the way Wyman had responded perfectly under scop.

O.N.I.'s building was two stories and an attic, wood-framed, beginning to rot already in the eternal Irish damp.

"We've got her on the third floor, Commander," the lieutenant said, "You get there by a ladder."

"In God's name, why?" They walked past the Charge of Quarters, who snapped to a guilty and belated attention, and through the deserted offices of the first and second floors.

"Frankly, we've had a little trouble hanging on to her."

"She runs away?"

"No, nothing like that—not yet, at least. Marine G-2 and Guard Intelligence School have both tried to snatch her from us. First with requisitions, then with muscle. We hope to keep her until the word gets to Iceland. Then, naturally, we'll be out in the cold."

The lieutenant laughed. Grinnel, puffing up the ladder, did not.

The door and lock on Lee Bennet's quarters were impressive. The lieutenant rapped. "Are you awake, Lee? There's an officer here who wants to talk to you."

"Come in," she said.

The lieutenant's hands flew over the lock and the door sprang open. The girl was sitting in the dark.

"I'm Commander Grinnel, my dear," he said. After eight hours in the joint, he could feel authentically fatherly to her. "If the time isn't quite convenient—"

"It's all right," she said listlessly. "What do you want to know?"

"The man you identify as Orsino—it was quite a shock to me. Commander Van Dellen, who died a hero's death only days ago accepted him as authentic and so, I must admit, did I. He passed both scop and polygraph."

"I can't help that," she said. "He came right up to me and told me who he was. I recognized him, of course. He's a polo player. I've seen him play on Long Island often enough, the damned snob. He's not much in the Syndic, but he's close to F. W. Taylor. Orsino's an orphan. I don't know whether Taylor's actually adopted him or not, I think not."

"No—possible—mistake?"

"No possible mistake." She began to tremble. "My God, Commander Whoever-You-Are, do you think I could forget one of those damned sneering faces. Or what those people did to me? Get the lie detector again! Strap me into the lie detector! I insist on it! I won't be called a liar! Do you hear me? Get the lie detector!"

"Please," the Commander soothed. "I do believe you, my dear. Nobody could doubt your sincerity. Thank you for helping us, and good night," He backed out of the room with the lieutenant. As the door closed he snapped at him, "Well, mister?"

The lieutenant shrugged. "The lie detector always bears her out. We've stopped using it on her. We're convinced that she's on our side. Almost deserving of citizenship."

"Come, now," the Commander said. "You know better than that."

Behind the locked door, Lee Bennet had thrown herself on the bed, dry-eyed. She wished she could cry, but tears never came. Not since those three roistering drunkards had demonstrated their 'virility' as males and their immunity as Syndics on her...she couldn't cry any more.

Charles Orsino—another one of them. She hoped they caught him and killed him, slowly. She knew all this was true. Then why did she feel like a murderess? Why did she think incessantly of suicide? Why, why, why?

Dawn came imperceptibly. First Charles could discern the outline of treetops against the sky and then a little of the terrain before him and at last two twisted shadows that slowly became sprawling half-naked bodies. One of them was a woman's, mangled by fifty-caliber slugs. The other was the body of a bearded giant—the one with whom they had struggled in the dark.

Charles crawled out stiffly. The woman was—had been—a stringy, white haired crone. Some animal's skull was tied to her pate with sinews as a headdress, and she was tattoed with blue crescents. The jaygee joined him standing over her and said, "One of their witches. Part of the religion, if you can call it that."

"A brand-new religion?" Charles asked dubiously, "Made up out of whole cloth?"

"No," the jaygee said. "I understand it's an *old* religion—pre-Christian. It kept going underground until the time of the Troubles. Then it flared up again all over Europe. A filthy business. Animal sacrifices every new moon. Human sacrifices twice a year. What can you expect from people like that?"

Charles reminded himself that the jaygee's fellow-citizens boiled recalcitrant slaves. "I'll see what I can do about the jeep," he said.

The jaygee sat down on the wet grass. "What the hell's the use?" he mumbled wearily. "Even if you get it running again. Even if we get back to the base. They'll be gunning for you.

Maybe they'll be gunning for me if they killed my father." He tried to smile. "You got any aces in the hole, gangster?"

"Maybe," Orsino said slowly. "What do you know about a woman named Lee—Bennet? Works with O.N.I.?"

"Smuggled over here by the D.A.R. A gold mine of information. She's a little nuts, too. What have you got on her?"

"Does she swing any weight? *Is she a citizen?*"

"No weight. They're just using her over at Intelligence to fill out the picture of the Syndic. And she couldn't be a citizen. A woman has to marry a citizen to be naturalized. What have you got to do with her for heaven's sake? Did you know her on the other side? She's death to the Syndic; she can't do anything for you."

Charles barely heard him. That had to be it. The trigger on Lee Falcaro's conditioning had to be the oath of citizenship as it was for his. And it hadn't been tripped because this pirate gang didn't particularly want or need women as first-class, all-privileges citizens. A small part of the Government's cultural complex—but one that could trap Lee Falcaro forever in the shell of her synthetic substitute for a personality. Lie-tests, yes. Scopolamine, yes. But for a woman, no subsequent oath.

"I ran into her in New Portsmouth. She knew me from the other side. She turned me in…" He knelt at a puddle and drank thirstily; the water eased hunger cramps a little. "I'll see what I can do with the jeep."

He lifted the hood and stole a look at the jaygee. Van Dellen was dropping off to sleep on the wet grass. Charles pried a shear pin from the jeep's winch, punched out the shear pin that had given way in the transmission and replaced it. It involved some hammering. Cracked block, he thought contemptuously. An officer and he couldn't tell whether the block was cracked or not. If I ever get out of this we'll sweep them from the face of the earth—or more likely just get rid of their tom-fool Sociocrats and Constitutionists. The rest are probably all right. Except maybe for those Guardsmen. A bad lot. Let's hope they get killed in the fighting.

The small of his back tickled; he reached around to scratch it and felt cold metal.

"Turn slowly or you'll be spitted like a pig;" a voice growled.

He turned slowly. The cold metal now at his chest, was the leaf-shaped blade of a spear. It was wielded by a red-haired, red-bearded, barrel-chested giant whose blue-green eyes were as cold as death.

"Tie that one," somebody said. Another half-naked man jerked his wrists behind him and lashed them together with cords.

"Hobble his feet." It was a woman's voice. A length of cord or sinew was knotted to his ankles with a foot or two of play. He could walk but not run. The giant lowered his spear and stepped aside.

The first thing Charles saw was that Lieutenant (j.g.) Van Dellen of the North American Navy had escaped forever from his doubts and confusions. They had skewered him to the turf while he slept. Charles hoped he had not felt the blow.

The second thing he saw was a supple and coltish girl of perhaps 20 tenderly removing the animal skull from the head of the slain witch and knotting it to her own red-tressed head. Even to Orsino's numbed understanding, it was clearly an act of the highest significance. It subtly changed the composition of the six-man group in the little glade. They had been a small mob until she put on the skull, but the moment she did they moved instinctively—one a step or two, the other merely turning a bit, perhaps—to orient on her. There was no doubt that she was in charge.

A witch, Orsino thought. It *kept going underground until the Troubles. A filthy business—human sacrifices twice a year.*

She approached him and, like the shifting of a kaleidoscope, the group fell into a new pattern of which she was still the focus. Charles thought he had never seen a face so humorlessly conscious of power. The petty ruler of a few barbarians, she carried herself as though she were empress of the universe. Nor did a large gray louse that crawled from her hairline across her forehead and back again affect her in the slightest. She wore a greasy animal hide as though it was royal purple. It added up to either insanity or a limitless pretension to religious authority. And her eyes were not mad.

"You," she said coldly. "What about the jeep and the guns? Do they go?"

He laughed suddenly and idiotically at these words from the

mouth of a stone-age goddess. A raised spear sobered him instantly. "Yes," he said.

"Show my men how," she said, and squatted regally on the turf.

"Please," he said, "could I have something to eat first?"

She nodded indifferently and one of the men loped off into the brush.

His hands untied and his face greasy with venison fat, Charles spent the daylight hours instructing six savages in the nomenclature, maintenance and operation of the jeep and the twin-fifty machine gun.

They absorbed it with utter lack of curiosity. They more or less learned to start and steer and stop the jeep. They more or less learned to load, point and fire the gun.

Through the lessons the girl sat absolutely motionless, first in shadow, then in noon and afternoon sun and then in shadow again. But she had been listening. She said at last, "You are telling them nothing new now. Is there no more?"

Charles noted that a spear was poised at his ribs. "A great deal more," he said hastily. "It takes months."

"They can work them now. What more is there to learn?"

"Well, what to do if something goes wrong."

She said, as though speaking from vast experience, "When something goes wrong, you start over again. That is all you can do. When I make death-wine for the spear blades and the death-wine does not kill, it is because something went wrong—a word or a sign or picking a plant at the wrong time. The only thing to do is make the poison again. As you grow in experience you make fewer mistakes. That is how it will be with my men when they work the jeep and the guns."

She nodded ever so slightly at one of the men and he took a firmer grip on his spear.

Death swooped low.

"No!" Charles exploded, "You don't understand! This isn't like anything you do at all!" He was sweating, even in the late afternoon chill. "You've got to have somebody who knows how to repair the jeep and the gun. If they're busted they're busted and no amount of starting over again will make them work!"

She nodded and said, "Tie his hands. We'll take him with us." Charles was torn between relief and wonder at the way she spoke. He realized that he had never, literally *never*, seen any person concede a point in quite that fashion. There had been no hesitation, there had been no reluctance in the voice, not a flicker of displeasure in the face. Simply, without forcing, she had said, "We'll take him with us." It was as though—as though she had remade the immediate past, un-making her opposition to the idea, nullifying it. She was a person who was not at war with herself in any respect whatever, a person who knew exactly who she was and what she was—

The girl rose in a single flowing motion, startling after her day spent in immobility. She led the way, flanked by two of the spearmen. The other four followed in the jeep, at a crawl. Last of all came Charles, and nobody had to urge him. In his portable trap his hours would be numbered if he got separated from his captors.

Stick with them, he told himself, stumbling through the brush. Just stay alive and you can outsmart these savages. He fell, cursed, picked himself up stumbled on after the growl of the jeep.

Dawn brought them to a collection of mud-and-wattle huts, a corral enclosing a few dozen head of wretched diseased cattle, a few adults and a few children. The girl was still clear-eyed and supple in her movements. Her spearmen yawned and stretched stiffly. Charles was a walking dead man, battered by countless trees and stumbles on the long trek. With red and swollen eyes he watched while half-naked brats swarmed over the jeep and grownups made obeisances to the girl—all but one.

This was an evil-faced harridan who said to her with cool insolence, "I see you claim the power of the goddess now, my dear. Has something happened to my sister?"

"The guns killed a certain person. I put on the skull. You know what I am; do not say 'claim to be'. I warn you once."

"Liar!" shrieked the harridan. "You killed her and stole the skull! St. Patrick and St. Bridget shrivel your guts! Abaddon and Lucifer pierce your eyes!"

An arena formed about them as the girl said coldly, "I warn you the second time."

The harridan made signs with her fingers, glaring at her; there was a moan from the watchers; some turned aside and a half-grown girl fainted dead away.

The girl with the skull on her pate said, as though speaking from a million years and miles away, "This is the third warning; there are no more. Now the worm is in your backbone gnawing. Now the maggots are at your eyes, devouring them. Your bowels turn to water; your heart pounds like the heart of a bird; soon it will not beat at all." As the eerie, space-filling whisper drilled on, the watchers broke and ran, holding their hands over their ears, white-faced, but the harridan stood as if rooted to the earth. Charles listened dully as the curse was droned, nor was he surprised when the harridan fell, blasted by it. Another sorceress, aided it is true by Pentothal, had months ago done the same to him.

The people trickled back, muttering and abject.

Just stay alive and you can outsmart these savages, he repeated ironically to himself. It had dawned on him that these savages lived by an obscure and complicated code harder to master than the intricacies of the Syndic or the Government.

A kick roused him to his feet. One of the spearmen grunted, "I'm putting you with Kennedy."

"All right," Charles groaned. "You take these cords off me?"

"Later." He prodded Charles to a minute, ugly blockhouse of logs from which came smoke and an irregular metallic clanging. He cut the cords, rolled great boulders away from a crawl-hole and shoved him through.

The place was about six by nine feet, hemmed in by ten-inch logs. The light was very bad and the smell was too. A few loop-holes let in some air. There was a latrine pit and an open stone hearth and a naked brown man with wild hair and a beard.

Rubbing his wrists, Charles asked uncertainly, "Are you Kennedy?"

The man looked up and croaked, "Are you from the Government?"

"Yes," Charles said, hope rekindling. "Thank God they put us together. There's a jeep. Also a twin-fifty. If we play this right the two of us can bust out—"

He stopped, disconcerted. Kennedy had turned to the hearth

and the small, fierce fire glowing on it and began to pound a red-hot lump of metal. There were spearheads and arrowheads about in various stages of completion, as well as files and a hone.

"What's the matter?" he demanded. "Aren't you interested?"

"Of course I'm interested," Kennedy said. "But we've got to begin at the beginning. You're too *general.*" His voice was mild, but reproving.

"You're right," Charles said. "I guess you've made a try or two yourself. But now that there are two of us, what do you suggest? Can you drive a jeep? Can you fire a twin-fifty?"

The man poked the lump of metal into the heart of the fire again, picked up a black-scaled spearhead and began to file an edge into it. "Let's get down to essentials," he suggested apologetically. "What is escape? Getting from an undesirable place to a desirable place, opposing and neutralizing things or persons adverse to the change of state in the process. But I'm not being specific, am I? Let's say, then, escape is getting *us* from a relatively undesirable place to a relatively desirable place, opposing and neutralizing the aborigines." He put aside the file and reached for the hone, sleeking it along the bright metal ribbon of the new edge. He look-ed up with a pleased smile and asked, "How's that for a plan?"

"Fine," Charles muttered. Kennedy beamed proudly as he repeated, "Fine, fine," and sank to the ground, born down by the almost physical weight of his depression. His hoped-for ally was stark mad.

CHAPTER THIRTEEN

Kennedy turned out to have been an armorer-artificer of the North American Navy, captured two years ago while deer hunting too far from the logging-camp road to New Portsmouth. Fed on scraps of gristle, isolated from his kind, beaten when he failed to make his daily task of spear heads and arrow points, he had shyly retreated into beautifully interminable labyrinths of abstraction. Now and then, Charles Orsino got a word or two of sense from him before the rosy clouds closed in. When attempted conversation with the lunatic palled, Charles could watch the aborigines through chinks in the palisade. There were about fifty of them. There would have been more if they hadn't been given to infanticide—for what reason, Charles could not guess.

He had been there a week when the boulders were rolled away one morning and he was roughly called out. He said to Kennedy before stooping to crawl through the hole, "Take it easy, friend. I'll be back, I hope."

Kennedy looked up with a puzzled smile, "That's such a *general* statement, Charles. Exactly what are you implying—"

The witch girl was there, flanked by spearmen. She said abruptly, "I have been listening to you. Why are you untrue to your brothers?"

He gawked. The only thing that seemed to fit was: "That's such a *general* statement," but he didn't say it.

"Answer," one of the spearmen growled.

"I—I don't understand. I have no brothers."

"Your brothers in Portsmouth, on the sea. Whatever you call them, they are your brothers, all children of the mother called Government. Why are you untrue to them?"

He began to understand. "They aren't my brothers. I'm not a child of the government. I'm a child of another mother far away, called Syndic."

She looked puzzled—and almost human—for an instant. Then the visor dropped over her face again as she said, "That is true. Now you must teach a certain person the jeep and the guns. Teach her well. See that she gets her hands on the metal and into the grease." To a spearman she said, "Bring Martha."

The spearman brought Martha, who was trying not to cry. She was a half-naked child of ten!

The witch girl abruptly left them. Her guards took Martha and bewildered Charles to the edge of the village where the jeep and its mounted guns stood behind a silly little museum exhibit rope of vine. Feathers and bones were knotted into the vine. The spearmen treated it as though it were a high-tension transmission line.

"*You* break it," one of them said to Charles. He did, and the spearmen sighed with relief. Martha stopped scowling and stared.

The spearman said to Charles, "Go ahead and teach her. The firing pins are out of the guns, and if you try to start the jeep you get a spear through you. Now teach her." He and the rest squatted on the turf around the jeep. The little girl shied violently as he took her hand and tried to run away. One of the spearmen slung her back into the circle. She brushed against the jeep and froze, white-faced.

"Martha," Charles said patiently, "there's nothing to be afraid of. The guns won't go off and the jeep won't move. I'll teach you how to work them so you can kill everybody you don't like with the guns and go faster than a deer in the jeep—"

He was talking into empty air as far as the child was concerned. She was muttering, staring at the arm that had brushed the jeep. She said, "That did it, I guess. There goes the power. May the goddess blast her—no. The power's out of me now. I felt it go." She looked up at Charles, quite calmly, and said, "Go on. Show me all about it. Do a good job."

"Martha, what are you talking about?"

"She was afraid of me, my sister, so she's robbing me of the power. Don't you know? I guess not. The goddess hates iron and machines. I had the power of the goddess in me, but it's gone now; I felt it go. Now nobody'll be afraid of me any more." Her face contorted and she said, "Show me how you work the guns."

He taught her what he could while the circle of spearmen looked on and grinned, cracking raw jokes about the child as anybody anywhere would about a tyrant deposed. She pretended to ignore them, grimly repeating names after him and imitating his practiced movements in loading drill. She was very bright, Charles realized. When he got a chance he muttered, "I'm sorry about this, Martha. It isn't my idea."

She whispered bleakly, "I know. I liked you. I was sorry when the other outsider took your dinner." She began to sob uncontrollably. "I'll never see anything again! Nobody'll ever be afraid of me again!" She buried her face against Charles' shoulder.

He smoothed her tangled hair mechanically and said to the watching, grinning circle, "Look; hasn't this gone far enough? Haven't you got what you wanted?"

The headman stretched and spat. "Guess so," he said. "Come on, girl." He yanked Martha from the seat and booted her toward the huts.

Charles scrambled down just ahead of a spear. He let himself be led back to the smithy blockhouse and shoved through the crawl hole.

"I was thinking about what you said the other day," Kennedy beamed, rasping a file over an arrowhead. "When I said that to change one molecule in the past you'd have to change every molecule in the past, and you said, 'Maybe so.' I've figured that what you were driving at was—"

"Kennedy," Charles said, "please shut up just this once. I've got to think."

"In what sense do you mean that, Charles? Do you mean that you're a rational animal and therefore that your *being* rather than *essence* is—"

"*Shut up or I'll pick up a rock and bust your head in with it!*" Charles roared. He more than half meant it. Kennedy hunched down before his hearth looking offended and scared. Charles squatted with his head in his hands.

I have been listening to you.

Repeated drives of the Government to wipe out the aborigines. Drives that never succeeded.

I'll never see anything again.

The way the witch girl had blasted her rival—but that was suggestion. But—

I have been listening to you. Why are you untrue to your brothers?

He'd said nothing like that to anybody, not to her or poor Kennedy.

He thought vaguely of *psi* force, a fragment in his memory. An old superstition, like the id-ego-superego triad of the sick-minded psychologists. Like vectors of the mind, exploded nonsense. But—

I have been listening to you. Why are you untrue to your brothers?

Charles smacked one fist against the sand floor in impotent rage. He was going as crazy as Kennedy. Did the witch girl—and Martha—have hereditary *psi* power? He mocked himself savagely—that's such a *general* question!

Neurotic adolescent girls in kerosene-lit farmhouses, he thought vaguely. Things that go bump—and crash and blooie and *whoo-oo-oo!* in the night. Not in electric lit city apartments. Not around fleshed-up middle-aged men and women. You take a hyperthyroid virgin, isolate her from power machinery and electric fields, put on the pressures that make her feel alone and tense to the bursting point—and naturally enough, something bursts. A chamberpot sails from under the bed and shatters on the skull of stepfather-tyrant. The wide-gilt-framed portrait of thundergod-grandfather falls with a crash. Sure, the nail crystallized and broke—*who crystallized?*

Neurotic adolescent girls speaking in tongues, reading face-down cards and closed books, screaming aloud when sister or mother dies in a railroad wreck fifty miles away, of cancer a hundred miles away, in a bombing overseas.

Sometimes they made saints of them. Sometimes they burned them. Burned them and *then* made saints of them.

A blood-raw hunk of venison came sailing through one of the loopholes and flopped on the sand.

I was sorry when the other outsider took your dinner.

Three days ago he'd dozed off while Kennedy broiled the meat over the hearth. When he woke, Kennedy had gobbled it all and was whimpering with apprehension. But he'd done nothing and said nothing; the man wasn't responsible. He'd said nothing, and yet somehow the child knew about it.

His days were numbered; soon enough the jeep would be out of gas and the guns would be out of ammo or an unreplaceable part lost or broken. Then, according to the serene logic that ruled the witch girl, he'd be surplus.

But there was a key to it somehow.

He got up and slapped Kennedy's hand away from the venison. "Naughty," he said, and divided it equally with a broad spear blade.

"Naughty," Kennedy said morosely. "The naught-class, the null-class. I'm the null-class. I plus the universe equal one, the universe-class. If you could transpose—but you can't transpose." Silently they toasted their venison over the fire.

It was a moonless night with one great planet, Jupiter he supposed, reigning over the star powdered sky. Kennedy slept muttering feebly in a corner. The hearthfire was out. It had to be out by dark. The spearmen took no chance of their trying to burn down the place. The village had long since gone to sleep, campfires doused, skin flaps pulled to across the door holes. From the corral one of the spavined, tick-ridden cows mooed uneasily and then fell silent.

Charles then began the hardest job of his life. He tried to think, straight and uninterrupted, of Martha, the little girl. Some of the things that interrupted him were:

The remembered smell of fried onions; they didn't have onions here;

Salt;

I wonder how the old 101st Precinct's getting along;

That fellow who wanted to get married on a hundred dollars;

Lee Falcaro, damn her!

This is damn foolishness; it can't possibly work;

Poor old Kennedy;

I'll starve before I eat another mouthful of that greasy deer-meat;

The Van Dellen kid, I wonder if I could have saved him;

Reiner's right; we've got to clean up the Government and then try to civilize these people;

There must be something wrong with my head, I can't seem to concentrate;

That terrific third-chukker play in the Finals, my picture all over town;

Would Uncle Frank laugh at this?

It was hopeless. He sat bolt upright, his eyes squeezed tensely together, trying to visualize the child and call her and it couldn't be done. Skittering images of her zipped through his mind, only to be shoved aside. It was damn foolishness, anyway...

He unkinked himself, stretched and lay down on the sand floor thinking bitterly...*why try?* You'll be dead in a few days or a few weeks; kiss the world goodbye. Back in Syndic Territory, fat, sloppy, happy Syndic Territory, did they know how good they had it? He wished he could tell them to cling to their good life. But

Uncle Frank said it didn't do any good to cling; it was a matter of tension and relaxation. When you stiffen up a way of life and try to fossilize it so it'll stay that way forever, then you find you've lost it.

Little Martha wouldn't understand it. Magic, ritual, the power of the goddess, fear of iron, fear of the jeep's vine enclosure—cursed, no doubt—what went on in such a mind? Could she throw things like a poltergeist-girl? They didn't have 'em any more; maybe it had something to do with electric fields or even iron. Or were they all phonies? An upset adolescent girl is a hell of a lot likelier to fake phenomena that produce them. Little Martha hadn't been faking her despair, though. The witch-girl (her sister, wasn't she?) didn't fake her icy calm and power. Martha'd be better off without such stuff—

"Charles," a whisper said.

He muttered stupidly, "My God. She heard me," and crept to the palisade. Through a chink between the logs she was just visible in the starlight.

She whispered, "I thought I wasn't going to see anything or hear anything ever again but I sat up and I heard you calling and you said you wanted to help me if I'd help you so I came as fast as I could without waking anybody up—you *did* call me, didn't you?"

"Yes, I did. Martha, do you want to get out of here? Go far away with me?"

"You bet I do. *She's* going to take the power of the goddess out of me and marry me to Dinny, he stinks like a goat and he has a cockeye, and then she'll kill all our babies. Just tell me what to do and I'll do it." She sounded very grim and decided.

"Can you roll the boulders away from the hole there?" He was thinking vaguely of teleportation; each boulder was a two-man job."

She said no.

He snarled, "Then why did you bother to come here?"

"Don't talk like that to me," the child said sharply—and he remembered what she thought she was.

"Sorry," he said.

"What I came about," she said calmly, "was the explosion. Can you make an explosion like you said? Back there at the jeep?"

What in God's name was she talking about?

"Back there," she said with exaggerated patience, "You was thinking about putting all the cartridges together and blowing up the whole damn shebang. Remember?"

He did, vaguely. One of a hundred schemes that had drifted through his head.

"I'd sure like to see that explosion," she said. "The way she got things figured, I'd almost just as soon get exploded myself as not."

"I might blow up the logs here and get out," he said slowly. "I think you'd be a mighty handy person to have along, too. Can you get me about a hundred of the machine gun cartridges?"

"They'll miss 'em."

"Sneak me a few at a time. I'll empty them, put them together again and you sneak them back."

She said, slow and troubled, "*She* set the power of the goddess to guard them."

"Listen to me, Martha," he said. "I mean *listen.* You'll be doing it for me and they told me the power of the goddess doesn't work on outsiders. Isn't that right?"

There was a long pause, and she said at last with a sigh, "I sure wish I could see your eyes, Charles. I'll try it, but I'm damned if I would if Dinny didn't stink so bad." She slipped away and Charles tried to follow her with his mind through the darkness, to the silly little rope of vine with the feathers and bones knotted in it—but he couldn't. Too tense again.

Kennedy stirred and muttered complainingly as an icy small breeze cut through the chinks of the palisade, whispering.

His eyes, tuned to the starlight, picked up Martha bent almost double, creeping toward the smithy-prison. She wore a belt of fifty-caliber cartridges around her neck like a stole. Looked like about a dozen of them. He hastily scooped out a bowl of clean sand and whispered, "Any trouble?"

He couldn't see the grin on her face, but knew it was there. "It was easy," she bragged. "One bad minute and then I checked with you and it was okay."

"Good kid. Pull the cartridges out of the links the way I showed you and pass them through."

She did. It was a tight squeeze.

He fingered one of the cartridges. The bullet fitted nicely into the socket of an arrowhead. He jammed the bullet in and wrenched at the arrowhead with thumb and forefinger—all he could get onto it. The brass neck began to spread. He dumped the powder into his little basin in the sand and reseated the bullet.

Charles shifted hands on the second cartridge. On the third he realized that he could put the point of the bullet on a hearthstone and press on the neck with both thumbs. It went faster then; in perhaps an hour he was passing the reassembled cartridges back through the palisade.

"Time for another load?" he asked.

"Nope," the girl said. "Tomorrow night."

"Good kid."

She giggled. "It's going to be a hell of a big bang, ain't it, Charles?"

CHAPTER FOURTEEN

"Leave the fire alone," Charles said sharply to Kennedy. The little man was going to douse it for the night.

There was a flash of terrified sense: "They beat you. If the fire's on after dark they beat you. Fire and dark are equal and opposite." He began to smile. "Fire is the negative of dark. You just change the sign, in effect rotate it through 180 degrees. But to rotate it through 180 degrees you have to first rotate it through one degree. And to rotate it through one degree you first have to rotate it through half a degree." He was beaming now, having forgotten all about the fire. Charles banked it with utmost care, heaping a couple of flat stones for a chimney that would preserve the life of one glowing coal invisibly.

He stretched out on the sand, one hand on the little heap beneath which five pounds of smokeless powder was buried, Kennedy continued to drone out his power-series happily.

Through the chinks in the palisade a man's profile showed, against the twilight. "Shut up," he said.

Kennedy, shivering, rolled over and muttered to himself. The spearman laughed and went on.

Charles hardly saw him. His whole mind was concentrated on the spark beneath the improvised chimney. He had left such a spark seven nights running. Only twice had it lived more than an hour. Tonight—tonight, it had to last. Tonight was the last night of the witch-girl's monthly courses, and during them she lost —or thought she lost, which was the same thing—the power of the goddess.

Primitive aborigines, he jeered silently at himself. A lifetime wasn't long enough to learn the intricacies of their culture—as occasional executions among them for violating magical law proved to the hilt. His first crude notion—blowing the palisade apart and running like hell was replaced by a complex escape plan hammered out in detail between him and Martha.

Martha assured him that the witch girl could track him through the dark by the power of the goddess except for four days a month—and he believed it. Martha herself laid a matter-of-fact claim to keener second sight than her sister because of her virginity. With Martha to guide him through the night and the witch-girl's power disabled, they'd get a day's head start. His hand strayed to a pebble under which jerked venison was hidden and ready.

"But Martha. Are you sure you're not—not kidding yourself? Are you *sure?*"

He felt her grin on the other side of the palisade. "You're sure wishing Uncle Frank was here so you could ask him about it, don't you, Charles?"

He sure was. He wiped his brow, suddenly clammy.

Kennedy couldn't come along. One, he wasn't responsible. Two, he might have to be Charles' cover story. They weren't too dissimilar in build, age, or coloring. Charles had a beard by now that sufficiently obscured his features, and two years absence should have softened recollections of Kennedy. Interrogated, Charles could take refuge in an imitation of Kennedy's lunacy.

"Charles, the one thing I don't get is this Lee dame. She got a spell on her? You don't want to mess with that."

"Listen, Martha, we've *got* to mess with her. It isn't a spell— exactly. Anyway I know how to take it off and then she'll be on our side."

"Can I set off the explosion? If you let me set off the explosion, I'll quit my bitching."

"We'll see," he said.

She chuckled very faintly in the dark. "Okay," she told him, "If I can't, I can't."

He thought of being married to a woman who could spot your smallest lie or reservation, and shuddered.

Kennedy was snoring by now and twilight was deepening into blackness. There was a quarter-moon, obscured by overcast. He hitched along the sand and peered through a chink at a tiny noise. It was the small scuffling feet of a woods-rat racing through the grass from one morsel of food to the next. It never reached it. There was a soft rush of wings as a great dark owl plummeted to earth and struck talons into the brown fur. The rat squealed its life away while the owl lofted silently to a tree branch where it stood on one leg, swaying drunkenly and staring with huge yellow eyes.

As sudden as that, it'll be. Charles thought abruptly weighted with despair. A half-crazy kid and yours truly trying to outsmart and out-Tarzan these wild men. If only the little dope would let me take the jeep! But the jeep was out. She rationalized her retention of the power even after handling iron by persuading herself that she was only acting for Charles; there was some obscure precedent in a long, memorized poem, which served her as a textbook of magic. But riding in the jeep was *out*.

By now she should be stringing magic vines across some of the huts and trails. "They'll see 'em when they get torches and it'll scare 'em. Of course I don't know how to do it right, but they don't know that. It'll slow 'em down. If *she* comes out of her house—and maybe she won't—she'll know they don't matter and send the men after us. But we'll be on our way. Charles, you sure I can't set off the explosion? Yeah, I guess you are. Maybe I can set off one when we get to New Portsmouth?"

"If I can possibly arrange it."

She sighed, "I guess that'll have to do."

It was too silent; he couldn't bear it. With feverish haste he uncovered the caches of powder and meat. Under the sand was a fat clayey soil. He dug up handfuls of it, wet it with the only liquid available and worked it into paste. He felt his way to the logs decided on for blasting, dug out a hole at their bases in the clay. After five careful trips from the powder cache to the hole, the mine was filled. He covered it with clay and laid on a roof of flat stones from the hearth. The spark of fire still glowed, and he nursed it with twigs.

She was there, whispering, "Charles?"

"Right here. Everything set?"

"All set. Let's have that explosion."

He took the remaining powder and with minute care, laid a train across the stockade to the mine. He crouched into a ball and flipped a burning twig onto the black line that crossed the white sand floor.

The blast seemed to wake up the world. Kennedy charged out of sleep, screaming, and a million birds woke with a squawk. Charles was conscious more of the choking reek than the noise as he scooped up the jerked venison and rushed through the ragged gap in the wall. A hand caught his—a small hand.

"You're groggy," Martha's voice said, sounding far away. "Come on—fast. *Man*…that was a great explosion!"

She towed him through the woods and underbrush—fast. As long as he hung on to her he didn't stumble or run into a tree once. Irrationally embarrassed by his dependence on a child, he tried letting go for a short time—very short—and was quickly battered into changing his mind. He thought dizzily of the spearmen trying to follow through the dark and could almost laugh again.

Their trek to the coast was marked by desperate speed. For twenty-four hours they stopped only to gnaw at their rations or snatch a drink at a stream. Charles kept moving because it was unendurable to let a ten-year-old girl exceed him in stamina. Both of them paid terribly for the murderous pace they kept. The child's face became skull-like and her eyes red; her lips dried and cracked. He gasped at her as they pulled their way up a bramble-covered 45-degree slope: "How do you do it? Isn't this ever going to end?"

"Ends soon," she croaked at him. "You know we dodged 'em three times?"

He could only shake his head. She stared at him with burning red eyes. "This ain't hard," she croaked. "You do this with a gut full of poison, *that's* hard."

"*Did* you?"

She grinned crookedly and chanted something he did not understand:

"Nine moons times thirteen is the daughter's age
"When she drinks the death-cup.
"Three leagues times three she must race and rage
"Down hills and up—"

She added matter-of-factly:

"Last year. Prove I have the power of the goddess. Run, climb, with your guts falling out. This year, starve for a week and run down a deer of seven points."

He had lost track of days and nights when they stood on the brow of a hill at dawn and looked over the sea. The girl gasped, "It's all right now. *She* wouldn't let them go on. She's a witch, but she's no fool." The child fell in her tracks. Charles, too tired for panic, slept too.

Charles woke with a wonderful smell in his nostrils. He followed it hungrily down the reverse slope of the hill to a grotto.

Martha was crouched over a fire on which rocks were heating. Beside it was a bark pot smeared with clay. As he watched, she lifted a red-hot rock with two green sticks and rolled it into the Pot. It boiled up and continued to boil for an astonishing number of minutes. That was the source of the smell.

"Breakfast?" he asked unbelievingly.

"Rabbit stew," she said. "Plenty of runways, plenty of bark, plenty of green branches. I made snares. Two tough old bucks cooking in there for an hour."

They chewed the meat from the bones in silence. She said at last, "We can't settle down here. Too near to the coast. And if we move further inland, there's *her*. And others. I been thinking." She spat a string of tough meat out. "There's England. Work our way around the coast. Make a raft or steal a canoe and cross the water. Then we could settle down. You can't have me for three times thirteen moons yet or I'd lose the power. But I guess we can wait. I heard about England and the English. They have no hearts left. We can take as many slaves as we want. They cry a lot but they don't fight. And none of their women has the power." She looked up anxiously. "You wouldn't want one of their women, would you? Not if you could have somebody with the power just by waiting for her?"

He looked down the hill and said slowly, "You know that's not what I had in mind, Martha. I have my own place with people far away. I want to get back there. I thought—I thought you'd like it too." Her face twisted. He couldn't bear to go on, not in words. "Look into my mind, Martha," he said. "Maybe you'll see what it means to me."

She stared long and deep. At last she rose, her face inscrutable, and spat into the fire. "Think I saved you for that?" she asked. "And for *her?* Not me. Save yourself from now on, mister. I'm going to beat my way south around the coast. England for me, and I don't want any part of you."

She strode off down the hill, gaunt and ragged, but with arrogance in her swinging, space-eating gait. Charles sat looking after her, stupefied, until she had melted into the underbrush. "Think I saved you for that? And for her?" She'd made some kind of mistake. He got up stiffly and ran after her, but he could not pick up an inch of her woods-wise trail. Charles slowly climbed to the grotto again and sat in its shelter.

He spent the morning trying to concoct simple springs out of bark strips and whippy branches. He got nowhere. The branches broke or wouldn't bend far enough. The bark shredded, or wouldn't hold a knot. Without metal, he couldn't shape the trigger to fit the bow so that it would be both sensitive and reliable.

At noon he drank enormously from a spring and looked morosely for plants that might be edible. He decided on something with a bulbous, onion-like root. For a couple of hours after that he propped rocks on sticks here and there. When he stepped back and surveyed them, he decided that any rabbit he caught with them would be, even for a rabbit, feeble-minded. He could think of nothing else to do.

First he felt a slight intestinal qualm and then a far from slight nausea. Then the root he had eaten took over with drastic thoroughness. He collapsed, retching, and only after the first spasms had passed was he able to crawl to the grotto. The shelter it offered was mostly psychological, but he had need of that. Under the ancient, mossy stones, he raved with delirium until dark.

Sometimes he was back in Syndic Territory, Charles Orsino of the two-goal handicap and the flashing smile. Sometimes he was back in the stinking blockhouse with Kennedy spinning interminable, excruciatingly boring strands of iridescent logic. Sometimes he was back in the psychology laboratory with the pendulum beating, the light blinking, the bell ringing and sense-impressions flooding him and drowning him with lies. Sometimes he raced in panic down the streets of New Portsmouth with sweatered Guardsmen pounding after him, their knives flashing fire.

But at last he was in the grotto again, with Martha sponging his head and cursing him in a low, fluent undertone for being seven times seven kinds of fool.

She said tartly, as recognition came into his eyes, "Yes, for the fifth time, I'm back. I should be making my way to England and a band of my own, but I'm back and I don't know why. I heard you in pain and I thought it served you right for not knowing deathroot when you see it, but I turned around and came back."

"Don't go," he said hoarsely.

She held a bark cup to his lips and made him choke down some nauseating brew. "Don't worry," she told him bitterly. "I won't go. I'll do everything you want, which shows that I'm as big a fool as you are, or bigger because I know better. I'll help you find her and take the spell off her. And may the goddess help me because I can't help myself."

"...things like sawed tree-trunks, shells you call them...a pile of them...he looks at them and he thinks they're going bad and they ought to be used soon...under a wooden roof they are...a thin man with death on his face and hate in his heart...he wears blue and gold...he sticks the gold, you call a coat's wrist the cuff, he sticks the cuff under the nose of a fellow and yells his hate out and the fellow feels ready to strangle on blood it's about a boat that sank this fellow, he's a fat little man and he kills and kills, he'd kill the man if he could..."

A picket boat steamed by the coast twice a day, north after dawn and south before sunset. They had to watch out for it; it swept the coast with powerful glasses.

"...it's the man with the bellyache again but now he's sleepy...he's cursing the skipper...sure there's nothing on the coast to trouble us...eight good men aboard and that one bastard of a skipper..."

Sometimes it jumped erratically, like an optical lever disturbed by the weight of a hair.

"...board over the door painted with a circle, a zigzag on its side, an up-and-down line...they call it office of intelligent navels...the lumber camp...machine goes chug-rip, chug-rip...and the place where they cut metal like wood on machines that spin around...a deathly-sick little fellow loaded down and chained...fell on his face, he can't get up, his bowels are water, his muscles are stiff, like dry branches and he's afraid...they curse him, they beat him, they take him to a machine that spins...*they...they—they—*"

She sat bolt upright, screaming. Her eyes didn't see Charles. He drew back one hand and slammed it across her cheek in a slap that reverberated like a pistol shot. Her head rocked to the blow and her eyes snapped back from infinity-focus.

She never told Charles what they had done to the sick slave in the machine shop, and he never asked her.

Without writing equipment Charles doubted profoundly that he'd be able to hang onto any of the material she supplied. He surprised himself; his memory developed with exercise.

The shadowy ranks of the New Portsmouth personnel became solider daily in his mind; the chronically-fatigued ordnance-man whose mainspring was to get by with the smallest possible effort; the sex-obsessed little man in Intelligence, who lived only for the brothels where he selected older women—women who looked like his mother; the human weasel in BuShips who was impotent in bed and a lacerating tyrant in the office; the admiral who knew he was dying and hated his juniors proportionally to their youth and health.

And—

"...this woman of yours...she ain't at home there...she ain't at...at home...*anywhere*...the fat man, the one that kills, he's talking to her but she isn't…yes she is…no she isn't—she's answering him, talking about over-the-sea…"

"Lee Falcaro," Charles whispered. "Lee Bennet."

The trance-frozen face didn't change; the eerie whisper went on without interruption: "…Lee Bennet on her lips, Lee Falcaro down deep in her guts…and the face of Charles Orsino down there too…"

An unexpected pang went through him.

He sorted and classified endlessly what he had learned. He formed and rejected a dozen plans. At last there was one he could not reject.

CHAPTER FIFTEEN

Commander Grinnel was officer of the day, and sore as a boil about it. O.N.I. wasn't supposed to catch the duty. You risked your life on cloak-and-dagger missions; let the shore-bound fancy dans do the drudgery. But there he was, nevertheless, in the guard house office with a .45 on his hip, the interminable night stretching before him, and the ten-man main guard snoring away outside.

He eased his bad military conscience by reflecting that there wasn't anything to guard, that patrolling the shore establishment was just worn out tradition. The ships and boats had their own watch. At the very furthest stretch of the imagination, a tarzan-type might sneak into town and try to steal some ammo. Well, if he got caught, he got caught. And if he didn't, who'd know the difference with the accounting as sloppy as it was here? They did things differently in Iceland.

They crept through the midnight dark of New Portsmouth's outskirts. As before, she led with her small hand. Lights flared on a wharf where perhaps a boat was being serviced. A slave screamed somewhere under the lash or worse.

"Here's the doss house," Martha whispered. It was smack between paydays—part of the plan—and the house was dark except for the hopefully lit parlor. They ducked down the alley that skirted it and around the back of Bachelor Officer Quarters. The sentry, if he were going his rounds at all, would be at the other end of his post when they passed—part of the plan.

Lee Falcaro was quartered alone in a locked room of the O.N.I. building. Martha had, from seventy miles away, frequently watched the lock being opened and closed.

They dove under the building's crumbling porch two minutes before a late crowd of drinkers roared down the street and emerged when they were safely gone. There was a charge of quarters, a little yeoman, snoozing under a dim light in the O.N.I. building's lobby.

"Anybody else?" Charles whispered edgily.

"No. Just her. She's asleep. Dreaming about—never mind. Come on Charles. He's out."

The little yeoman didn't stir as they passed him and crept up the stairs. Lee Falcaro's room was part of the third-floor attic, finished off specially. You reached it by a ladder from a second-floor one-man office.

The lock was an eight-button piccolo—very rare in New Portsmouth and presumably loot from the mainland. Charles' fingers flew over it: 1-7-5-4-, 2-2-7-3-, 8-2-6-6- and it flipped open silently.

But the door squeaked.

"She's waking up!" Martha hissed in the dark. "She'll yell!"

Charles reached the bed in two strides and clamped his hand over Lee Falcaro-Bennet's mouth. Only a feeble "mmm!" came out, but the girl thrashed violently in his grip.

"Shut up, lady!" Martha whispered. "Nobody's going to rape you."

There was an astonished "mmm?" and she subsided, trembling.

"Go ahead," Martha told him. "She won't yell."

He took his hand away nervously. "We've come to administer the oath of citizenship," he said.

The girl answered in the querulous voice that was hardly hers, "You picked a strange time for it. Who are you? What's all the whispering for?"

He improvised. "I'm Commander Lister. Just in from Iceland aboard atom sub *Taft*. They didn't tell you in case it got turned down, but I was sent for authorization to give you citizenship. You know how unusual it is for a woman."

"Who's this child? And why did you get me up in the dead of night?"

He dipped deeply into Martha's probings of the past week. "Citizenship'll make the Guard Intelligence gang think twice before they try to grab you again. Naturally they'd try to block us if we administered the oath in public. Ready?"

"Dramatic," she sneered. "Oh, I suppose so. Get it over with."

"Do you, Lee Bennet, solemnly renounce all allegiances previously held by you and pledge your allegiance to the North American Government?"

"I do," she said.

There was a choked little cry from Martha. "Hell's fire," she said. "Like breaking a leg!"

"What are you talking about, little girl?" Lee asked, coldly alert.

"It's all right," Charles said wearily. "Don't you know my voice? I'm Orsino. You turned me in back there because they don't give citizenship to women and so your de-conditioning didn't get triggered off. I managed to break for the woods. A bunch of natives got me. I busted loose with the help of Martha here. Among her other talents, the kid's a mind reader. I remember the triggering shocked me out of a year's growth; how do you feel?"

Lee was silent, but Martha answered in a voice half-puzzled and half-contemptuous, "She feels fine, but she's crying."

"Am not," Lee Falcaro gulped.

Charles turned from her, embarrassed. In a voice that strove to be normal, he whispered to Martha, "What about the boat?"

"Still there," she said.

Lee Falcaro said tremulously, "Wh—wh—what boat?"

"Martha's staked out a reactor-driven patrol speedboat at a wharf. One guard aboard. She watched it in operation and I have some small-boat time. I really think we can grab it. If we get a good head start, they don't have anything based here that'll catch up with it. If we get a break on the weather, their planes won't be able to pick us up."

Lee Falcaro stood up, dashing tears from her eyes. "Then let's go," she said evenly.

"How's the C.Q.—that man downstairs, Martha?"

"Still sleepin'. The way's as clear now as it'll ever be."

They closed the door behind them and Charles worked the lock. The Charge of Quarters looked as though he couldn't be roused by anything less than an earthquake as they passed—but Martha stumbled on one of the rotting steps after they were outside the building.

"Patrick and Bridget rot my clumsy feet off!" she whispered. "He's awake."

"Under the porch," Charles said. They crawled into the dank space between porch floor and ground. Martha kept up a scarcely audible volley-fire of maledictions aimed at herself.

When they stopped abruptly Charles knew it was bad.

Martha held up her hand for silence, and Charles imagined in the dark that he could see the strained and eerie look of her face. After a pause she whispered, "He's using the—what do you call it? You talk and somebody hears you far away? A prowler, he says to them. A wild man from the woods. The bitches' bastard must have seen you in your handsome suit of skin and dirt, Charles. Oh, we're *for* it! May my toe that stumbled grow the size of a boulder! May my cursed eyes that didn't see the step fall out!"

They huddled down in the darkness and Charles took Lee Falcaro's hand reassuringly. It was cold. A moment later his other hand was taken, with grim possessiveness, by the child.

Martha whispered, "The fat little man. The man who kills, Charles."

He nodded. He thought he had recognized Grinnel from her picture.

"And ten men waking up. Charles, do you remember the way to the wharf?"

"Sure," he said. "But we're not going to get separated."

"They're mean, mad men," she said. "Bloody-minded. And the little man is the worst."

They heard the stomping feet and a babble of voices, and Commander Grinnel's clear, fat-man's tenor: "Keep it quiet, men. He may still be in the area." The feet thundered over their heads on the porch.

In the barest of whispers Martha said, "The man that slept tells them there was only one, and he didn't see what he was like except for the bare skin and the long hair. And the fat man says they'll find him and—and—and says they'll find him." Her hand clutched Charles' desperately and then dropped it as the feet thudded overhead again.

Grinnel was saying, "Half of you head up the street and half down. Check the alleys, check open window—hell, I don't have to tell you. If we don't find the bastard on the first run we'll have to wake up the whole Guard Battalion and patrol the whole base with them all the damn night, so keep your eyes open. Take off."

"Remember the way to the wharf, Charles," Martha said. "Goodbye lady. Take care of him. Take good care of him." She wrenched her hand away and darted out from under the porch.

Lee muttered some agonized monosyllable. Charles started out after the child instinctively and then collapsed weakly back onto the dirt. They heard the rest.

"Hey, you—it's him, by God! Get him! Get him!"

"Here he is, down here! Head him off!"

"Over there!" Grinnel yelled, "Head him off! Head him—good work!"

"For God's sake. It's a girl."

"Those damn yeomen and their damn prowlers,

Grinnel: "Where are you from, kid?"

"That's no kid from the base, commander. Look at her!"

"I just *was* looking, Sarge. Looks good to me, don't it to you?"

Grinnel, tolerant, fatherly, amused: "Now, men, have your fun but keep it quiet."

"Don't be afraid, kid—" There was an animal howl from Martha's throat that made Lee Falcaro shake hysterically and Charles grind his fingernails into his palms.

Grinnel: "Sergeant, you'd better tie your shirt around her head and take her into the O.N.I. building."

"Why, commander! And let that lousy little yeoman in on it?"

Grinnel, amused, a good Joe, a man's man: "That's up to you men. Just keep it quiet."

"Why, commander, sometimes I like to make a little noise—"

"Ow!" a man yelled. There was a scuffle of feet and babbling voices, "Get her, you damn fool!" "She bit my hand—" "There she goes—" and a single emphatic shot.

Grinnel's voice said into the silence that followed, "That's that, men."

"Did you *have* to shoot, Commander?" an aggrieved Guardsman said.

"Don't blame me, fellow. Blame the guy that let her go."

"Dammit, she bit me—"

Somebody said as though he didn't mean it, "We ought to take her someplace."

"The hell with that. Let 'em get her in the morning."

"Them as wants her." A cackle of harsh laughter.

Grinnel, tolerantly: "Back to the guardhouse, men. And keep it quiet."

They scuffled off and there was silence again for long minutes. Charles said at last, "We'll go down to the wharf." They crawled out and looked for a moment from the shelter of the building at the bundle lying in the road.

Lee muttered, "Grinnel."

"Shut up," Charles said. He led her down deserted alleys and around empty corners, strictly according to plan.

The speedboat was a twenty-foot craft at Wharf Eighteen, bobbing on the water safely removed from other moored boats and ships. Lee Falcaro let out a small, smothered shriek when she saw a uniformed sailor sitting in the cockpit, apparently staring directly at them.

"It's all right," Charles said. "He's a drunk. He's always out cold by this time of night." Smoothly Charles found the rope locker, cut lengths with the sailor's own knife and bound mid gagged him. The man's eyes opened, weary, glazed and red while this was going on and closed again. "Help me lug him ashore," Charles said. Lee Falcaro took the sailor's legs and they eased him onto the wharf.

They went back into the cockpit. "This is deep water," Charles said, "so you'll have no trouble with pilotage. You can read a compass and charts. There's an automatic dead reckoner. My advice is just to pull the moderator rods out quarter-speed, point the thing west, pull the rods out as far as they'll go—and relax.

Either they'll overtake you or they won't."

She was beginning to get the drift. She said nervously, "You're talking as though you're not coming along."

"I'm not," he said, playing the lock of the arms rack. The bar fell aside and he pulled a .45 pistol from its clamp. He thought back and remembered where the boat's diminutive magazine was located, broke the feeble lock and found a box of short, fat, heavy little cartridges. He began to snap them into the pistol's magazine.

"What do you think you're up to?" Lee Falcaro demanded.

"Appointment with Commander Grinnel," he said. He slid the heavy magazine into the pistol's grip and worked the slide to jack a cartridge into the chamber.

"Shall I cast off for you?" he asked.

"Don't be a fool," she said. "You sound like a revival of a Mickey Spillane comedy. You can't bring her back to life and you've got a job to do for the Syndic."

"You do it," he said, and snapped another of the blunt, fat, little cartridges into the magazine.

She cast off, reached for the moderator-rod control and pulled it hard.

"Gee," he gasped, "you'll sink us!" and dashed for the controls. You had seconds before the worm gears turned, the cadmium rods withdrew from their slots, the reactor seethed and sent boiling metal cycling through the turbine—

He slammed down manual levers that threw off the fore and aft mooring lines, spun the wheel, bracing himself, and saw Lee Falcaro go down to the deck in a tangle, the .45 flying from her hand and skidding across the knurled plastic planking. But by then the turbine was screaming an alarm to the whole base and they were cutting white water through the buoy-marked gap in the harbor net.

Lee Falcaro got to her feet. "I'm not proud of myself," she said to him. "But she told me to take care of you."

He said grimly, "We could have gone straight to the wharf without that little layover to pick you up. Take the Wheel."

"Charles, I—"

He snarled at her.

"Take the Wheel."

She did, and he went aft to stare through the darkness. The harbor lights were twinkling pinpoints; then his eyes misted so he could not see them at all. He didn't give a damn if a dozen corvettes were already slicing the bay in pursuit. He had failed.

CHAPTER SIXTEEN

It was a dank fog-shrouded morning. Sometime during the night the quill of the dead reckoner had traced its fine red line over the 30th meridian. Roughly halfway, Charles Orsino thought, rubbing the sleep from his eyes. But the line was straight as a string for the last four hours of their run. The damn girl must have fallen asleep on watch. He glared at her in the bow and broke open a ration. Blandly oblivious to the glare, she said, "Good morning."

Charles swallowed a mouthful of chocolate, half-chewed, and choked on it. He reached hastily for water and found the tall plastic column of the ion-exchange apparatus empty. "Damn it," he snarled, "why didn't you refill this thing when you emptied it? And why didn't you zigzag overnight? You're utterly irresponsible." He hurled the bucket over-side, hauled it up and slopped seawater into the apparatus. Now there'd be a good twenty minutes before a man-sized drink accumulated.

"Just a minute," she told him steadily. "Let's straighten this out. I haven't had any water on the night watch so I didn't have any occasion to refill the tube. You must have taken the last of the water with your dinner. And as for the zigzag, you said we should run a straightaway now and then to mix it up. I decided that last night was as good a time as any."

He took a small drink from the reservoir, stalling. There was something—yes; he had *meant* to refill the apparatus after his dinner ration. And he *had* told her to give it a few hours of straightaway some night...

He said formally, "You're quite right on both counts, I apologize." He bit into a ration.

"That's not good enough," she said. "I'm not going to have you tell me you're sorry and then go scowling and sulking about the boat. In fact I don't like your behavior at all."

He said, enormously angry, *"Oh, you don't do you?"* and hated her, the world, and himself for the stupid inadequacy of the comeback.

"No. I don't. I'm seriously worried. I'm afraid the conditioning you got didn't fall away completely when they swore you in. You've been acting irrationally and inconsistently."

"What about you?" he snapped. "You got conditioned too."

"That's right," she said, "That's another reason why you're worrying me. I find impulses in myself that have no business there. I simply seem to do a better job of controlling them than you're doing. For instance, we've been quarreling and at cross-purposes ever since you and Martha picked me up. That couldn't be unless I were contributing to the friction."

The wheel was fixed; she took a step or two aft and said professorially, "I've never had trouble getting along with people. I've had differences, of course, and at times I've allowed myself displays of temper when it was necessary to assert myself. But I find that you upset me; that for some reason or other your opinion on a matter is important to me; that if it differs with mine there should be a reconciliation."

He put down the ration and said wonderingly, "Do you know, that's the way I feel about you? And you think it's the conditioning or—or something?" He took a couple of steps forward, hesitantly.

"Yes," she said in a rather tremulous voice. "The conditioning or something. For instance, you're inhibited. You haven't made an indecent proposition to me, not even as a matter of courtesy. Not that I care, of course, but—" In stepping aft, she tripped over the water bucket and went down to the deck with a faint scream. He said, "Here, let me help you." He picked her up and didn't let go.

"Thanks," she said faintly, "The conditioning technique can't be called faulty, but it has inherent limitations..." She trailed off and he kissed her. She kissed back and said more faintly still, "Or it might be the drugs we used... Oh, Charles, what *took* you so long?"

He said, brooding, "You're way out of my class, you know, I'm just a bagman for the New York police. I wouldn't even be that if it weren't for Uncle Frank, and you're a Falcaro. It's just barely thinkable that I could make a pass at you. I guess that held me off and I didn't want to admit it so I got mad at you instead. Hell—I could have swum back to the base and made a damned fool of myself trying to find Grinnel, but down inside I knew better. The kid's *gone.*"

"We'll make a psychologist of you yet," she said.

"Psychologist? Why? You're joking."

"No. It's not a joke. You'll *like* psychology, darling. You can't go on playing polo forever, you know."

Darling! What was he getting into? Old man Gilby was four-goal at sixty, wasn't he? Good lord, was he hooked into marriage at twenty-three? Was she married already? Did she know or care whether he was? Had she been promiscuous? Would she continue to be? He'd never know; that was the one thing you never asked; your only comfort, if you needed comfort, was that she could never dream of asking you. What went on here? Let me out!

It went through his mind in a single panicky flash and then he said, "The hell with it, "and kissed her again.

She wanted to know: "The hell with what, darling?"

"Everything. Tell me about psychology, I can't go on playing polo forever."

It was an hour before she got around to telling him about psychology: "The neglect has been criminal—and inexplicable. For about a century it's been assumed that psychology is a dead fallacy. Why?"

"All right," he said amiably, playing with a lock of her hair. "Why?"

"Lieberman," she said, "Lieberman of Johns-Hopkins. He was one of the old-line topological psychology men—don't let the lingo throw you, Charles; it's just the name of a system. He wrote an attack on the mengenlehre psychology school—point-sets of emotions, class-inclusions of reactions and so on. He blasted them to bits by proving that their constructs didn't correspond to the emotions and reactions of random-sampled populations. And then came the payoff: he tried the same acid test on his *own* school's constructs and found out that they didn't correspond either. It didn't frighten him; he was a scientist. He published, and then the jig was up. Everybody, from full professors to undergraduate students went down the roster of the schools of psychology and wrecked them so comprehensively that the field was as dead as palmistry in twenty years. The miracle is that it hadn't happened before. The flaws were so glaring! Textbooks of the older kind solemnly described syndromes, psychoses, neuroses that simply couldn't be found in the real world! And that's the way it was all the way down the line."

"So where does that leave us?" Charles demanded, "Is it or isn't it a science?"

"It is," she said simply, "Lieberman and his followers went too far. It became a kind of hysteria. The experimenters must have been too eager. They misread results, they misinterpreted statistics, they misunderstood the claims of a school and knocked down not its true claims but straw-man claims they had set up themselves."

"But—*psychology!*" Charles protested, obscurely embarrassed at the thought that man's mind was subject to scientific study—not because he knew the first thing about it, but because *everybody* knew psychology was phony.

She shrugged, "I can't help it. We were doing physiology of the sensory organs, trying to settle the oldie about focusing the eye, and I got to grubbing around the pre-Lieberman texts looking for light in the darkness. Some of it sounded so...not sensible, yet *positive*...that I ran off one of Lieberman's population checks. And the old boy had been dead wrong. M*engenlehre* constructs correspond quite nicely to the actual way people's minds work, I kept checking and the schools that were destroyed as hopelessly fallacious a century ago checked out, some closely and some not so closely, as good descriptions of the way the mind works. Some have predictive value. I used *mengenlehre* psychology algorisms to compute the conditioning on you and me, including the trigger release. It worked. You see, Charles? We're on the rim of something tremendous!"

"When did this Lieberman flourish?"

"I don't have the exact dates in my head. The breakup of the schools corresponded roughly with the lifetime of John G. Falcaro."

That pinpointed it rather well. John G. succeeded Rafael, who succeeded Amadeo Falcaro, first leader of the Syndic in revolt. Under John G., the hard-won freedom was enjoyed, the bulging store-houses were joyously emptied, craft union rules went joyously out the window and builders *worked*, the dollar went to an all-time high and there was an all-time number of dollars in circulation. It had been an exuberant time still fondly remembered; just the time for over-enthusiastic rebels against a fusty scholasticism to joyously smash old ways of thought without too much exercise of the conscience. It all checked out.

She started and he got to his feet. A hardly-noticed discomfort was becoming acute; the speedboat was pitching and rolling quite seriously, for the first time since their escape. "Dirty weather coming up," he said. *We've been too damned lucky so far,* he thought, but didn't remark out loud, that there was much to worry about in the fact that there seemed to have been no pursuit. The meager resources of the North American Navy wouldn't be spent on chasing a single minor craft—not if the weather could be counted on to finish her off.

"I thought we were unsinkable?"

"In a way. Seal the boat and she's unsinkable the way a corked bottle is. But the boat's made up of a lot of bits and pieces that go together just so. Pound her for a few hours with waves and the bits and pieces give way. She doesn't sink, but she doesn't steam or steer either. I wish the Syndic had a fleet on the Atlantic."

"Sorry," she said. "The nearest fleet I know of is the Mob ore boats on the Great Lakes and they aren't likely to pick us up."

The sea-search radar pinged and they flew to the screen, "*Something* at 273 degrees, about eight miles," he said. "It can't be pursuit. They couldn't have any reason at all to circle around us and come at us from ahead," He strained his eyes into the west and thought he could see a black speck on the gray.

Lee Falcaro tried a pair of binoculars and complained, "These things won't work."

"Not on a rolling, pitching platform they won't—not with an optical lever eight miles long. I don't suppose this boat would have a gyro-stabilized signal glass." He spun the wheel to 180; they staggered and clung as the bow whipped about, searched and steadied on the new course. The mounting waves slammed them broadside-to and the rolling increased. They hardly noticed; their eyes were on the radarscope. Fogged as it was with sea return, they nevertheless could be sure after several minutes that the object had changed course to 135. Charles made a flying guess at her speed, read their own speed off and scribbled for a moment.

He said nothing, but spun the wheel to 225 and went back to the radarscope. The object changed course to 145. Charles scribbled again and said at last, flatly, "They're running collision courses on us. Automatically computed, I suppose, from a radar. We're through."

He spun the wheel to 180 again, and studied the crawling green spark on the radarscope. "This way we give 'em the longest run for their money and can pray for a miracle. The only way we can use our speed to outrun them is to turn around and head back into Government Territory—which isn't what we want. Relax, Lee. Maybe if the weather thickens they'll lose us—no, not with radar."

They sat together on a bunk, wordlessly, for hours while the spray dashed higher and the boat shivered to hammering waves. Briefly they saw the pursuer, three miles off, low, black and ugly, before fog closed in again.

At nightfall there was the close, triumphant roar of a big reaction turbine and a light stabbed through the fog, flooding the boat with blue-white radiance. A cliff-like black hull loomed alongside as a bullhorn roared at them, "Cut your engines and come about into the wind."

Lee Falcaro read White-painted letters on the black hull; "*Hon. James J. Regan, Chicago.*" She turned to Charles and said wonderingly, "It's an ore boat. From the Mob Great Lakes fleet."

CHAPTER SEVENTEEN

"Here?" Charles demanded, *"Here?"*

"No possible mistake," she said, stunned. "When you're a Falcaro you travel. I've seen 'em in Duluth, I've seen 'em in Quebec, I've seen 'em in Buffalo."

The bullhorn voice roared again, dead in the shroud of fog; "Come into the wind and cut your engines or we'll put a shell into you."

Charles turned the wheel and wound in the moderator rod; the boat pitched like a splinter on the waves. There was a muffled double explosion and two grapnels crunched into the plastic hull, bow and stern. As the boat steadied, sharing the inertia of the ore ship, a dark figure leaped from the blue-white eye of the searchlight to their deck. And another. And another.

"Hello, Jim," Lee Falcaro said almost inaudibly. "Haven't met since Las Vegas, have we?"

The first boarder studied her cooly. He was built for football or any other form of mayhem. He ignored Charles completely, "Lee Falcaro as advised. Do you still think twenty reds means a black is bound to come up? You always were a fool, Lee. And now you're in real trouble."

"What's going on, mister?" Charles snapped. "We're Syndics and I presume you're Mobsters. Don't you recognize the treaty?"

The boarder turned to Charles inquiringly. "Some confusion," he said. "Max Wyman? Charles Orsino? Or just some wild man from outback?"

"Orsino," Charles said formally. "Second cousin of Edward Falcaro, under the guardianship of Francis W. Taylor."

The boarder bowed slightly, "James Regan IV," he said, "No need to list my connections. It would take too long and I feel no need to justify myself to a small-time dago chiseler. Watch him gentlemen!"

Charles found his arms pinned by Regan's two companions. There was a gun muzzle in his ribs.

Regan shouted to the ship and a ladder was let down. Lee Falcaro and Charles climbed it with guns at their backs. He said to her, "Who is this lunatic?" It did not even occur to him that the young man was who he claimed to be—the son of the Mob Territory opposite number of Edward Falcaro.

"He's Regan," she said. "And I don't know who's the lunatic, him or me. Charles, I'm sorry, terribly sorry, I got you into this."

He managed to smile, "I volunteered," he said.

"Enough talk," Regan said, following them onto the deck. Dull-eyed sailors watched them incuriously, and there were a couple of anvil-jawed men with a stance and swagger Charles had come to know, Guardsmen—he would have staked his life on it. Guardsmen of the North American Government Navy—aboard a Mob Territory ship and acting as if they were passengers or high-rated crewmen.

Regan smirked and said, "I'm on the horns of a dilemma. There are no accommodations that are quite right for you. There are storage compartments that are worse than you deserve and there are passenger quarters that are too good for you. I'm afraid it will have to be one of the compartments. Your consolation will be that it's only a short run to Chicago."

Chicago—headquarters for Mob Territory. The ore ship had been on a return trip to Chicago when alerted somehow by the Navy to intercept the fugitives. *Why?*

"Down there," one of the men gestured briskly with a gun. They climbed down a ladder into a dark, oily cavern fitfully lit by a flash in Regan's hand.

"Make yourselves comfortable," Regan told them. "If you get a headache, don't worry. We were carrying some a-v-gas on the outward run." The flash winked out and a door clanged on them.

"I can't believe it," Charles said. "That's a top Mob man? Couldn't you be mistaken?" He groped in the dark and found her. The place did reek of gasoline.

She clung to him and said, "Hold me, Charles... Yes that's Jimmy Regan.

"That's what will become top man in the mob. Jimmy's a charmer at a Las Vegas Hotel. Jimmy's a gourmet when he orders at the Pump Room and he's trying to overawe you. Jimmy plays polo too, but he's crippled three of his own teammates because he's not very good at it, I kept telling myself whenever I ran into him that he was just an accident, the Mob could survive him. But his father acts—funny. There's something wrong with them there's something wrong with them, there's some—

"They roll out the carpet when you show up but the people around them are afraid of them. There's a story I never believed— but I believe it now. What would happen if my uncle pulled out a pistol and began screaming and shot a waiter? Jimmy's father did it, they tell me. And nothing happened except that the waiter was dragged away and everybody said it was a good thing Mr. Regan saw him reach for his gun and shot him first. Only the waiter didn't have a gun.

"I saw Jimmy last three years ago. I haven't been in Mob

Territory since. I didn't like it there. Now I know why. Give Mob Territory enough time and it'll be like New Portsmouth. Something went wrong with them. We have the Treaty of Las Vegas and a hundred years of peace and there aren't many people going back and forth between Syndic and Mob except for a few high-ups like me who have to circulate. Manners. So you pay duty calls—and shut your eyes to what they're really like.

"*This* is what they're like. This dark, damp stinking compartment. And my uncle—and all the Falcaros—and you— and I—we aren't like them. Are we? *Are we?*" Her fingers bit into his arms. She was shaking.

"Easy," he soothed her. "Easy, easy. We're all right. We'll be all right. I think I've got it figured out. This must be some private gunrunning Jimmy's gone in for. Loaded an ore boat with a-v-gas and ammo and ran it up the Seaway. If anybody in Syndic Territory gave a damn they thought it was a load of ore for New Orleans via the Atlantic and the Gulf. But Jimmy ran his load to Ireland or Iceland, H.Q. A little private flier of his. He wouldn't dare harm us. There's the Treaty and you're a Falcaro."

"Treaty," she said. "I tell you they're all in it. Now that I've seen the Government in action I understand what I saw in Mob Territory. They've gone rotten, that's all. They've gone rotten. The way he treated you, because he thought you didn't have his rank! Sometimes my uncle's high-handed, sometimes he tells a person off, sometimes he lets him know he's top man in the Syndic and doesn't propose to let anybody teach him how to suck eggs. But the spirit's different. In the Syndic it's parent to child. In the Mob it's master to slave. Not based on age, not based on achievement, but based on the accident of birth. You tell me 'You're a Falcaro' and that packs weight. Why? Not because I was born a Falcaro, but because they let me stay a Falcaro. If I hadn't been brainy and quick, they'd have adopted me out before I was ten. They don't do that in Mob Territory. Whatever chance sends a Regan is a Regan then and forever. Even if it's a paranoid constitutional inferior like Jimmy's father. Even if it's a giggling pervert like Jimmy.

She paused and looked at Orsino. "God, Charles, I'm scared.

She continued, "At last I know these people and I'm scared.

113

You'd have to see Chicago to know why. The lake front palaces, finer than anything in New York, Regan Memorial Plaza, finer than Scratch Sheet Square—great gilded marble figures, a hundred running yards of heroic frieze. But the hovels you see only by chance! Gray brick towers dating from the Third Fire! The children with faces like weasels, the men with faces like hogs, the women with figures like beer barrels and all of them glaring at you when you drive past as if they could cut your throat with joy. I never understood the look in their eyes until now, and you'll never begin to understand what I'm talking about until you see their eyes..."

Charles revolted against the idea. It was too gross to go down. It didn't square with his acquired picture of life in North America and therefore Lee Falcaro must be somehow mistaken or hysterical. "There," he murmured, stroking her hair. "We'll be all right. We'll be all right." He tried to soothe her.

She twisted out of his arms and raged: "I *won't* be humored. They're mad, I tell you. Dick Reiner was right. We've got to wipe out the Government. But Frank Taylor was right too. We've got to blast the Mob before they blast us. They've died and decayed into something too horrible to bear. If we let them stay on the continent with us their stink will infect us and poison us to death. We've got to do something. We've got to do something."

"What?"

It stopped her cold. After a minute she uttered a shaky laugh. "The fat, sloppy, happy Syndic," she said, "sitting around while the wolves overseas and the maniacs across the Mississippi are waiting to jump. Yes—do what?"

Charles Orsino was not good at arguments or indeed at any abstract thinking. He knew it. He knew the virtues that had commended him to F. W. Taylor were his energy and an off-hand talent for getting along with people. But something rang terribly false in Lee's words.

"That kind of thinking doesn't get you anywhere, Lee," he said slowly. "I didn't absorb much from Uncle Frank, but I did absorb this—you run into trouble if you make up stories about the world and then act as if they're true. The Syndic isn't somebody sitting around. The Government isn't wolves. The Mobsters aren't maniacs. And they aren't waiting to jump on the Syndic. The Syndic isn't anything that's jumpable. It's some people and their morale and credit."

"Faith is a beautiful thing," Lee Falcaro said bitterly. "Where'd you get yours?"

"From the people I knew and worked with. Numbers-runners, bookies, sluts. Decent citizens."

"And what about the scared and unhappy ones in Riveredge? That sow of a woman in the D.A.R. who smuggled me aboard a coast raider? The neurotics and psychotics I found more and more of when I invalidated the Lieberman findings? Charles, the North American Government didn't scare me especially. But the thought that they're lined up with a continental power does. It scares me damnably because it'll be three against one. Against the Syndic will be the Mob, the Government—and our own unbalanced citizens."

Uncle Frank never let that word "citizens" pass without a tirade. "We are not a government!" he always yelled. "We are not a government! We must not think like a government! We must not think in terms of duties and receipts and disbursements. We must think in terms of the old loyalties that bound the Syndic together!" Uncle Frank was sedentary, but he had roused himself once to the point of wrecking a bright young man's newly installed bookkeeping system for the Medical Center. He had used a cane, most enthusiastically; and then bellowed, "The next wise guy who tries to sneak punch-cards into this joint will get them down his throat! What the hell do we need punch cards for? Either there's room enough and doctors enough for the patients or there isn't. If there is, we take care of them. If there isn't, we put 'em in an ambulance and take them someplace else. And if I hear one damned word about 'efficiency'—" he glared the rest and strode out, puffing and leaning on Charles' arm, "Efficiency," he growled in the corridor. "Every so often a wise guy comes to me whimpering that people are getting away with murder, collections are ten per cent below what they ought to be, the Falcaro Fund's being milked because fifteen per cent of the dough goes to people who aren't in need at all, eight per cent of the people getting old-age pensions aren't really past sixty. Get efficient, these people tell me. Save money by triple-checking collections. Save money by tightening up the Fund Rules. Save money by a nice big vital statistics system so we can check on pensioners. Yeah! Have people Who might be *working* check on collections instead, and make enemies to boot whenever we catch somebody short. Make the Fund a grudging Scrooge instead of an open-handed sugar daddy—and let people worry about their chances of making the Fund instead of knowing it'll take care of them if they're caught short. Set up a vital statistics system from birth to death, with numbers and fingerprints and house registration and maybe the gas chamber if you forget to report a change of address. You know what's wrong with the wise guys, Charles? Constipation. And they want to constipate the universe," Charles remembered his uncle restored to chuckling good humor by the time he had finished embroidering his spur-of-the-moment theory with elaborate scatological details.

"The Syndic will stand," he said to Lee Falcaro, thinking of his uncle who knew what he was doing, thinking of Edward Falcaro who did the right thing without knowing why, thinking of his good friends in the 101st Precinct, the roaring happy crowds in Scratch Sheet Square, the good-hearted men of Riveredge Breakdown Station 26 who had borne with his sullenness and intolerance simply because that was the way things were and that was the way you acted. "I don't know what the Mob's up to, and I got a shock from the Government, and I don't deny that we have a few miserable people who can't seem to be helped. But you've seen too much of the Mob and Government and our abnormals. Maybe you don't know as much as you should about our ordinary people. Anyway, all we can do is wait."

"Yes," she said. "All we can do is wait. Until Chicago we have each other."

CHAPTER EIGHTEEN

They were too sick with gasoline fumes to count the passing hours or days. Food was brought to them from time to time, but it tasted like a-v-gas. They could not think for the sick headaches that pounded incessantly behind their eyes. When Lee developed vomiting spasms that would not stop, Charles Orsino pounded on the bulkhead with his fists and yelled, his voice thunderous in the metal compartment, for an hour.

Somebody came at last—Regan. The light stabbed Charles' eyes when he opened the door, "Trouble?" Regan asked, smirking.

"Miss Falcaro may be dying," Charles said. His own throat felt as though it had been gone over with a cobbler's rasp. "I don't have to tell you your life won't be worth a dime if she dies and it gets back to Syndic Territory. She's got to be moved and she's got to have medical attention."

"Death threat from the dago?" Regan was amused. "I have it on your own testimony that the Syndic is merely morale and people and credit—not a formidable organization. Yes, there was a mike in here. One reason for your discomfort. You'll be gratified to learn that I thought most of your conversation decidedly dull. However, the lady will be of no use to us dead and we're now in the seaway entering Lake Michigan. I suppose it can't do any harm to move you two. Pick her up, will you? I'll let you lead the way— and I'll remind you that I may not, as the lady said, be a four-goal polo player but I am a high expert with the handgun. Get moving."

Charles did not think he could pick his own feet up, but the thought of pleading weakness to Regan was unbearable. He could try. Staggering, he got Lee Falcaro over his shoulder and through the door. Regan courteously stood aside and murmured, "Straight ahead and up the ramp. I'm giving you my own cabin. We'll be docking soon enough; I'll make out."

Charles dropped her onto a sybaritic bed in a small but lavishly-appointed cabin. Regan whistled up a deckhand and a ship's officer of some sort, who arrived with a medicine chest. "Do what you can for her, mister," he told the officer. And to the deckhand: "Just watch them. They aren't to touch anything. If they give you trouble, you're free to punch them around a bit." He left, whistling.

The officer fussed unhappily over the medicine chest and stalled by sponging off Lee Falcaro's face and throat. The deckhand watched impassively. He was a six-footer, and he hadn't spent days inhaling casing-head fumes. The trip-hammer pounding behind Charles's eyes seemed to be worsening with the fresher air.

THE SYNDIC

He collapsed into a seat and croaked, with shut eyes, "While you're trying to figure out the vomiting, can I have a handful of aspirins?"

"Eh? Nothing was said about you. You were in Number Three with her? I suppose it'll be all right. Here." He poured a dozen tablets into Charles' hand. "Get him some water, you." The deckhand brought a glass of water from the adjoining lavatory and Charles washed down some of the tablets. The officer was reading a booklet, worry written on his face, "Do you know any medicine?" he finally asked.

The hard-outlined, kidney-shaped ache was beginning to diffuse through Charles' head, more general now and less excruciating. He felt deliciously sleepy, but roused himself to answer, "Some athletic trainer stuff, I don't know—morphine? Curare?"

The officer ruffled through the booklet. "Nothing about vomiting," he said. "But it says curare for muscular cramp and I guess that's what's going on. A liqoid suspension to release it slowly into the bloodstream and give the irritation time to subside. Anyway, I can't kill her if I watch the dose…"

Charles, through half-opened eyes, saw Lee Falcaro's arm reach behind the officer's back to his medicine chest. The deckhand's eyes were turning to the bed—Charles heaved himself to his feet, skyrockets going off again through his head, and started for the lavatory. The deckhand grabbed his arm, "Rest, mister! Where do you think you're going?"

"Another glass of water—"

"*I'll* get it. You heard my orders."

Charles subsided. When he dared to look again, Lee's arm lay alongside her body and the officer was triple checking dosages in his booklet against a pressurized hypodermic spray. The officer sighed and addressed Lee: "You won't even feel this. Relax." He read his setting on the spray again, checked it again against the booklet. He touched the syringe to the skin of Lee's arm and thumbed open the valve. It hissed for a moment and Charles knew submicroscopic particles of the medication had been blasted under Lee's skin too fast for nerves to register the shock.

His glass of water came and he gulped it greedily. The officer packed the pressurized syringe away, folded the chest and said to both of them, rather vaguely, "That should do it. If, uh, if anything happens—or if it doesn't work—call me and I'll try something else. Morphine, maybe."

He left and Charles slumped in the chair, the pain ebbing and sleep beginning to flow over him. Not yet, he told himself. She hooked something from the chest. He said to the deckhand, "Can I clean the lady and myself up?"

"Go ahead, mister. You can use it. Just don't try anything."

The man lounged in the doorframe of the lavatory alternately studying Charles at the washbasin and Lee on the bed. Charles took off a heavy layer of oily grease from himself and then took washing tissues to the bed. Lee Falcaro's spasms were tapering off. As he washed her, she managed a smile and an unmistakable wink.

"You folks married?" the deckhand asked.

"No," Charles said. Weakly she held up her right arm for the washing tissue. As he scrubbed the hand, he felt a small cylinder smoothly transferred from her palm to his. He slid it into a pocket and finished the job.

The officer popped in again with a carton of milk, "Any better, miss?" he asked.

"Yes," she whispered.

"Good. Try to drink this." Immensely set up by his success in treatment, he hovered over her for a quarter of an hour getting the milk down a sip at a time. It stayed down. He left trailing a favorable prognosis. Meanwhile, Charles had covertly examined Lee's booty: a pressurized syringe labeled *morphine sulfate sol.* It was full and ready. He cracked off the protective cap and waited his chance.

It came when Lee grimaced at him and called the deckhand in a feeble murmur. She continued to murmur so indistinctly that he bent over trying to catch the words. Charles leaned forward and emptied the syringe at one-inch range into the taut seat of the deckhand's pants. He scratched absently and said to Lee, "You'll have to talk up, lady." Then he giggled, looked bewildered and collapsed on the floor, staring, coked to the eyebrows.

Lee painfully sat up on the bed. "Porthole," she said.

Charles went to it and struggled with the locking lugs. It opened—and an alarm bell began to clang through the ship. *Now* he saw the hair-fine, broken wire. An alarm trip-wire.

Feet thundered outside and the glutinous voice of Jimmy Regan was heard: "Wait, you damn fools! You in there—is everything all right? Did they try to pull something?"

Charles kept silent and shook his head at the girl. He picked up a chair and stood by the door. The glutinous voice again, in a mumble that didn't carry through—and the door sprang open, Charles brought the chair down in a murderous chop, conscious only that it seemed curiously light. There was an impact and the head fell.

It was Regan, with a drawn gun. It had been Regan. His skull was smashed before he knew it. Charles felt as though he had all the time in the world. He picked up the gun to a confused roar like a slowed-down sound track and emptied it into the corridor. It had been a full automatic, but the fifteen shots seemed as well spaced as a ceremonial salute. Regan, in his vanity, wore two guns, Charles scooped up the other and said to Lee, "Come on."

He knew she was following as he raced down the cleared corridor and down the ramp, back to the compartment in which they had been locked. Red danger lights burned on the walls, Charles flipped the pistol to semiautomatic as they passed a red-painted bulkhead with valves and gages sprouting from it. He turned and fired three deliberate shots into it. The last was drowned out by a dull roar as gasoline fumes exploded. Pipe fittings and fragments of plate whizzed about them like bullets as they raced on.

Somebody ahead loomed, yelling querulously, "What the hell was that, Mac? What blew?"

"Where's the reactor room?" Charles demanded, jamming the pistol into his chest. The man gulped and pointed.

"Take me there. Fast!"

"Now *look*, Mac—"

Charles told him in a few incisive details where and how he was going to be shot. The man went white and led them down the corridor and into the reactor room. Three white-coated men with the aloof look of reactor specialists stared at them as they bulled into the spotless chamber.

The oldest sniffed; "And what, may I ask, are you crewmen doing in—"

Lee slammed the door behind them and said, "Sound the radiation alarm."

"Certainly not! You must be the couple we—"

"Sound the radiation alarm." She picked up a pair of dividers from the plot board and approached the technician with murder on her face. He gaped until she poised the needle points before his eyes and repeated, *"Sound the radiation alarm."* Nobody in the room, including Charles, had the slightest doubt that the points would sink into the technician's eyeballs if he refused.

"Do what she says, Will," he mumbled, his eyes crossing on the dividers. "For God's sake, do what she says. She's crazy."

One of the men moved very cautiously—watching Charles and the gun—to a red handle and pulled it down. A ferro-concrete barrier rose to wall off the chamber and the sine-curve wail of a standard radioactivity warning began to howl mournfully through the ship.

"Dump the reactor metal," Charles said. His eyes searched for the exit, and found it—a red-painted breakaway panel standard for a hot lab.

A technician wailed, "We *can't* do that! We can't *do* that! A million bucks of thorium with a hundred years of life in it—have a heart, mister! They'll crucify us!"

"They can dredge for it," Charles said, "Dump the metal."

"Dump the metal," Lee said. She hadn't moved.

The senior technician's eyes were still on the bright needle points. He was crying silently. "Dump it," he said.

"Okay, chief. Your responsibility, remember."

"Dump it!" wailed the senior.

The technician did something technical at the control board. After a moment the steady rumbling of the turbines ceased and the ship's deck began to wallow underfoot.

"Hit the panel, Lee," Charles said. She did, running. He followed her through the oval port. It was like an open-bottomed diving bell welded to the hull. There were large, luminous cleats for pulling yourself down through the water, under the rim of the bell. He dropped the pistol into the water, breathed deeply a couple of times and began to climb down. There was no sign of Lee.

He kicked up through the dark water on a long slant away from the ship. It might be worse. With a fire and a hot-lab alarm and a dead chief aboard, the crew would have things on their mind besides looking for bobbing heads.

He broke the surface and treaded water to make a minimum target. He did not turn to the ship. His dark hair would be less visible than his white face. And if he was going to get a burst of machine-gun bullets through either, he didn't want to know about it. Ahead he saw Lee's blonde hair spread on the water for a moment and then it vanished. He breathed hugely, ducked and swam under water toward it.

When he rose next a sheet of flame was lightening the sky and the oily reek of burning hydrocarbons tainted the air. He dove again, and this time caught up with Lee. Her face was bone-white and her eyes blank. Where she was drawing her strength from he could not guess. Behind them the ship sent up an oily plume and the sine curve wail of the radioactivity warning could be faintly heard. Before them a dim shore stretched.

He gripped her naked arm, roughened by the March waters of Lake Michigan, bent it around his neck and struck off for the shore. His lungs were bursting in his chest and the world was turning gray-black before his burning eyes. He heaved his tired arm through the water as though each stroke would be his last, but the last stroke, by some miracle, never was the last.

CHAPTER NINETEEN

It hadn't been easy to get time off from the oil-painting factory. Ken Oliver was a little late when he slid into the aseptic-smelling waiting room of the Michigan City Medical Center. A parabolic mike in the ceiling trained itself on the heat he radiated and followed him across the floor to a chair. A canned voice said, "State your business, please."

He started a little and said in the general direction of the mike, "I'm Ken Oliver. A figure man in the Blue Department, Picasso Oils and Etching Corporation. Dr. Latham sent me here for—what do you call it—a biopsy?"

"Thank you, please be seated."

He smiled because he was seated already and picked up a magazine, the current copy of the *Illinois Sporting News*, familiarly known as the Green Sheet. Everybody in Mob Territory read it. The fingers of the blind spelled out its optimism and its selections at Hawthorne in Braille. If you were not only blind but fingerless, there was a talking edition that read itself aloud to you from tape.

He riffled through the past performances and selections to the articles. This month's lead was—*Thank God I am dying of Throat Cancer.*

He leaned back in the chair dizzily, the waiting room becoming gray mist around him. *No,* he thought. *No.* It couldn't be that. All it could be was a little sore on the back of his throat—no more than that. Just a little sore on the back of his throat. He'd been a fool to go to Latham. The fees were outrageous and he was behind, always a little behind, on his bills. But cancer—so much of it around—and the drugs didn't seem to *help* any more... But Latham had almost promised him it was non-malignant.

"Mr. Oliver," the loudspeaker said, "please go to Dr. Riordan's office, Number Ten."

Riordan was younger than he was. That was supposed to be bad in a general practitioner, good in a specialist. And Riordan was a specialist—pathology. A sour-faced young specialist.

"Good morning. Sit here. Open your mouth. Wider than that, and relax. *Relax;* your glottis is locked."

Oliver couldn't protest around the plastic-and-alcohol taste of the tongue depressor. There was a sudden coldness and a metallic snick that startled him greatly; then Riordan took the splint out of his mouth and ignored him as he summoned somebody over his desk set. A young man, even younger than Riordan, came in, "Freeze, section, and stain this right away," the pathologist said, handing him a forceps from which a small blob dangled. "Have them send up the Rotino charts, three hundred to nine hundred inclusive."

He began to fill out charts, still ignoring Oliver, who sat and sweated bullets for ten minutes. Then he left and was back in five minutes more.

"You've got it," he said shortly, "It's operable and you won't lose much tissue." He scribbled quickly on a blank sheet of typing paper and handed it to Oliver. The painter numbly read, "...anterior...epithelioma...metastases...giant cells..."

Riordan was talking again: "Give this to Latham. It's my report. Have him line up a surgeon. As to the operation, I say the sooner the better unless you care to lose your larynx. That will be fifty dollars."

"Fifty dollars," the painter said blankly. "But Dr. Latham told me—" He trailed off and got out his checkbook. Only thirty-two in the account, but he would deposit his paycheck today which would bring it up. It was after three so his check wouldn't go in today—he wrote out the slip slowly and carefully.

Riordan took it, read it suspiciously, put it away and said, "Good day, Mr. Oliver."

Oliver wandered from the Medical Center into the business heart of the art colony. The Van Gogh Works on the left must have snagged the big order from Mexico—their chimneys were going full blast and the reek of linseed oil and turps was strong in the air. But the poor beggars on the line at Rembrandts, Ltd. across the square were out of luck. They'd been laid off for a month now, with no sign of a work call yet. Somebody jostled him off the sidewalk, somebody in a great hurry. Oliver sighed. The place was getting more like Chicago every day. He sometimes thought he had made art his line not because he had any special talent, but because artists were relatively easy-going people, not so quick to pop you in the nose, not such aggressive drunks when they *were* drunks.

Quit the stalling, a thin, cold voice inside him said. Get over to Latham. The man said "The sooner the better."

He went over to Latham whose waiting room was crowded with irascible women. After an hour, he got to see the old man and hand him the slip.

Latham said, "Don't worry about a thing. Riordan's a good man. If he says it's operable, it's operable. Now we want Finsen to do the whittling. With Finsen operating, you won't have to worry about a thing. He's a good man. His fee's fifteen hundred."

"Oh, my God!" Oliver gulped.

"What's the matter—haven't you got it?"

To his surprise and terror, Oliver found himself giving Dr.

Latham a hysterical stump speech about how he didn't have it and who did have it and how could anybody get ahead with the way prices were shooting up and everybody gouged you every time you turned around and yes, that went for doctors too and if you did get a couple of bucks in your pocket the salesmen heard about it and battered at you until you put down an installment on some piece of junk you didn't want to get them out of your hair and what the hell kind of world was this anyway.

Latham listened, smiling and nodding, with, as Oliver finally realized, his hearing aid turned off. His voice ran down and Latham said briskly, "All right, then. You just come around when you've arranged the financial details and I'll contact Finsen. He's a good man; you won't have to worry about a thing. And remember...the sooner, the better."

Oliver slumped out of the office and went straight to the Mob Building, office of the Regan Benevolent Fund. An acid-voiced woman there turned him down indignantly, "You should be ashamed of yourself trying to draw on the Fund when there are people in actual want who can't be accommodated. No, I don't want to hear any more about it if you please. There are others waiting."

Waiting for what? The same treatment?

Oliver realized with a shock that he hadn't phoned his foreman as promised, and it was four minutes to five. He did a dance of agonized impatience outside a telephone booth occupied by a fat woman. She noticed him, pursed her lips, hung up—and stayed in the booth. She began a slow search of her handbag, found coins and slowly dialed a new number. She gave him a malevolent grin as he walked away, crushed. He had a good job record, but that was no way to keep it good. One black mark, another black mark, and one day—bingo.

General Advances was open, of course. Through its window you could see handsome young men and sleek young women just waiting to help you, whatever the fiscal jam. He went in and was whisked to a booth where a big-bosomed honey-voiced blonde oozed sympathy over him. He walked out with a check for fifteen hundred dollars after signing countless papers, with the creamy hand of the girl on his to help guide the pen. What was printed on the papers, God and General Advances alone knew. There were men on the line who told him with resignation that they had been paying off to G.A. for the better part of their lives. There were men who said bitterly that G.A. was owned by the Regan Benevolent Fund, which must be a lie.

The street was full of people—strangers who didn't look like your run-of-the-mill artist. Muscle men, with the Chicago style and if anybody got one in the gut, too dammed bad about it. They were peering into faces as they passed.

He was frightened. He stepped onto the slidewalk and hurried home, hoping for temporary peace there. But there was no peace for his frayed nerves. The apartment house door opened obediently when he told it, "Regan," but the elevator stood stupidly still when he said, "Seventh Floor." He spat bitterly and precisely, *"Sev-enth Floor."* The doors closed on him with a faintly derisive, pneumatic moan and he was whisked up to the eighth floor. He walked down wearily and said, "Cobalt blue" to his own door after a furtive look up and down the hall. It worked and he went to his phone to flash Latham, but didn't. Oliver sank instead into a dun-colored pneumatic chair, his 250-dollar Hawthorne Electric Stepsaver door mike following him with its mindless snout. He punched a button on the chair and the 600-dollar hi-fi selected a random tape. A long, pure melodic trumpet line filled the room. It died for two beats and then the strings and woodwinds picked it up and tossed it—

Oliver snapped off the music, sweat starting from his brow. It was the Gershwin *Lost Symphony*, and he remembered how Gershwin had died. There had been a little nodule in his brain as there was a little nodule in Oliver's throat.

Time, the Great Kidder. The years drifted by. Suddenly you were middle-aged, running to the medics for this and that. Suddenly they told you to have your throat whittled out or die disgustingly. And what did you, have to show for it? A number, a travel pass, a payment book from General Advance, a bunch of junk you never wanted, a job that was a heavier ball and chain than any convict ever wore in the barbarous days of Government. Was this what Regan and Falcaro had bled for?

He defrosted some hamburger, fried it and, ate it and then went mechanically down to the tavern. He didn't like to drink every night, but you had to be one of the boys, or word would get back to the plant and you might be on your way to another black mark. They were racing under the lights at Hawthorne too, and he'd be expected to put a couple of bucks down. He never seemed to win. Nobody he knew ever seemed to win. Not at the horses, not at the craps table, not at the numbers.

He stood outside the neon-bright saloon for a long moment, and then turned and walked into the darkness away from town, possessed by impulses he did not understand or want to understand. He had only a vague hope that standing on the Dunes and looking out across the dark lake might somehow soothe him.

In half an hour he had reached the deciduous forest, then the pine, then the scrubby brushes, then the grasses, then the bare white sand. And lying in it he found two people—a man so hard and dark he seemed to be carved from oak and a woman so white and gaunt she seemed to be carved from ivory.

He turned shyly from the woman.

"Are you all right?" he asked the man. "Is there anything I can do?"

The man opened red-rimmed eyes, "Better leave us alone," he said, "We'd only get you into trouble."

Oliver laughed hysterically. "Trouble?" he said, "Don't think of it."

The man seemed to be measuring him with his eyes, and said at last, "You'd better go and not talk about us. We're enemies of the Mob."

Oliver said after a pause, "So am I. Don't go away, I'll be back with some clothes and food for you and the lady. Then I can help you to my place. I'm an enemy of the Mob too, I just never knew it until now."

He started off and then turned, "You won't go away? I mean it. I want to help you, I can't seem to help myself, but perhaps there's something—"

The man said tiredly, "We won't go away."

Oliver hurried off. There was something mingled with the scent of the pine forest tonight. He was halfway home before he identified it—oil smoke.

CHAPTER TWENTY

Lee swore and said, "I can get up if I want to."

"You'll stay in bed whether you want to or not," Charles told her, "You're a sick woman."

"I'm a very bad-tempered woman and that means I'm convalescent. Ask anybody."

"I'll go right out into the street and do that, darling."

She got out of bed and wrapped Oliver's dressing gown around her, "I'm hungry again," she said.

"He'll be back soon. You've left nothing but some frozen—worms, looks like. Shall I defrost them?"

"Please don't trouble, I can wait."

"Window!" he snapped.

She ducked back and swore again, this time at herself, "Sorry," she said. "Which will do us a whole hell of a lot of good if somebody saw me and started wondering."

Oliver came in with packages. Lee kissed him and he grinned shyly. "Trout," he whispered. She grabbed the packages and flew to the kitchenette.

"The way to Lee Falcaro's heart," Charles mused. "How's your throat, Ken?"

"No pain, today," Oliver whispered. "Latham says I can talk as much as I like. And I've got things to talk about." He opened his coat and hauled out a flat package that had been stuffed under his belt. "Stolen from the factory. Brushes, pens, tubes of ink, drawing instruments. My friends, you are going to return to Syndic Territory in style, with passes and permits galore."

Lee returned. "Trout's frying," she said, "I heard that about the passes. Are you sure you can fake them?"

His face fell. "Eight years at the Chicago Art Institute," he whispered, "Three years at Original Reproductions; Inc. Eleven years at Picasso Oils and Etchings, where I am now third figure man in the Blue Department. I really think I deserve your confidence."

"Ken, we trust and love you. If it weren't for the difference in your ages I'd marry you *and* Charles. Now what about the Chicagoans? Hold it—the fish!"

Dinner was served and cleared away before they could get more out of Oliver. His throat wasn't ready for more than one job at a time. He told them at last, "Things are quieting down. There are still some strangers in town and the road patrols are still acting very hard-boiled. But nobody's been pulled in today. Somebody told me on the line that the whole business is a lot of foolishness. He said the ship must have been damaged by somebody's stupidity and Regan must have been killed in a brawl—everybody knows he was half-crazy; like his father. So my friend figures they made up the story about two wild Europeans to cover up a mess. I said I thought there was a lot in what he said." Oliver laughed silently.

"Good man!" Charles tried not to act over-eager. "When do you think you can start on the passes, Ken?"

Oliver's face dropped a little, "Tonight," he whispered. "I don't suppose the first couple of tries will be any good so—let's go."

Lee put her hand on his shoulder, "We'll miss you too," she said, "But don't ever forget this—we're coming back. Hell won't stop us. We're coming back."

Oliver was arranging stolen instruments on the table, "You have a big order," he whispered sadly, "I guess you aren't afraid of it because you've always been rich and strong. Anything you want to do you think you can do. But those Government people? And after them the Mob? Maybe it would be better if you just let things take their course, Lee. I've found out a person can be happy even here."

"We're coming back," Lee said.

Oliver took out his own Michigan City-Chicago travel permit. As always, the sight of it made Charles wince. Americans under such a yoke! Oliver whispered, "I got a good long look today at a Michigan City Buffalo permit. The foreman's. He buys turps from Carolina at Buffalo. I sketched it from memory as soon as I got by myself. I don't swear to it, not yet, but I have the sketch to practice from and I can get a few more looks later."

He pinned down the drawing paper, licked a ruling pen and filled it, and began to copy the border of his own pass.

"I don't suppose there's anything I can do?" Lee asked.

"You can turn on the audio," Oliver whispered. "They have it going all the time at the shop, I don't feel right working unless there's some music driving me out of my mind."

Lee turned on the big Hawthorne Electric set with a wave of her hand; imbecilic music filled the air and Oliver grunted and settled down.

Lee and Charles listened, fingers entwined, to half an hour of slushy ballads while Oliver worked. The news period announcer came on with some anesthetic trial verdicts, sports results and society notes about which of the Regans had gone where. Then—

"The local Mobsters of Michigan City, Indiana, today welcomed Maurice Regan to their town. Mr. Regan will assume direction of efforts to apprehend the two European savages who murdered James Regan IV last month aboard the ore boat *Hon. John Regan* in waters off Michigan City. You probably remember that the Europeans did some damage to the vessel's reactor room before they fled from the ship. How they boarded the ship and their present whereabouts are mysteries—but they probably won't be mysteries long, Maurice Regan is little-known to the public, but he has built an enviable record in the administration of the Chicago Police Department. Mr. Regan, on taking charge of the case, said this: "We know by traces found on the Dunes that they got away. We know from the logs of highway patrols that they didn't get out of the Michigan City area. The only way to close the books on this matter fast is to cover the city with a fine-tooth comb. Naturally and unfortunately this will mean inconvenience to many citizens, I hope they will bear with the inconveniences gladly for the sake of confining those two savages in a place where they can no longer be a menace. I have methods of my own and there may be complaints. Reasonable suggestions will be needed, but with crackpots I have no patience."

The radio began to spew more sports results. Oliver turned and waved at it to be silent. "I don't like that," he whispered. "I never heard of this Regan in the Chicago Police."

"They said he wasn't in the public eye."

"I wasn't the public. I did some posters for the police and I knew who was who. And that bit at the end. I've heard things like

130

it before. The Mob doesn't often admit it's in the wrong, you know. When they try to disarm criticism in advance...well...this Regan must be a rough fellow."

Charles and Lee Falcaro looked at each other in sudden fear, "We don't want to hurry you, Ken," she said. "But it looks as though you'd better do a rush job."

Nodding, Oliver bent over the table. "Maybe a week," he said hopefully. With the finest pen he traced the curlicues that an engraving lathe had evolved to make the passes foolproof. Odd, he thought—the lives of these two hanging by such a weak thing as the twisted thread of color that feeds from pen to paper. And, as an afterthought—I suppose mine does too.

Oliver came back the next day to work with concentrated fury, barely stopping to eat and not stopping to talk. Lee got it out of him, but not easily. After being trapped in a half dozen contradictions about feeling well and having a headache, about his throat being sore and the pain having gone, he put down his pen and whispered steadily, "I didn't want you to worry friends. But it looks bad. There is a new crowd in town. Twenty couples have been pulled in by them—couples to prove who they were. Maybe fifty people have been pulled in for questioning—what do you know about this, what do you know about that. And they've begun house searches. Anybody you don't like, you tell the new Regan about him. Say he's sheltering Europeans. And his people pull them in. Why...everybody wants to know...are they pulling in couples who are obviously American if they're looking for Europeans? And everybody says they've never seen anything like it. Now—I think I'd better get back to work."

"Yes," Lee said. "I think you had."

Charles was at the window, peering around the drawn blind, "Look at that," he said to Lee. She came over. A big-man on the street below was walking, very methodically down the street.

"I will bet you," Charles said, "that he'll be back this way in ten minutes or so—and so on through the night."

"I won't take the bet," she said. "He's a sentry, all right. The Mob's learning from their friends across the water. Learning too damned much. They must be all over town."

They watched at the window and the sentry was back in ten

minutes. On his fifth tour he stopped a young couple going down the street studied their faces, drew a gun on them and blew a whistle. A patrol came and took them away; the girl was hysterical. At two in the morning, the sentry was relieved by another, just as big and just as dangerous looking. At two in the morning they were still watching and Oliver was still hunched over the table tracing exquisite filigree of color.

In five days, virtually without sleep, Oliver finished two Michigan City-Buffalo travel permits. The apartment house next door was hit by raiders while the ink dried; Charles and Lee Falcaro stood waiting grotesquely armed with kitchen knives. But it must have been a tip rather than part of the search plan crawling nearer to their end of town. The raiders did not hit their building.

Oliver had bought clothes according to Lee's instructions—including two men's suits, Oliver's size. One she let out for Charles; the other she took in for herself. She instructed Charles minutely in how he was to behave on the outside. First he roared with incredulous laughter. Lee, wise in psychology assured him that she was perfectly serious. Oliver, puzzled by his naivete, assured him that such things were not uncommon—not at least in Mob Territory. Charles then roared with indignation and Lee roared him down. His last broken protest was, "But what'll I do if somebody takes me up on it?"

She shrugged, washing her hands of the matter, and went on trimming and dying her hair.

It was morning when she kissed Oliver goodbye, said to Charles, "See you at the station. Don't say goodbye," and walked from the apartment, a dark-haired boy with a slight limp. Charles watched her down the street. A cop turned to look after her and then went on his way.

Half an hour later Charles shook hands with Oliver and went out.

Oliver didn't go to work that day. He sat all day at the table, drawing endless slow sketches of Lee Falcaro's head.

Time the Great Kidder, he thought. He opens the door that shows you in the next room tables of goodies, colorful and tasty, men and women around the tables pleasantly surprised to see you, beckoning to you to join the feast. We have roast beef if you're serious, we have caviar if you're experimental, we have Baked Alaska if you're frivolous—join the feast; try a little bit of everything. So you start toward the door.

Time, the Great Kidder, pulls the rug from under your feet and slams the door while the guests at the feast laugh their heads off at your painful but superficial injuries.

Oliver slowly drew Lee's head for the fifteenth time and wished he dared to turn on the audio for the news. Perhaps, he thought, the next voice you hear will be the cops at the door.

CHAPTER TWENTY-ONE

Charles walked down the street and ran immediately into a challenge from a police sergeant.

"Where you from, mister?" the cop demanded, balanced and ready to draw.

Charles gulped and let Lee Falcaro's drilling take over. "Oh, around, sergeant, I'm from around here."

"What're you so nervous about?"

"Why, sergeant, you're such an exciting type, really. Did anybody ever tell you that you look great in uniform?

The cop glared at him and said, "If I wasn't in uniform, I'd hang one on you sister. And if the force wasn't all out hunting the lunatics that killed Mr. Regan, I'd pull you in for spitting on the sidewalk. Get to hell off my beat and stay off. I'm not forgetting your face."

Charles scurried on. It had worked.

It worked once more with a uniformed policeman. One of the Chicago plainclothes imports was the third and last. He socked Charles in the jaw and sent him on his way with a kick in the rear. He had been thoroughly warned that it would probably happen: "Count on them to overreact. That's the key to it. You'll make them so eager to assert their own virility, that it'll temporarily bury their primary mission. It's quite likely that one or more pokes will be taken at you. All you can do is take them. If you get—*when* you get through, they'll be cheap at the price."

The sock in the jaw hadn't been very expert. The kick in the pants was negligible, considering the fact that it had propelled him through the gate of the Michigan City Transport Terminal.

By the big terminal clock, the Chicago-Buffalo Express was due in fifteen minutes. Its gleaming single rail, as tall as a man, crossed the far end of the concourse. Most of the fifty-odd people in the station were probably Buffalo-bound...safe geldings who could be trusted to visit Syndic Territory, off the leash and return obediently. Well-dressed, of course, and many past middle age, with a stake in the Mob Territory stronger than hope of freedom. One youngster, though—oh. It was Lee, leaning, slack-jawed, against a pillar and reading the Green Sheet.

Who were the cops in the crowd? The thickset man with restless eyes, of course. The saintly-looking guy who kept moving and glancing into faces.

Charles went to the newsstand and put a coin in the slot for *The Mob—A Short History*, by the same Arrowsmith Hunde who had brightened and misinformed his youth.

Nothing to it, he thought. Train comes in, put your money in the turnstile, show your permit to the turnstile's eye, get aboard and that-is-that, Unless the money is phony, or the pass is phony in which case the turnstile locks and all hell breaks loose. His money was just dandy, but the permit now—there hadn't been anyway to test it against a turnstile's template, or time to do it if there had been a way. Was the probability of boarding two to one?

The probability abruptly dropped to zero as a round little man flanked by two huge men entered the station.

Commander Grinnel.

The picture puzzle fell into a whole as the two plainclothesmen circulating in the station eyed Grinnel and nodded to him. The big one absent-mindedly made a gesture that was the start of a police salute.

Grinnel was Maurice Regan the Maurice Regan mysteriously unknown to Oliver, who knew the Chicago police, Grinnel was a bit of a lend-lease from the North American Navy, called in because of his unique knowledge of Charles Orsino and Lee Falcaro, their faces, voices and behavior. Grinnel was the expert in combing the city without any nonsense about rights and mouthpieces. Grinnel was the expert who could set up a military interior guard of the city. Grinnel was the specialist temporarily invested with the rank of a Regan so he could do his job.

The round little man with the halo of hair walked briskly to the turnstile and there stood at a military parade rest with a look of resignation on his face.

How hard on me it is, he seemed to be saying, that I have such dull damn duty. How hard that an officer of my brilliance must do sentry-go for every train to Syndic Territory.

The slack-jawed youth who was Lee Falcaro looked at him over her Green Sheet and nodded before dipping into the Tia Juana past performances again. She knew.

Passengers were beginning to line up at the turnstile, smoothing out their money and fiddling with their permits. In a minute he and Lee Falcaro would have to join the line or stand conspicuously on the emptying floor. The thing was dead for twenty-four hours now, until the next train—and then Grinnel headed across the floor looking very impersonal. The look of a man going to the men's room. The station cops and Grinnel's two bruisers drifted together at the turnstile and began to chat.

Charles followed Grinnel, wearing the same impersonal look, and entered the room almost on his heels.

Grinnel saw him in a washbowl mirror; simultaneously he half turned, opened his mouth to yell and whipped his hand into his coat. A single roundhouse right from Charles crunched into the soft side of his neck. He fell with his head twisted at an odd angle. Blood began to run from the corner of his mouth onto his shirt.

"Remember Martha?" Charles whispered down at the body, "That was for murder," He looked around the tiled room. There was a mop closet with the door ajar, and Grinnel's flabby body fitted in it.

Charles walked from the washroom to the line of passengers across the floor. It seemed to go on for miles. Lee Falcaro was no longer lounging against the past. He spotted her in line, still slack-jawed, still gaping over the magazine. The monorail began to sing shrilly with the vibration of the train braking a mile away, and the turnstile "unlocked" light went on.

There was the usual number of fumblers, the usual number of "please unfold your currency" flashes. Lee carried through to the

135

end with her slovenly pose. For her the sign said, "incorrect denominations." Behind her a man snarled, "for Christ's sake, kid, we're all waiting on you!" The cops only half noticed; they were talking. When Charles got to the turnstile one of the cops was saying, "Maybe it's something he ate. How'd *you* like somebody to barge in—"

The rest was lost in the clicking of the turnstile that let him through.

He settled in a very pneumatic chair as the train accelerated evenly to a speed of three hundred and fifty miles per hour. A sign in the car said that the next stop was Buffalo. And there was Lee, lurching up the aisle against the acceleration. She spotted him, tossed the Green Sheet in the Air and fell into his lap.

"Disgusting!" snarled a man across the aisle, "Simply disgusting!"

"You haven't seen anything yet," Lee told him, and kissed Charles on the mouth.

The man choked, "I shall certainly report this to the authorities when we arrive in Buffalo!"

"Mmm," said Lee, preoccupied, "Do that, mister. Do that."

CHAPTER TWENTY-TWO

"I didn't like his reaction," Charles told her in the anteroom of F. W. Taylor's office. "I didn't talk to him long on the phone, but I don't like his reaction at all. He seemed to think I was exaggerating. Or all wet. Or a punk kid."

"I can assure him you're not that," Lee Falcaro said warmly. "Call on me any time."

He gave her a worried smile. The door opened then and they went in.

Uncle Frank looked up. "We'd just about written you two off," he said. "What's it like?"

"Bad," Charles said. "Worse than anything you've imagined. There's an underground, all right, and they are practicing assassination."

"Too bad," the old man said. "We'll have to shake up the bodyguard organization. Make 'em de rigeur at all hours, screen 'em and see that they really know how to shoot. I hate to meddle, but we can't have the Government knocking our people off."

"It's worse than that," Lee said, "There's a tie-up between the Government and the Mob. We got away from Ireland aboard a speedboat and we were picked up by a Mob Great Lakes ore ship. It had been running gasoline and ammunition to the Government. Jimmy Regan was in charge of the deal. We jumped into Lake Michigan and made our way back here. We were in Mob Territory—down among the small-timers—long enough to establish that the Mob and Government are hand in glove. One of these days they're going to jump us."

"Ah," Taylor said softly. "I've thought so for a long time."

Charles burst out, "Then for God's sake, Uncle Frank, why haven't you *done* anything? You don't know what it's like out there. The Government's a nightmare. They have slaves. And the Mob's not much better. Numbers! Restrictions! Permits! Passes! And they don't call it that, but they have taxes!"

"They're mad," Lee said. "Quite mad. And I'm talking technically. Neurotics and psychotics swarm in the streets of Mob Territory. The Government, naturally—but the Mob was a shock. We've got to get ready, Mr. Taylor. Every psychotic or severe neurotic in Syndic Territory is a potential agent of theirs."

"Don't just check off the Government, darling," Charles said tensely. "They've got to be smashed. They're no good to themselves or anybody else. Life's a burden there if only they knew it. And they're holding down the natives by horrible cruelty."

Taylor leaned back and asked, "What do you recommend?"

Charles said, "A fighting fleet and an army."

Lee said, "Mass diagnosis of the unstable. Screening of severe cases and treatment where it's indicated. Riveredge must be a plague-spot of agents."

Taylor shook his head and told them, "It won't do."

Charles was aghast. "It won't *do*? Uncle Frank, what the hell do you mean, it won't do? Didn't we make it clear? They want to invade us and loot us and subject us!"

"It won't do," Taylor said. "I choose the devil we know. A

137

fighting fleet is out. We'll arm our merchant vessels and hope for the best. A full-time army is out. We'll get together some kind of militia. And a roundup of the unstable is out."

"Why?" Lee demanded. "My people have worked out perfectly effective techniques—"

"Let me talk, please. I have a feeling that it won't be any good, but hear me out.

"I'll take your black art first, Lee. As you know, I have played with history. To a historian, your work has been very interesting. The sequence was this—study of abnormal psychology collapsed under Lieberman's findings, study of abnormal psychology revived by you when you invalidated Lieberman's findings. I suggest that Lieberman and his followers were correct—and that you were correct, I suggest that what changed was the makeup of the population. That would mean that before Lieberman there were plenty of neurotics and psychotics to study, that in Lieberman's time there were so few that earlier generalizations were invalidated, and that now—in our time, Lee—neurotics and psychotics are among us again in increasingly ample numbers."

The girl opened her mouth, shut it again and thoughtfully studied her nails.

"I will not tolerate," Taylor went on, "a roundup or a registration, or mass treatment or any such violation of the Syndic's spirit."

Charles exploded, "Damn it, this is a matter of life or death to the Syndic!"

"No, Charles. Nothing can be a matter of life or death to the Syndic. When anything becomes a matter of life or death to the Syndic, the Syndic is already dead, its morale, is already disintegrated, its credit already gone. What is left is not the Syndic but the Syndic's dead shell. I am not in a position to say objectively now whether the Syndic is dead or alive. I fear it is dying. The rising tide of neurotics is a symptom. The suggestion from you two, who should be imbued with the old happy-go-lucky, we-can't-miss esprit of the Syndic that we cower behind mercenaries instead of trusting the people who made us—that's another symptom. Dick Reiner's rise to influence on a policy of driving the Government from the seas is another symptom.

"I mentioned the devil we know as my choice. That's the status quo, even though I have reason to fear it's crumbling beneath our feet. If it is, it may last out our time. We'll shore it up with armed merchantmen and a militia. If the people are with us now as they always have been, that'll do it. The devil we don't know is what we'll become if we radically dislocate Syndic life and attitudes.

"I can't back a fighting fleet. I can't back a regular army. I can't back any restrictive measure on the freedom of anybody but an apprehended criminal. Read history. It has taught me not to meddle, it has taught me that no man should think himself clever enough or good enough to dare it. *That* is the lesson history teaches us.

"Who can know what he's doing when he doesn't even know why he does it? Bless the bright Cro-Magnon for inventing the bow and damn him for inventing missile warfare. Bless the stubby little Sumerians for miracles in gold and lapis lazuli and damn them for burying a dead queen's handmaidens living in her tomb. Bless Shih Hwang-Ti for building the Great Wall between northern barbarism and southern culture, and damn him for burning every book in China. Bless King Minos for the ease of Cnossian flush toilets and damn him for his yearly tribute of Greek sacrificial victims. Bless Pharaoh for peace and damn him for slavery. Bless the Greeks for restricting population so the well-fed few could kindle a watchtower in the west, and damn the prostitution and sodomy and wars of colonization by which they did it. Bless the Romans for their strength to smash down every wall that hemmed their building genius, and damn them for their weakness that never broke the bloody grip of Etruscan savagery on their minds. Bless the Jews who discovered the fatherhood of God and damn them who limited it to the survivors of a surgical operation. Bless the Christians who abolished the surgical preliminaries and damn them who substituted a thousand cerebral quibbles. Bless Justinian for the Code of Law and damn him for his countless treacheries that were the prototype of the wretched Byzantine millennium. Bless the churchmen for teaching and preaching, and damn them for drawing a line beyond which they could only teach and preach in peril of the stake.

"Bless the navigators who opened the New World to famine-ridden Europe, and damn them for syphilis. Bless the redskins who bred maize, the great preserver of life and damn them for breeding maize the great destroyer of topsoil. Bless the Virginia planters for the solace of tobacco and damn them for the red gullies they left where forests had stood. Bless the obstetricians with forceps who eased the agony of labor and damn them for bringing countless monsters into the world to reproduce their kind. Bless the Point Four boys who slew the malaria mosquitoes of Ceylon and damn them for letting more Sinhalese be born then five Ceylons could feed.

"Who knows what he is doing, why he does it or what the consequences will be?

"Let the social scientists play with their theories if they like; I'm fond of poetry myself. The fact is that they have not so far solved what I call the two-billion-body problem. With brilliant hindsight some of them tell us that more than a dozen civilizations have gone down into the darkness before us. I see no reason why ours should not go down into the darkness with them, nor do I see any reason why we should not meanwhile enjoy ourselves collecting sense-impressions to be remembered with pleasure in old age. No; I will not agitate for extermination of the Government and hegemony over the Mob. Such a policy would automatically, inevitably and immediately entail many, many violent deaths and painful wounds. The wrong kind of sense-impressions. I shall, with fear and trembling, recommend the raising of a militia—a purely defensive, extremely sloppy militia—and pray that it will not involve us in a war of aggression."

He looked at the two of them and shrugged. "Lee, so stern, Charles so grim," he said, "I suppose you're dedicated now." He looked at the desk.

He thought: *I have a faint desire to take the pistol from my desk and shoot you both. I nave a nervous feeling that you're about to embark on a crusade to awaken Syndic Territory to its perils. You think the fate of civilization hinges on you. You're right, of course. The fate of civilization hinges on every one of us at any given moment. We are all components in the two-billion-body problem. Somehow for a century we've achieved in Syndic Territory for almost everybody the civil liberties, peace of mind and living standards that were enjoyed by the middle classes before 1914—plus longer life, better health, a more generous morality, increased command over nature; minus the servant problem and certain superstitions. A handful of wonderfully pleasant decades. When you look back over history you wonder who in his right mind could ask for more. And you wonder who would dare to presume to tamper with it.*

He studied the earnest young faces. There was so much that he might say—but he shrugged again.

"Bless you," he said, "Gather ye sense impression while ye may. Some like pointer readings, some like friction on the mucous membranes. Now go about your business; I have work to do."

He didn't really. When he was alone he leaned back and laughed and laughed.

Win, lose or draw, those two would go far and enjoy themselves mightily along the way, which was what counted.

THE END

If you've enjoyed this book, you will not want to miss these terrific titles…

ARMCHAIR SCI-FI & HORROR DOUBLE NOVELS, $12.95 each

D-11 **PERIL OF THE STARMEN** by Kris Neville
THE FORGOTTEN PLANET by Murray Leinster

D-12 **THE STAR LORD** by Boyd Ellanby
CAPTIVES OF THE FLAME by Samuel R. Delaney

D-13 **MEN OF THE MORNING STAR** by Edmund Hamilton
PLANET FOR PLUNDER by Hal Clement and Sam Merwin, Jr.

D-14 **ICE CITY OF THE GORGON** by Chester S. Geier and Richard S. Shaver
WHEN THE WORLD TOTTERED by Lester Del Rey

D-15 **WORLDS WITHOUT END** by Clifford D. Simak
THE LAVENDER VINE OF DEATH by Don Wilcox

D-16 **SHADOW ON THE MOON** by Joe Gibson
ARMAGEDDON EARTH by Geoff St. Reynard

D-17 **THE GIRL WHO LOVED DEATH** by Paul W. Fairman
SLAVE PLANET by Laurence M. Janifer

D-18 **SECOND CHANCE** by J. F. Bone
MISSION TO A DISTANT STAR by Frank Belknap Long

D-19 **THE SYNDIC** by C. M. Kornbluth
FLIGHT TO FOREVER by Poul Anderson

D-20 **SOMEWHERE I'LL FIND YOU** by Milton Lesser
THE TIME ARMADA by Fox B. Holden

ARMCHAIR SCIENCE FICTION CLASSICS, $12.95 each

C-3 **INTO PLUTONIAN DEPTHS**
by Stanton A. Coblentz

C-4 **CORPUS EARTHLING**
by Louis Charbonneau

C-5 **THE TIME DISSOLVER**
by Jerry Sohl

C-6 **WEST OF THE SUN**
by Edgar Pangborn

ARMCHAIR SCI-FI & HORROR GEMS SERIES, $12.95 each

G-1 **SCIENCE FICTION GEMS, Vol. One**
Isaac Asimov and others

G-2 **HORROR GEMS, Vol. One**
Carl Jacobi and others

HURTLING THROUGH TIME!

It was one man pitted against the limitless wastes of Time. His name was Martin Saunders, and he fought the strange, inhuman civilizations of Earth's unguessable future before finally finding his one true love in all the universe. Her name was Taury, an Empress of a dying empire, and a creature of ultimate virtue and beauty; and Martin Saunders knew that everything from his past was of nothing compared to the love he found for her. A love that would last literally for eternity, as he searched hopelessly among the never-ending tomorrows for the road to one unforgettable yesterday!

We're sure you'll find "Flight to Forever" to be one of the most memorable time travel novels you have ever read. It is a true forgotten masterpiece, penned by one of the most heralded science fiction writers of all time, Poul Anderson.

CAST OF CHARACTERS

MARTIN SAUNDERS

A great scientist and the country's first time traveler, but was he destined to be lost in the future forever?

EMPRESS TAURY

She commanded the remains of a crumbling empire, but her heart belonged to a man from 40 thousand years ago!

VARGOR ALFRI

A fierce warrior and prince of the Empire, he betrayed the man who saved the empire from destruction.

BELGOTAI

He was an alien mercenary from the future, but he turned out to be the best friend an Earthman could have.

THE DREAMER

Incredibly old and wise, he was the last remaining counselor from the glory days of the old Empire.

SAM HULL

He was basically along for the ride—thousands of years into the future, and it got him more than he bargained for.

FLIGHT TO FOREVER

By
POUL ANDERSON

ARMCHAIR FICTION
PO Box 4369, Medford, Oregon 97501-0168

For more information about Armchair Books and products, visit our website at…

www.armchairfiction.com

Or email us at…

armchairfiction@yahoo.com

CHAPTER ONE
No Return

THAT morning it rained, a fine, summery mist blowing over the hills and hiding the gleam of the river and the village beyond. Martin Saunders stood in the doorway letting the cool, wet air blow in his face and wondered what the weather would be like a hundred years from now.

Eve Lang came up behind him and laid a hand on his arm. He smiled down at her, thinking how lovely she was with the raindrops caught in her dark hair like small pearls. She didn't say anything; there was no need for it, and he felt grateful for silence.

He was the first to speak. "Not long now, Eve." And then, realizing the banality of it, he smiled. "Only why do we have this airport feeling? It's not as if I'll be gone long."

"A hundred years," she said.

"Take it easy, darling. The theory isn't foolproof. I've been on time jaunts before, remember? Twenty years ahead and twenty back. The projector works, it's been proven in practice. This is just a little longer trip, that's all."

"But the automatic machines, that went a hundred years ahead, never came back—"

"Exactly. Some damn fool thing or other went wrong with them. Tubes blew their silly heads off, or some such thing. That's why Sam and I have to go, to see what went wrong. We can repair our machine. We can compensate for the well-known perversity of vacuum tubes."

"But why the two of you? One would be enough. Sam—"

"Sam is no physicist. He might not be able to find the trouble. On the other hand, as a skilled mechanic he can do

things I never could. We supplement each other."
Saunders took a deep breath. "Look, darling—"

Sam Hull's bass shout rang out to them. "All set, folks!
Any time you want to go, we can ride!"

"Coming." Saunders took his time, bidding Eve a proper
farewell, a little in advance. She followed him into the house
and down to the capacious underground workshop.

The projector stood in a clutter of apparatus under the
white radiance of fluoro-tubes. It was unimpressive from the
outside, a metal cylinder some ten feet high and thirty feet
long with the unfinished look of all experimental setups. The

FLIGHT TO FOREVER

*One man against the limitless wastes of Time, he fought
the strange, inhuman civilizations of Earth's unguessable future, searching hopelessly among the never-
ending tomorrows—for the road to one unforgettable
yesterday!*

A Novel by POUL ANDERSON

The place pulsed and
throbbed with incredible
forces . . .

outer shell was simply protection for the battery banks and the massive dimensional projector within. A tiny space in the forward end was left for the two men.

Sam Hull gave them a gay wave. His massive form almost blotted out the gray-smocked little body of MacPherson. "All set for a hundred years ahead," he exclaimed. "Two thousand seventy-three, here we come!"

MacPherson blinked owlishly at them from behind thick lenses. "It all tests out," he said. "Or so Sam here tells me. Personally, I wouldn't know an oscillograph from a klystron. You have an ample supply of spare parts and tools. There should be no difficulty."

"I'm not looking for any, Doc," said Saunders. "Eve here won't believe we aren't going to be eaten by monsters with stalked eyes and long fangs. I keep telling her all we're going to do is check your automatic machines, if we can find them, and make a few astronomical observations, and come back."

"There'll be people in the future," said Eve.

"Oh, well, if they invite us in for a drink we won't say no," shrugged Hull. "Which reminds me—" He fished a pint out of his capacious coverall pocket. "We ought to drink a toast or something, huh?"

Saunders frowned a little. He didn't want to add to Eve's impression of a voyage into darkness. She was worried enough, poor kid, poor, lovely kid. "Hell," he said, "we've been back to nineteen fifty-three and seen the house standing. We've been ahead to nineteen ninety-three and seen the house standing. Nobody home at either time. These jaunts are too dull to rate a toast."

"Nothing," said Hull, "is too dull to rate a drink." He poured and they touched glasses, a strange little ceremony in the utterly prosaic laboratory. "Bon voyage!"

"Bon voyage." Eve tried to smile, but the hand that lifted the glass to her lips trembled a little.

"Come on," said Hull. "Let's go, Mart. Sooner we set out, the sooner we can get back."

"Sure." With a gesture of decision, Saunders put down his glass and swung toward the machine. "Goodbye, Eve, I'll see you in a couple of hours—after a hundred years or so."

"So long—Martin." She made the name a caress.

MacPherson beamed with avuncular approval.

Saunders squeezed himself into the forward compartment with Hull. He was a big man, long-limbed and wide-shouldered, with blunt, homely features under a shock of brown hair and wide-set gray eyes lined with crow's feet from much squinting into the sun. He wore only the plain blouse and slacks of his work, stained here and there with grease or acid.

The compartment was barely large enough for the two of them, and crowded with instruments—as well as the rifle and pistol they had along entirely to quiet Eve's fears. Saunders swore as the guns got in his way, and closed the door. The clang had in it an odd note of finality.

"Here goes," said Hull unnecessarily.

Saunders nodded and started the projector warming up. Its powerful thrum filled the cabin and vibrated in his bones. Needles flickered across gauge faces, approaching stable values.

Through the single porthole he saw Eve waving. He waved back and then, with an angry motion, flung down the main switch.

The machine shimmered, blurred, and was gone. Eve drew a shuddering breath and turned back to MacPherson.

GRAYNESS swirled briefly before them, and the drone of the projectors filled the machine with an enormous song. Saunders watched the gauges, and inched back the switch that controlled their rate of time advancement. A hundred years ahead—less the number of days since they'd sent the first automatic, just so that no dunderhead in the future would find it and walk off with it…

He slapped down the switch and the noise and vibration came to a ringing halt.

Sunlight streamed in through the porthole. "No house?" asked Hull.

"A century is a long time," said Saunders. "Come on, let's go out and have a look."

They crawled through the door and stood erect. The machine lay in the bottom of a half-filled pit above which grasses waved. A few broken shards of stone projected from the earth. There was a bright blue sky overhead, with fluffy white clouds blowing across it.

"No automatics," said Hull, looking around.

"That's odd. But maybe the ground-level adjustments—let's go topside." Saunders scrambled up the sloping walls of the pit.

It was obviously the half-filled basement of the old house, which must somehow have been destroyed in the eighty years since his last visit. The ground-level machine in the projector automatically materialized it on the exact surface whenever it emerged. There would be no sudden falls or sudden burials under risen earth. Nor would there be disastrous materializations inside something solid; mass-sensitive circuits prevented the machine from halting whenever solid matter occupied its own space. Liquid or gas molecules could; get out of the way fast enough.

Saunders stood in tall, wind-rippled grass and looked over the serene landscape of up pet New York State. Nothing had changed, the river and the forested hills beyond it were the same, the sun was bright and clouds shone in the heavens.

No—no, before God! Where was the village?

House gone, town gone—what had happened? Had people simply moved, away, or…?

He looked back down to the basement. Only a few minutes ago—a hundred years in the past—he had stood there in a tangle of battered apparatus, and Doc and Eve— and now it was a pit with wild grass covering the raw earth. An odd desolation tugged at him.

Was *he* still alive today? Was Eve? The gerontology of 1973 made it entirely possible, but one never knew. And he didn't want to find out.

"Musta' give the country back to the Indians," grunted Sam Hull.

The prosaic wisecrack restored a sense of balance. After all, any sensible man knew that things changed with time. There would be good and evil in the future as there had been in the past. "—And they lived happily ever after" was pure myth. The important thing was change, an unending flux out of which all could come. And right now there was a job to do.

They scouted around in the grass, but there was no trace of the small automatic projectors. Hull scowled thoughtfully. "You know," he said, "I think they started back and blew out on the way."

"You must be right," nodded Saunders. "We can't have arrived more than a few minutes after their return-point." He started back toward the big machine. "Let's take our observation and get out."

They set up their astronomical equipment and took readings on the declining sun. Waiting for night, they cooked a meal on a camp stove and sat while" a cricket-chirring dusk deepened around them.

"I like this future," said Hull. "It's peaceful. Think I'll retire here—or now—in my old age."

The thought of transtemporal resorts made Saunders grin. But—who knew? Maybe!

The stars wheeled grandly overhead. Saunders jotted

down figures on right ascension, declination and passage times. From that, they could calculate later, almost to the minute, how far the machine had taken them. They had not moved in space at all, of course, relative to the surface of the earth. "Absolute Space" was an obsolete fiction, and as far as the projector was concerned Earth was the immobile center of the universe.

They waded through dew-wet grass back down to the machine. "We'll try ten-year stops, looking for the automatics," said Saunders. "If we don't find 'em that way, to hell with them. I'm hungry."

2063—it was raining into the pit.

2053—sunlight and emptiness.

2043—the pit was fresher now, and a few rotting timbers lay half-buried in the ground.

Saunders scowled at the meters. "She's drawing more power than she should," he said.

2023—the house had obviously burned, charred stumps of wood were in sight. And the projector had roared with a skull-cracking insanity of power; energy drained from the batteries like water from a squeezed sponge; a resistor was beginning to glow.

They checked the circuits, inch by inch, wire by wire. Nothing was out of order.

"Let's go." Hull's face was white.

It was a battle to leap the next ten years; it took half an hour of bawling, thundering, tortured labor for the projector to fight backward. Radiated energy made the cabin unendurably hot.

2013—the fire-blackened basement still stood. On its floor lay two small cylinders, tarnished with some years of weathering.

"The automatics got a little further back," said Hull. "Then they quit, and just lay here."

Saunders examined them. When he looked up from his instruments, his face was grim with the choking fear that was rising within him. "Drained," he said. "Batteries completely dead. They used up all their energy reserves."

"What in the devil is this?" It was almost a snarl from Hull.

"I—don't—know. There seems to be some kind of resistance which increases the further back we try to go—"

"Come on!"

"But—"

"Come on, gawd damn it!"

Saunders shrugged hopelessly.

It took two hours to fight back five years. Then Saunders stopped the projector. His voice shook.

"No go, Sam. We've used up three-quarters of our stored energy—and the farther back we go, the more we use per year. It seems to be some sort of high-order exponential function."

"So—".

"So we'd never make it. At this rate, our batteries will be dead before we get back another ten years." Saunders looked ill. "It's some effect the theory didn't allow for, some accelerating increase in power requirements the farther back into the past we go. For twenty-year hops or less, the energy increases roughly as the square of the number of years traversed. But it must actually be something like an exponential curve, which starts building up fast and furious beyond a certain point. We haven't enough power left in the batteries!"

"If we could recharge them—"

"We don't have such equipment with us. But maybe—"

They climbed out of the ruined basement and looked eagerly towards the river. There was no sign of the village. It must have been torn down or otherwise destroyed still further back in the past at a point they'd been through.

"No help there," said Saunders.

"We can look for a place. There must be people somewhere!"

"No doubt." Saunders fought for calm. "But we could spend a long time looking for them, you know. And—" his voice wavered. "Sam, I'm not sure even recharging at intervals would help. It looks very much to me as if the curve of energy consumption is approaching a vertical asymptote."

"Talk English, will you?" Hull's grin was forced.

"I mean that beyond a certain number of years an infinite amount of energy may be required. Like the Einsteinian concept of light as the limiting velocity. As. you approach the speed of light, the energy needed to accelerate increases ever more rapidly; You'd need infinite energy to get beyond the speed of light—which is just a fancy way of saying you can t do It. The same thing may apply to time as well as space.

"You mean—we can't ever get back?"

"I don't know." Saunders looked desolately around at the smiling landscape. "I could be wrong. But I'm horribly afraid I'm right."

Hull swore, "What're we going to do about it?"

"We've got two choices," Saunders said. "One, we can hunt for people, recharge our batteries, and keep trying. Two, we can go into the future."

"The future!"

"Uh-huh. Sometime in the future, they ought to know: more about such things than we do. They may know a way to get around this effect. Certainly they could give us a powerful enough engine so that, if energy is all that's needed, we can get back. A small atomic generator, for instance."

Hull stood with bent head, turning the thought over in his mind. There was a meadowlark singing somewhere, maddeningly sweet.

Saunders forced a harsh laugh. "But the very first thing on the agenda," he said, "is breakfast!"

CHAPTER TWO
Belgotai of Syrtis

THE food was tasteless. They ate in a heavy silence, choking the stuff down. But in the end they looked at each other with a common resolution.

Hull grinned and stuck out a hairy paw. "It's a hell of a roundabout way to get home, "he said, "but I'm for it."

Saunders clasped hands with him, wordlessly. They went back to the machine.

"And now where?" asked the mechanic.

"It's two thousand eight," said Saunders. "How about—well—two-thousand five-hundred A. D.?"

"Okay. It's a nice round number. Anchors aweigh!"

The machine thrummed and shook. Saunders was gratified to notice the small power consumption as the years and decades fled by. At that rate, they had energy enough to travel to the end of the world.

Eve, Eve, I'll come back. I'll come back if I have to go ahead to Judgment Day…

2500 A. D. The machine blinked into materialization on top of a low hill—the pit had filled in during the intervening centuries. Pale, hurried sunlight flashed through wind-driven rain clouds into the hot interior.

"Come," said Hull. "We haven't got all day."

He picked up the automatic rifle. "What's the idea?" exclaimed Saunders.

"Eve was right the first time," said Hull grimly. "Buckle, on that pistol, Mart."

Saunders strapped the heavy weapon to his thigh. The metal was cold under his fingers.

They stepped out and swept the horizon. Hull's voice

rose in a shout of glee. "People!"

There was a small town beyond the river, near the site of old Hudson. Beyond it lay fields of ripening grain and clumps of trees. There was no sign of a highway. Maybe surface transportation was obsolete now.

The town looked—odd. It must have been there a long time, the houses were weathered. They were tall peak-roofed buildings, crowding narrow streets. A flashing metal tower reared some five hundred feet into the lowering sky, near the center of town.

Somehow, it didn't look the way Saunders had visualized communities of the future. It had an oddly stunted appearance, despite the high buildings and—sinister? He couldn't say. Maybe it was only his depression.

Something rose from the center of the town, a black ovoid that whipped into the sky and lined out across the river. *Reception committee*, thought Saunders. His hand fell on his pistol butt.

It was an airjet, he saw as it neared, an egg-shaped machine with stubby wings and a flaring tail. It was flying slowly now, gliding ground ward, toward them.

"Hello, there!" bawled Hull. He stood erect with the savage wind tossing his flame-red hair, waving. "Hallo, people!"

The machine dove at them. Something stabbed from its nose, a line of smoke—tracers!

Conditioned reflex flung Saunders to the ground. The bullets whined over his head, exploding with a vicious crash behind him. He saw Hull blown apart.

The jet rushed overhead and banked for another assault. Saunders got up and ran, crouching low, weaving back and forth. The line of bullets spanged past him again, throwing up gouts of dirt where they hit. He threw himself down again.

Another try…Saunders was knocked off his feet by the bursting of a shell. He rolled over and hugged the ground, hoping the grass would hide him. Dimly, he thought that the jet was too fast for strafing a single man; it overshot its mark.

He heard it whine overhead, without daring to look up. It circled vulture-like, seeking him. He had time for a rising tide of bitter hate.

Sam—they'd killed him, shot him without provocation— Sam, red-haired Sam with his laughter and his comradeship. Sam was dead and they had killed him.

He risked turning over. The jet was settling to earth; they'd hunt him from the ground. He got up and ran again.

A shot wailed past his ear. He spun around, the pistol in his hand, and snapped a return shot. There were men in black uniforms coming out of the jet. It was long range, but his gun was a heavy war model, it carried. He fired again and felt a savage joy at seeing one of the black-clad figures spin on its heels and lurch to the ground.

The time machine lay before him. No time for heroics; he had to get away—fast! Bullets were zinging around him.

He burst through the door and slammed it shut. A slug whanged through the metal wall. Thank God the tubes were still warm!

He threw the main switch. As vision wavered, he saw the pursuers almost on him. One of them was aiming something like a bazooka.

They faded into grayness. He lay back, shuddering. Slowly, he grew aware that his clothes were torn and that a metal fragment had scratched his hand.

And Sam was dead. Sam was dead.

He watched the dial creep upward. Let it be 3000 A. D. Five-hundred years was not too much to put between himself and the men in black.

HE CHOSE nighttime. A cautious look outside revealed that he was among tall buildings with little if any light. Good!

He spent a few moments bandaging his injury and changing into the extra clothes Eve had insisted on providing—a heavy wool shirt and breeches, boots, and a raincoat that should help make him relatively inconspicuous. The holstered pistol went along, of course, with plenty of extra cartridges. He'd have to leave the machine while he reconnoitered and chance its discovery. At least he could lock the door.

Outside, he found himself standing in a small cobbled courtyard between high houses with shuttered and darkened windows. Overhead was utter night, the stars must be clouded, but he saw a vague red glow to the north, pulsing and flickering. After a moment, he squared his shoulders and started down an alley that was like a cavern of blackness.

Briefly, the incredible situation rose in his mind. In less than an hour he had leaped a thousand years past his own age, had seen his friend murdered and now stood in an alien city more alone than man had ever been. *And Eve, will I see you again!*

A noiseless shadow, blacker than the night, slipped past him. The dim light shone greenly from its eyes—an alley cat! At least man still had pets. But he could have wished for a more reassuring one.

Noise came from ahead, a bobbing light flashing around at the doors of houses. He dropped a hand through the slit in his coat to grasp the pistol butt.

Black against the narrowed skyline four men came abreast, filling the street. The rhythm of their footfalls was military— a guard of some kind. He looked around for shelter; he didn't want to be taken prisoner by unknowns.

No alleys to the side—he sidled backward. The flashlight

beam darted ahead, crossed his body, and came back. A voice shouted something, harsh and peremptory.

Saunders turned and ran. The voice cried again behind him. He heard the slam of boots after him. Someone blew a horn, raising echoes that hooted between the high dark walls.

A black form grew out of the night. Fingers like steel wires closed on his arm, yanking him to one side. He opened his mouth, and a hand slipped across it. Before he could recover balance, he was pulled down a flight of stairs in the street.

"In heah." The hissing whisper was taut in his ear. "Quickly."

A door slid open just a crack. They burst through, and the other man closed it behind them. An automatic lock clicked shut.

"Ih don' tink dey vised use," said the man grimly. "Dey better not ha'!"

Saunders stared at him. The other man was of medium height, with a lithe, slender build shown by the skin-tight gray clothes under his black cape. There was a gun at one hip, a pouch at the other. His face was sallow, with a yellowish tinge, and the hair was shaven. It was a lean, strong face, with high cheekbones and narrow jaw, straight nose with flaring nostrils, dark, slant eyes under Mephistophelean brows. The mouth, wide and self-indulgent, was drawn into a reckless grin that showed sharp white teeth. Some sort of white-Mongoloid half-breed, Saunders guessed.

"Who are *you?*" he asked roughly.

The stranger surveyed him shrewdly. "Belgotai of Syrtis," he said at last. "But yuh don' belong heah."

"I'll say I don't." Wry humor rose in Saunders. "Why did you snatch me that way?"

"Yuh didn' wanna fall into de Watch's hands, did yuh?" asked Belgotai. "Don' ask mih why Ih ressued a stranger. Ih happened to come out, see yuh running, figgered anybody running fro de Watch desuhved help, an' pulled yuh back in." He shrugged. "Of course, if yuh don' wanna be helped, go back upstaiahs."

"I'll stay here, of course," he said. "And—thanks for rescuing me."

"De nada," said Belgotai. "Come, le's ha' a drink."

It was a smoky, low-ceilinged room, with a few scarred wooden tables crowded about a small charcoal fire and, big barrels in the rear—a tavern of some sort, an underworld hangout. Saunders reflected that he might have done worse. Crooks wouldn't be as finicky about his antecedents as officialdom might be. He could ask his way around, learn.

"I'm afraid I haven't any money," he said. "Unless—" He pulled a handful of coins from his pocket.

Belgotai looked sharply at them and drew a whistling breath between his teeth. Then his face smoothed into blankness. "Ih'll buy," he said genially. "Come, Hennaly, gi' us whissey."

Belgotai drew Saunders into a dark corner seat, away from the others in the room. The landlord brought tumblers of rotgut remotely akin to whiskey, and Saunders gulped his with a feeling of need.

"Wha' name do yuh go by?" asked Belgotai.

"Saunders. Martin Saunders."

"Glad to see yuh. Now—" Belgotai leaned closer, and his voice dropped to a whisper—"Now, Saunders, *when're* yuh from?"

Saunders started. Belgotai smiled thinly. "Be frank," he said. "Dese're mih frien's heah. Dey'd think nawting of slitting yuh troat and dumping yuh in de alley. But Ih mean well."

With a sudden great weariness, Saunders relaxed. What the hell, it had to come out sometime. "Nineteen hundred seventy-three," he said.

"Eh? De future?"

"No—the past."

"Oh. Diff'ent chronning, den. How far back?"

"One thousand and twenty-seven years."

Belgotai whistled. "Long ways! But Ih were sure yuh mus' be from de past. Nobody eve' came fro' de future. "

Sickly: "You mean—it's impossible?"

"Ih do' know."   Belgotai's grin was wolfish. "Who'd visit dis era fro' de future, if dey could? But wha's yuh story?"

Saunders bristled. The whiskey was coursing hot in his veins now. "I'll trade information," he said coldly. "I won't give it."

"Faiah enawff. Blast away, Mahtin Saundahs. "

Saunders told his story in a few words. At the end, Belgotai nodded gravely. "Yuh ran into de Fanatics, five hundred yeahs ago," he said. "Dey was deat' on time travelers. Or on most people, for dat matter."

"But what's happened?   What sort of world is this, anyway?"

Belgotai's slurring accents were getting easier to follow. Pronunciation had changed a little, vowels sounded different, the "r" had shifted to something like that in twentieth-century French or Danish, other consonants were modified. Foreign words, especially Spanish, had crept in. But it was still intelligible. Saunders listened. Belgotai was not too well versed in history, but his shrewd brain had a grasp of the more important facts.

The time of troubles had begun in the twenty-third century with the revolt of the Martian colonists against the increasingly corrupt and tyrannical Terrestrial Directorate. A century later the folk of Earth were on the move, driven by famine, pestilence and civil war, a chaos out of which rose the religious enthusiasm of the Armageddonists—the Fanatics, as

they were called later. Fifty years after the massacres on
Luna, Huntry was the military dictator of Earth, and the rule
of the Armageddonists endured for nearly three hundred
years. It was a nominal sort of rule, vast territories were
always in revolt and the planetary colonists were building up a
power which kept the Fanatics out of space, but wherever
they did have control they ruled with utter ruthlessness.

Among other things they forbade was time travel. But it
had never been popular with anyone since the Time War,
when a defeated Directorate army had leaped from the
twenty-third to the twenty-fourth century and wrought havoc
before their attempt at conquest was smashed. Time travelers
were few anyway, the future was too precarious—they were
apt to be killed or enslaved in one of the more turbulent
periods.

In the late twenty-seventh century, the Planetary League
and the African Dissenters had finally ended Fanatic rule.
Out of the postwar confusion rose the Pax Africana, and for
two hundred years man had enjoyed an era of comparative
peace and progress which was wistfully looked back on as a
golden age; indeed, modern chronology dated from the
ascension of John Mteza, I. Breakdown came through
internal decay and the onslaughts of barbarians from the
outer planets, the Solar System split into a multitude of small
states and even independent cities. It was a hard, brawling
period, not without a brilliance of its own, but it was drawing
to a close now.

"Dis is one of de city-states," said Belgotai. "Liung-Wei,
it's named—founded by Sinese invaders about tree centuries
ago. It's under de dictatorship of Krausmann now, a
stubborn old buzzard who'll no surrender dough de armies of
de Atlantic Master're at ouah very gates now. Yuh see de red
glow? Dat's deir projectors working on our energy screen.
When dey break it down, day'll take de city and punish it for

holding out so long. Nobody looks happily to dat day."

HE ADDED a few remarks about himself. Belgotai was of a dying age, the past era of small states who employed mercenaries to fight their battles. Born on Mars, Belgotai had hired out over the whole Solar System. But the little mercenary companies were helpless before the organized levies of the rising nations, and after the annihilation of his band Belgotai had fled to Earth where he dragged out a weary existence as thief and assassin. He had little to look forward to.

"Nobody wants a free comrade now," he said ruefully. "If de Watch don't catch me first, Ih'll hang when de Atlantics take de city."

Saunders nodded with a certain sympathy.

Belgotai leaned close with a gleam in his slant eyes. "But yuh can help me, Mahtin Saundahs," he hissed. "And help yuhself too."

"Eh?" Saunders blinked wearily at him.

"Sure, sure. Take me wid yuh, out of dis damned time. Dey can't help yuh here, dey know no more about time travel dan yuh do—most likely dey'll trow yuh in de calabozo and smash yuh machine. Yuh have to go on. Take me!"

Saunders hesitated, warily. What did he really know? How much truth was in Belgotai's story? How far could he trust—

"Set me off in some time when a free comrade can fight again. Meanwhile Ih'll help. Ih'm a good man wid gun or vibrodagger. Yuh can't go batting alone into de future."

Saunders wondered. But what the hell—it was plain enough that this period was of no use to him. And Belgotai had saved him, even if the Watch wasn't as bad as he claimed. And—well—he needed someone to talk to, if nothing else. Someone to help him forget Sam Hull and the gulf of centuries separating him from Eve.

Decision came. "Okay."

"Wonnaful! Yuh'll no be sorry, Mahtin." Belgotai stood up. "Come, le's be blasting off."

"Now?"

"De sooner de better. Someone may find yuh machine. Den it's too late."

"But—you'll want to make ready—say goodbye—"

Belgotai slapped his pouch. "All Ih own is heah." Bitterness underlay his reckless laugh. "Ih've none to say goodbye to, except mih creditors. Come!"

Half dazed, Saunders followed him out of the tavern. This time-hopping was going too fast for him, he didn't have a chance to adjust.

For instance, if he ever got back to his own time he'd have descendants in this age. At the rate at which lines of descent spread, there would be men in each army who had his own and Eve's blood, warring on each other without thought of the tenderness which had wrought their very beings. But then, he remembered wearily, he had never considered the common ancestors he must have with men he'd shot out of the sky in the war he once had fought.

Men lived in their own times, a brief flash of light ringed with an enormous dark, and it was not in their nature to think beyond that little span of years. He began to realize why time travel had never been common.

"Hist!" Belgotai drew him into the tunnel of an alley. They crouched there while four black-caped men of the Watch strode past. In the wan red light, Saunders had a glimpse of high cheekbones, half-Oriental features, the metallic gleam of guns slung over their shoulders.

They made their way to the machine where it lay between lowering houses crouched in a night of fear and waiting. Belgotai laughed again, a soft, joyous ring in the dark.

"Freedom!" he whispered.

They crawled into it and Saunders set the controls for a hundred years ahead. Belgotai scowled. "Most like de world'll be very tame and quiet den," he said.

"If I get a way to return," said Saunders, "I'll carry you on whenever you want to go."

"Or yuh could carry me back a hundred years from now," said the warrior. "Blast away, den!"

3100 A. D. A waste of blackened, fused rock. Saunders switched on the Geiger counter and it clattered crazily. Radioactive! Some hellish atomic bomb had wiped Liung-Wei from existence. He leaped another century, shaking.

3200 A. D. The radioactivity was gone, but the desolation remained, a vast vitrified crater under a hot, still sky, dead and lifeless. There was little prospect of walking across it in search of man, nor did Saunders want to get far from the machine. If he should be cut off from it...

By 3500, soil had drifted back over the ruined land arid a forest was growing. They stood in a drizzling rain and looked around them.

"Big trees;" said Saunders. "This forest has stood for a long time without human interference."

"Maybe man went back to de caves?" suggested Belgotai.

"I doubt it. Civilization was just too widespread for a lapse into total savagery. But it may be along ways to a settlement."

"Le's go ahead, den!" Belgotai's eyes gleamed with interest.

The forest still stood for centuries thereafter. Saunders scowled in worry. He didn't like this business of going farther and farther from his time, he was already too far ahead ever to get back without help. Surely, in all ages of human history—

4100 A. D. They flashed into materialization on a broad

grassy sward where low, rounded buildings of something that looked like tinted plastic stood between fountains, statues, and bowers. A small aircraft whispered noiselessly overhead, no sign of motive power on its exterior.

There were humans around, young men and women who wore long colorful capes over light tunics. They crowded forward with a shout. Saunders and Belgotai stepped out, raising hands in a gesture of friendship. But the warrior kept his hands close to his gun.

The language was a flowing, musical tongue with only a baffling hint of familiarity. Had times changed that much?

They were taken to one of the buildings. Within its cool, spacious interior, a grave, bearded man in ornate red robes stood up to greet them. Someone else brought in a small machine reminiscent of an oscilloscope with microphone attachments. The man set it on the table and adjusted its dials.

He spoke again, his own unknown language rippling from his lips. But words came out of the machine—English!

"Welcome, travelers, to this branch of the American College. Please be seated."

Saunders and Belgotai gaped. The man smiled. "I see the psychophone is new to you. It is a receiver of encephalic emissions from the speech centers. When one speaks, the corresponding thoughts are taken by the machine, greatly amplified, and beamed to the brain of the listener, who interprets them in terms of his own language.

"Permit me to introduce myself. I am Hamalon Avard, dean of this branch of the College." He raised bushy gray eyebrows in polite inquiry.

They gave their names and Avard bowed ceremoniously. A slim girl, whose scanty dress caused Belgotai's eyes to widen, brought a tray of sandwiches and a beverage not unlike tea. Saunders suddenly realized how hungry and tired he was. He collapsed into a seat that molded itself to his contours and looked dully at Avard.

Their story came out, and the dean nodded. "I thought you were time travelers," he said. "But this is a matter of great interest. The archeology departments will want to speak to you, if you will be so kind—"

"Can you help us?" asked Saunders. "Can you fix our machine so it will reverse?"

"Alas, no. I am afraid our physics holds no hope for you. I can consult the experts, but I am sure there has been no change in spatiotemporal theory since reformulation. According to it, the energy needed to travel into the past increases tremendously with the period covered. The deformation of world lines, you see. Beyond a period of about seventy years, infinite energy is required."

Saunders nodded dully. "I thought so. Then there's no hope?"

"Not in this time, I am afraid. But science is advancing rapidly. Contact with alien culture in the Galaxy has proved an immense stimulant—"

"Yuh have interstellar travel?" exploded Belgotai. "Yuh can travel to de stars?"

"Yes, of course. The faster-than-light drive was worked out over five hundred years ago on the basis of Priogan's modified relativity theory. It involves warping through higher dimensions— But you have more urgent problems than scientific theories."

"Not Ih!" said Belgotai fiercely. "If Ih can get put among de stars—dere must be wars dere—"

"Alas, yes, the rapid expansion of the frontier has thrown the Galaxy into chaos. But I do not think you could get passage on a spaceship. In fact, the Council will probably order your temporal deportation as unintegrated individuals. The sanity of Sol will be in danger otherwise."

"Why, yuh—" Belgotai snarled and reached for his gun. Saunders clapped a hand on the warrior's arm.

"Take it easy, you bloody fool," he said furiously. "We can't fight a whole planet. Why should we? There'll be other ages."

Belgotai relaxed, but his eyes were still angry.

THEY stayed at the College for two days. Avard and his colleagues were courteous, hospitable, eager to hear what the travelers had to tell of their periods. They provided food and living quarters and much-needed rest. They even pleaded Belgotai's case to the Solar Council, via telescreen. But the answer was inexorable: the Galaxy already had too many barbarians. The travelers would have to go.

Their batteries were taken out of the machine for them and a small atomic engine with nearly limitless energy reserves installed in its place. Avard gave them a psychophone for communication with whoever they met in the future. Everyone was very nice and considerate. But Saunders found himself reluctantly agreeing with Belgotai. He didn't care much for these over-civilized gentlefolk. He didn't belong in this age.

Avard bade them grave goodbye. "It is strange to see you go," he said. "It is a strange thought that you will still be traveling long after my cremation, that you will see things I cannot dream of." Briefly, something stirred in his face. "In a way I envy you." He turned away quickly, as if afraid of the thought. "Goodbye and good fortune."

4300 A. D. The campus buildings were gone, but small, elaborate summerhouses had replaced them. Youths and girls in scanty rainbow hued dress crowded around the machine.

"You are time travelers?" asked one of the young men, wide-eyed.

Saunders nodded, feeling too tired for speech.

"Time travelers!" A girl squealed in delight.

"I don't suppose you have any means of traveling into the past these days?" asked Saunders hopelessly.

"Not that I know of. But please come, stay for a while, tell us about your journeys. This is the biggest lark we've had since the ship came from Sirius."

There was no denying the eager insistence. The women, in particular, crowded around, circling them in a ring of soft arms, laughing and shouting and pulling them away from the machine. Belgotai grinned. "Le's stay de night," he suggested.

Saunders didn't feel like arguing the point. There was time enough, he thought bitterly. All the time in the world.

It was a night of revelry. Saunders managed to get a few facts. Sol was a Galactic backwater these days, stuffed with mercantile wealth and guarded by nonhuman mercenaries against the interstellar raiders and conquerors. This region was one of many playgrounds for the children of the great merchant families, living for generations off inherited riches. They were amiable kids, but there was a mental and physical softness over them, and a deep inward weariness from a meaningless round of increasingly stale pleasure. Decadence.

Saunders finally sat alone under a moon that glittered with the diamond-points of domed cities, beside a softly lapping artificial lake, and watched the constellations wheel overhead—the far suns that man had conquered without mastering himself. He thought of Eve and wanted to cry, but the hollowness in his breast was dry and cold.

CHAPTER THREE
Trapped in the Time-Stream

BELGOTAI had a thumping hangover in the morning that a drink offered by one of the women removed. He argued for a while about staying in this age. Nobody would deny him passage this time; they were eager for fighting men out in the Galaxy. But the fact that Sol was rarely visited now, that he might have to wait years, finally decided him on continuing.

"Dis won' go on much longer," he said. "Sol is too tempting a prize, an' mercenaries aren' allays loyal. Sooner or later, dere'll be war on Earl' again."

Saunders nodded dispiritedly. He hated to think of the blasting energies that would devour a peaceful and harmless folk, the looting and murdering and enslaving, but history was that way. It was littered with the graves of pacifists.

The bright scene swirled into grayness. They drove ahead.

4400 A. D. A villa was burning, smoke and flame reaching up into the clouded sky. Behind it stood the looming bulk of a ray-scarred spaceship, and around it boiled a vortex of men, huge bearded men in helmets and cuirasses, laughing as they bore out golden loot and struggling captives. The barbarians had come!

The two travelers leaped back into the machine. Those weapons could fuse it to a glowing mass. Saunders swung the main-drive switch far over.

"I think we'd better make a longer jump," Saunders said, as the needle crept past the century mark. "Can't look for much scientific progress in a dark age. I'll try for five thousand A. D."

His mind carried the thought on: *Will there ever be progress of the sort we must have? Eve, will I ever see you again?* As if his yearning could carryover the abyss of millennia: *Don't mourn me too long, my dearest. In all the bloody ages of human history, your happiness is all that ultimately matters.*

AS THE needle approached six centuries, Saunders tried to ease down the switch. *Tried!*

"What's the matter?" Belgotai leaned over his shoulder.

With a sudden cold sweat along his ribs, Saunders tugged harder. The switch was immobile—the projector wouldn't stop.

"Out of order?" asked Belgotai anxiously.

"No—it's the automatic mass-detector. We'd be annihilated if we emerged in the same space with solid matter. The detector prevents the projector from stopping if it senses such a structure." Saunders grinned savagely. "Some damned idiot must have built a house right where we are!"

The needle passed its limit, and, still they droned on through a featureless grayness. Saunders reset the dial and noted the first half millennium. It was nice, though not necessary, to know what year it was when they emerged.

He wasn't worried at first. Man's works were so horribly impermanent; he thought with a sadness of the cities and civilizations he had seen rise and spend their little hour and sink back into the night and chaos of time. But after a thousand years…

Two thousand…

Three thousand…

Belgotai's face was white and tense in the dull glow of the instrument panel. "How long to go?" he whispered.

"I—don't—know."

Within the machine, the long minutes passed while the projector hummed its song of power and two men stared with hypnotized fascination at the creeping record of centuries.

For twenty thousand years that incredible thing stood. In the year 25,296 A. D., the switch suddenly went down under Saunders' steady tug. The machine flashed into reality, tilted, and slid down a few feet before coming to rest. Wildly, they opened the door.

The projector lay on a stone block big as a small house, whose ultimate slipping from its place had freed them. It was halfway up a pyramid.

A monument of gray stone, a tetrahedron a mile to a side and a half a mile high. The outer casing had worn away, or been removed, so that the tremendous blocks stood naked to the weather. Soil had drifted up onto it, grass and trees grew on its titanic slopes. Their roots, and wind and rain and frost, were slowly crumbling the artificial hill to earth again, but still it dominated the landscape.

A defaced carving leered out from a tangle of brush. Saunders looked at it and looked away, shuddering. No human being had ever carved that thing.

The countryside around was altered; he couldn't see the old river and, there was a lake glimmering in the distance that had not been there before. The hills seemed lower, and forest covered them. It was a wild, primeval scene, but there was a spaceship standing near the base, a monster machine with its nose rearing skyward and a sunburst blazon on its hull. And there were men working nearby.

Saunders' shout rang in the still air. He and Belgotai scram bled down the steep slopes of earth, clawing past trees and vines. Men!

No—not all men. A dozen great shining engines were toiling without supervision at the foot of the pyramid— robots. And of the group which turned to stare at the travelers, two were squat, blue-furred, with snouted faces and six-fingered hands.

Saunders realized with an unexpectedly eerie shock that he was seeing extraterrestrial intelligence. But it was to the men that he faced.

They were all tall, with aristocratically refined features and a calm that seemed inbred. Their clothing was impossible to describe; it was like a rainbow shimmer around them, never the same in its play of color and shape. So, thought Saunders, so must the old gods have looked on high Olympus, beings greater and more beautiful than man.

But it was a human voice that called to them, a deep, well-modulated tone in a totally foreign language. Saunders remembered exasperately that he had forgotten the psychophone. But one of the blue-furred aliens was already fetching a round, knob-studded globe out of which the familiar translating voice seemed to come: "…time travelers."

"From the very remote past, obviously," said another man. Damn him, damn them all, they weren't any more excited than at the bird which rose, startled, from the long grass. You'd think time travelers would at least be worth shaking by the hand.

"Listen," snapped Saunders, realizing in the back of his mind that his annoyance was a reaction against the awesomeness of the company, "we're in trouble. Our machine won't carry us back, and we have to find a period of time that knows how to reverse the effect. Can you do it?"

One of the aliens shook his animal head.

"No," he said. "There is no way known to physics of getting farther back than about seventy years. Beyond that, the required energy approaches infinity and—"

Saunders groaned. "We know it," said Belgotai harshly.

"At least you must rest," said one of the men in a more kindly tone. "It will be interesting to hear your story."

"I've told it to too many people in the last few millennia," rasped Saunders. "Let's hear yours for a change."

Two of the strangers exchanged low-voiced words. Saunders could almost translate them himself: *"Barbarians—- childish emotional pattern—well, humor them for a while."*

"This is an archeological expedition, excavating the pyramid," said one of the men patiently. "We are from the Galactic Institute, Sarlan-sector branch. I am Lord Arsfel of Astracyr, and these are my subordinates. The nonhumans, as you may wish to know, are from the planet Quulhan, whose sun is not visible from Terra."

Despite himself, Saunders' awed gaze turned to the stupendous mass looming over them. "Who built it?" he breathed.

"The Ixchulhi made such structures on planets they conquered, no one knows why. But then, no one knows what they were, or where they came from, or where they ultimately went. It is hoped that some of the answers may be found in their pyramids."

THE atmosphere grew more relaxed. Deftly, the men of the expedition got Saunders' and Belgotai's stories and what information about their almost prehistoric periods they cared for. In exchange, something of history was offered them.

After the Ixchulhi's ruinous wars the Galaxy had made a surprisingly rapid comeback. New techniques of mathematical psychology made it possible to unite the peoples of a billion worlds and rule them effectively. The Galactic Empire was egalitarian—it had to be, for one of its mainstays was the fantastically old and evolved race of the planet called Vro-Hi by men.

It was peaceful, prosperous, and colorful with diversity of races and cultures, expanding in science and the arts. It had already endured for ten thousand years, and there seemed no doubt in Arsfel's calm mind that it could endure forever. The barbarians along the Galactic periphery and out in the Magellanic Clouds? Nonsense! The Empire would get around to civilizing them in due course; meanwhile they were only a nuisance.

But Sol could almost be called one of the barbarian suns, though it lay within the Imperial boundaries. Civilization was concentrated near the center of the Galaxy, and Sol lay in what was actually a remote and thinly starred region of space. A few primitive landsmen still lived on its planets and had infrequent intercourse with the nearer stars, but they hardly counted. The human race had almost forgotten its ancient home.

Somehow the picture was saddening to the American. He thought of old Earth spinning on her lonely way through the emptiness of space, he thought of the great arrogant Empire and of all the mighty dominions that had fallen to dust through the millenia. But when he ventured to suggest that this civilization, too, was not immortal, he was immediately snowed under with figures, facts, logic, the curious paramathematical symbolism of modern mass psychology. It could be shown rigorously that the present setup was inherently stable—and already ten thousand years of history had given no evidence to upset that science…

"I give up," said Saunders. "I can't argue with you."

They were shown through the spaceship's immense interior, the luxurious apartments of the expedition, the looming intricate machinery that did its own thinking. Arsfel tried to show them his art, his recorded music, his psychobooks, but it was no use, they didn't have the understanding.

Savages! Could an Australian aborigine have appreciated Rembrandt, Beethoven, Kant, or Einstein? Could he have lived happily in sophisticated New York society?

"We'd best go," muttered Belgotai. "We don't belong

heah."

Saunders nodded. Civilization had gone too far for them, they could never be more than frightened pensioners in its hugeness. Best to get on their way again.

"I would advise you to leap ahead for long intervals," said Arsfel. "Galactic civilization won't have spread out this far for many thousands of years, and certainly whatever native culture Sol develops won't be able to help you." He smiled. "It doesn't matter if you overshoot the time when the process you need is invented. The records won't be lost, I assure you. From here on, you are certain of encountering only peace and enlightenment...unless, of course, the barbarians of Terra get hostile, but then you can always leave them behind. Sooner or later, there will be true civilization here to help you."

"Tell me honestly," said Saunders. "Do you think the negative time machine will ever be invented?"

One of the beings from Quulhan shook his strange head. "I doubt it," he said gravely. "We would have had visitors from the future."

"They might not have cared to see your time," argued Saunders desperately. "They'd have complete records of it. So they'd go back to investigate more primitive ages, where their appearance might easily pass unnoticed."

"You may be right," said Arsfel. His tone was disconcertingly like that with which an adult comforts a child by a white lie.

"Le's go!" snarled Belgotai.

IN 26,000 THE FORESTS still stood and the pyramid had become a high hill where trees nodded and rustled in the wind.

In 27,000 a small village of wood and stone houses stood among smiling grain fields.

In 28,000 men were tearing down the pyramid, quarrying

it for stone. But its huge bulk was not gone before 30,000 A. D., and a small city had been built from it.

Minutes ago, thought Saunders grayly, they had been talking to Lord Arsfel of Astracyr, and now he was five thousand years in his grave.

In 31,000, they materialized on one of the broad lawns that reached between the towers of a high and proud city. Aircraft swarmed overhead and a spaceship, small beside Arsfel's but nonetheless impressive, was standing nearby.

"Looks like de Empire's got heah," said Belgotai.

"I don't know," said Saunders. "But it looks peaceful, anyway. Let's go out and talk to people."

They were received by tall, stately women in white robes of classic lines. It seemed that the Matriarchy now ruled Sol, and would they please conduct themselves as befitted the inferior sex? No, the Empire hadn't ever gotten out here; Sol paid tribute, and there was an Imperial legate at Sirius, but the actual boundaries of Galactic culture hadn't changed for the past three millennia. Solar civilization was strictly homegrown and obviously superior to the alien influence of the Vro-Hi.

No, nothing was known about time theory. Their visit had been welcome and all that, but now would they please go on? They didn't fit in with the neatly regulated culture of Terra.

"I don't like it," said Saunders as they walked back toward the machine. "Arsfel swore the Imperium would keep expanding its actual as well as its nominal sphere of influence. But it's gone static now. Why?"

"Ih tink," said Belgotai, "dat spite of all his fancy mathematics, yuh were right. Nawthing lasts forever."

"But—my God!"

CHAPTER FOUR
End of Empire

34,000 A. D. The Matriarchy was gone. The city was a tumbled heap of fire-blackened rocks. Skeletons lay in the ruins.

"The barbarians are moving again," said Saunders bleakly. "They weren't here so very long ago, these bones are still fresh, and they've got a long ways to go to dead center. An empire like this one will be many thousands of years in dying. But it's doomed already."

"What'll we do?" asked Belgotai.

"Go on," said Saunders softly. "What else can we do?"

35,000 A. D. A peasant hut stood under huge old trees. Here and there a broken column stuck out of the earth, remnant of the city. A bearded man in coarsely woven garments fled wildly with his woman and brood of children as the machine appeared.

36,000 A. D. There was a village again, with a battered old spaceship standing hard by. There were half a dozen different races, including man, moving about, working on the construction of some enigmatic machine. They were dressed in plain, shabby clothes," with guns at their sides and the hard look of warriors in their eyes. But they didn't treat the new arrivals too badly.

Their chief was a young man in the cape and helmet of an officer of the Empire. But his outfit was at least a century old, and he was simply head of a small troop that had been hired from among the barbarian hordes to protect this part of Terra. Oddly, he insisted he was a loyal vassal of the Emperor.

The Empire! It was still a remote glory, out there among the stars. Slowly it waned, slowly the barbarians encroached while corruption and civil war tore it apart from the inside, but it was still the pathetic, futile hope of intelligent beings throughout the Galaxy. Some day it would be restored. Someday civilization would return to the darkness of the outer worlds, greater and more splendid than ever. Men dared not believe otherwise.

"But we've got a job right here," shrugged the chief. "Tautho of Sirius will be on Sol's necks soon. I doubt if we can stand him off for long."

"And what'll yuh do den?" challenged Belgotai.

The young-old face twisted in a bitter smile. "Die, of course. What else is there to do—these days?"

They stayed overnight with the troopers. Belgotai had fun swapping lies about warlike exploits, but in the morning he decided to go on with Saunders. The age was violent enough, but its hopelessness daunted even his tough soul.

Saunders looked haggardly at the control panel. "We've got to go a long ways ahead," he said. "A hell of a long ways."

50,000 A. D. They flashed out of the time drive and opened the door. A raw wind caught at them, driving thin sheets of snow before it. The sky hung low and gray over a landscape of high rocky hills where pine trees stood gloomily between naked crags. There was ice on the river that murmured darkly out of the woods.

Geology didn't work that fast, even fourteen thousand years wasn't a very long time to the slowly changing planets. It must have been the work of intelligent beings, ravaging and scoring the world with senseless wars of unbelievable forces.

A gray stone mass dominated the landscape. It stood enormous a few miles off, its black walls sprawling over incredible acres, its massive crenellated towers reaching gauntly into the sky. And it lay half in ruin, torn and tumbled stone distorted by energies that once made rock run molten, blurred by uncounted millennia of weather—old.

"Dead," Saunders' voice was thin under the hooting wind. "All dead."

"No!" Belgotai's slant eyes squinted against the flying snow. "No, Mahtin, Ih tink Ih see a banner flying."

The wind blew bitterly around them, searing them with its chill. "Shall we go on?" asked Saunders dully.

"Best we go find out wha's happened," said Belgotai. "Dey can do no worse dan kill us, and Ih begin to tink dat's not so bad."

Saunders put on all the clothes he could find and took the psychophone in one chilled hand. Belgotai wrapped his cloak tightly about him. They started toward the gray edifice.

The wind blew and blew. Snow hissed around them, covering the tough gray-green vegetation that hugged the stony ground. Summer on Earth, 50,000 A. D.

As they neared the structure, its monster size grew on them. Some of the towers that still stood must be almost half a mile high, thought Saunders dizzily. But it had a grim, barbaric look; no civilized race had ever built such a fortress.

Two small, swift shapes darted into the air from that cliff-like wall. "Aircraft," said Belgotai laconically. The wind ripped the word from his mouth.

They were ovoidal, without external controls or windows, apparently running on the gravitic forces which had long ago been tamed. One of them hovered overhead, covering the travelers, while the other dropped to the ground. As it landed, Saunders saw that it was old and worn and scarred. But there was a faded sunburst on its side. Some memory of the Empire must still be alive.

TWO came out of the little vessel and approached the travelers with guns in their hands. One was human, a tall well-built young man with shoulder-length black hair blowing under a tarnished helmet, a patched purple coat streaming from his cuirassed shoulders, a faded leather kilt and buskins. The other…

He was a little shorter than the man, but immensely broad of chest and limb. Four muscled arms grew from the massive shoulders, and a tufted tail lashed against his clawed feet. His head was big, broadskulled, with a round half-animal face and cat-like whiskers about the fanged mouth and the split-pupil yellow eyes. He wore no clothes except a leather harness, but soft blue-gray fur covered the whole great body.

The psychophone clattered out the man's hail: "Who comes?"

"Friends," said Saunders. "We wish only shelter and a little information."

"Where are you from?" There was a harsh, peremptory note in the man's voice. His face—straight, thin-boned, the countenance of a highly bred aristocrat—was gaunt with strain. "What do you want? What sort of spaceship is that you've got down there?"

"Easy, Vargor," rumbled the alien's bass. "That's no spaceship; you can see that."

"No," said Saunders. "It's a time projector."

"Time travelers!" Vargor's intense blue eyes widened. "I heard of such things once, but—time travelers!" Suddenly: "When are you from? Can you help us?"

"We're from very long ago," said Saunders pityingly. "And I'm afraid we're alone and helpless."

Vargor's erect carriage sagged a little. He looked away. But the other being stepped forward with an eagerness in him. "How far back?" he asked. "Where are you going?"

"We're going to hell, most likely. But can you get us

inside? We're freezing."

"Of course. Come with us. You'll not take it amiss if I send a squad to inspect your machine? We have to be careful, you know."

The four squeezed into the aircraft and it lifted with a groan of ancient engines. Vargor gestured at the fortress ahead and his tone was a little wild. "Welcome to the hold of Brontothor! Welcome to the Galactic Empire!"

"The Empire?"

"Aye, this is the Empire, or what's left of it. A haunted fortress on a frozen ghost world, last fragment of the old Imperium and still trying to pretend that the Galaxy is not dying—that it didn't die millennia ago, that there is something left besides wild beasts howling among the ruins." Vargor's throat caught in a dry sob. "Welcome!"

The alien laid a huge hand on the man's shoulder. "Don't get hysterical, Vargor," he reproved gently. "As long as brave beings hope, the Empire is still alive—whatever they say."

He looked over his shoulder at the others. "You really are welcome," he said. "It's a hard and dreary life we lead here. Taury and the Dreamer will both welcome you gladly." He paused. Then, unsurely, "But best you don't say too much about the ancient time, if you've really seen it. We can't bear too sharp a reminder, you know."

The machine slipped down beyond the wall, over a gigantic flagged courtyard to the monster bulk of the—the donjon, Saunders supposed one could call it. It rose up in several tiers, with pathetic little gardens on the terraces, toward a dome of clear plastic.

The walls, he saw, were immensely thick, with weapons mounted on them that he could see clearly through the drifting snow. Behind the donjon stood several long, barracks-like buildings, and a couple of spaceships that must have been held together by pure faith rested near what looked like an arsenal. There were guards on duty, helmeted men with energy rifles, their cloaks wrapped tightly against the wind, and other folk scurried around under the monstrous walls, men and women and children.

"There's Taury," said the alien, pointing to a small group clustered on one of the terraces. "We may as well land right there." His wide mouth opened in an alarming smile. "And forgive me for not introducing myself before. I'm Hunda of Haamigur, general of the Imperial armies, and this is Vargor Alfri, prince of the Empire."

"Yuh crazy?" blurted Belgotai. "What Empire?"

Hunda shrugged. "It's a harmless game, isn't it? At that, you know, we are the Empire—legally. Taury is a direct descendant of Maurco the Doomer, last Emperor to be anointed according to the proper forms. Of course, that was five thousand years ago and Maurco had only three systems left then, but the law is clear. These hundred or more barbarian pretenders, human and otherwise, haven't the shadow of a real claim to the title."

The vessel grounded and they stepped out. The others waited for them to come up. There were half a dozen old men, their long beards blowing wildly in the gale, there was a being with the face of a longbeaked bird and one that had the shape of a centauroid.

"The court of the Empress Taury," said Hunda.

"Welcome." The answer was low and gracious.

Saunders and Belgotai stared dumbly at her. She was tall, tall as a man, but under her tunic of silver links and her furred cloak she was such a woman as they had dreamed of without ever knowing in life. Her proudly lifted head had something of Vargor's looks, the same clean-lined, high-cheeked face, but it was the countenance of a woman, from the broad clear brow to the wide, wondrously chiseled mouth and the strong chin. The cold had flushed the lovely pale planes of her cheeks. Her heavy bronze-red hair was braided about her helmet, with one rebellious lock tumbling softly toward the level, dark brows. Her eyes, huge and oblique and gray as northern seas, were serene on them.

Saunders found tongue. "Thank you, your majesty," he said in a firm voice.

"If it please you, I am Martin Saunders of America, some forty-eight thousand years in the past, and my companion is Belgotai, free companion from Syrtis about a thousand years later. We're at your service for what little we'll be able to do."

She inclined her stately head, and her sudden smile was warm and human. "It is a rare pleasure," she said. "Come inside, please. And forget the formality. Tonight let us simply be alive."

THEY sat in what had been a small council chamber. The great hall was too huge and empty, a cavern of darkness and rustling relics of greatness, hollow with too many memories. But the lesser room had been made livable, hung with tapestries and carpeted with skins. Fluorotubes cast a white light over it, and a fire crackled cheerfully in the hearth. Had it not been for the wind against the windows, they might have forgotten where they were.

"—and you can never go back?" Taury's voice was sober. "You can never get home again?"

"I don't think so," said Saunders. "From our story, it doesn't look that way, does it?"

"No," said Hunda. "You'd better settle down in some time and make the best of matters."

"Why not with us?" asked Vargor eagerly.

"We'd welcome you with all our hearts," said Taury, "but I cannot honestly advise you to stay. These are evil times."

It was a harsh language they spoke, a ringing metallic tongue brought in by the barbarians. But from her throat

Saunders thought, it was utter music.

"We'll at least stay a few days," he said impulsively. "It's barely possible we can do something."

"I doubt that," said Hunda practically. "We've retrogressed, yes. For instance, the principle of the time projector was lost long ago. But still, there's a lot of technology left which was far beyond your own times."

"I know," said Saunders defensively. "But—well, frankly—we haven't fitted in any other time as well."

"Will there ever be a decent age again?" asked one of the old courtiers bitterly.

The avian from Klakkahar turned his eyes on Saunders. "It wouldn't be cowardice for you to leave a lost cause that you couldn't possibly aid," he said in his thin, accented tones. "When the Anvardi come, I think we will all die."

"What is de tale of de Dreamer?" asked Belgotai. "You've mentioned some such."

It was like a sudden darkness in the room. There was silence, under the whistling wind, and men sat wrapped in their own cheerless thoughts. Finally Taury spoke.

"He is the last of the Vro-Hi, counselors of The Empire. That one still lives—the Dreamer. But there can never really be another Empire, at least not on the pattern of the old one. No other race is intelligent enough to coordinate it."

Hunda shook his big head, puzzled. "The Dreamer once told me that might be for the best," he said. "But he wouldn't explain."

"How did you happen to come hereto Earth, of all planets?" Saunders asked.

Taury smiled with a certain grim humor. "The last few generations have been one of the Imperium's less fortunate periods," she said. "In short, the most the Emperor ever commanded was a small fleet. My father had even that shot away from him. He fled with three ships, out toward the

Periphery. It occurred to him that Sol was worth trying as a refuge."

The Solar System had been cruelly scarred in the dark ages. The great engineering works that had made the other planets habitable were ruined, and Earth herself had been laid waste. There had been a weapon used that consumed atmospheric carbon dioxide. Saunders, remembering the explanation for the Ice Ages offered by geologists of his own time, nodded in dark understanding. Only a few starveling savages lived on the planet now, and indeed the whole Sirius. Sector was so desolated that no conqueror thought it worth bothering with.

It had pleased the Emperor to make his race's ancient home the capital of the Galaxy. He had moved into the ruined fortress of Brontothor, built some seven thousand years ago by the nonhuman Grimmani and blasted out of action a millennium later. Renovation of numerous parts of it, installation of weapons programs and defensive works, institution of agriculture... "Why, he had suddenly acquired a whole planetary system!" said Taury with a half-sad smile.

SHE took them down into the underground levels the next day to see the Dreamer. Vargor went along too, walking close beside her, but Hunda stayed topside; he was busy supervising the construction of additional energy screen generators.

They went through immense vaulted taverns hewed out of the rock, dank tunnels of silence where their footfalls echoed weirdly and shadows flitted beyond the dull glow of fluorospheres. Now and then they passed a looming monstrous bulk, the corroded hulk of some old machine. The night and loneliness weighed heavily on them, they huddled together and did not speak for fear of rousing the jeering echoes.

"There were slideways here once," remarked Taury as they started, "but we haven't gotten around to installing new ones. There's too much else to do."

Too much else—a civilization to rebuild, with these few broken remnants. How can they dare even to keep trying in the face of the angry gods? What sort of courage is it they have?

Taury walked ahead with the long, swinging stride of a warrior, a red lioness of a woman in the wavering shadows. Her gray eyes caught the light with a supernatural brilliance. Vargor kept pace, but he lacked her steadiness, his gaze shifted nervously from side to side as they moved down the haunted, booming length of the tunnels. Belgotai went cat-footed, his own restless eyes had merely the habitual wariness of his hard and desperate lifetime. Again Saunders thought, what a strange company they were, four humans from the dawn and the dusk of human civilization, thrown together at the world's end and walking to greet the last of the gods. His past life, Eve, MacPherson, the world of his time, were dimming in his mind, they were too remote from his present reality. It seemed as if he had never been anything but a follower of the Galactic Empress.

They came at last to a door. Taury knocked softly and swung it open—yes, they were even back to manual doors now.

Saunders had been prepared for almost anything, but nonetheless the appearance of the Dreamer was a shock. He had imagined a grave white-bearded man, or a huge-skulled spider-thing, or a naked brain pulsing in a machine-tended case. But the last of the Vro-Hi was—a monster.

No—not exactly. Not when you discarded human standards, then he even had a weird beauty of his own. The gross bulk of him sheened with iridescence, and his many seven-fingered hands were supple and graceful, and the eyes—the eyes were huge pools of molten gold, lambent and wise, a stare too brilliant to meet directly.

He stood up on his stumpy legs as they entered, barely four feet high though the head-body unit was broad and massive. His hooked beak did not open, and the psychophone remained silent, but as the long delicate feelers pointed toward him Saunders thought he heard words, a deep organ voice rolling soundless through the still air: "Greeting, your majesty. Greeting your highness. Greeting, men out of time, and welcome!"

Telepathy—direct telepathy—so that was how it felt!

"Thank you...sir." Somehow, the thing rated the title, rated an awed respect to match his own grave formality. "But I thought you were in a trance of concentration till now. How did you know—" Saunders' voice trailed off and he flushed with sudden distaste.

"No, traveler, I did not read your mind as you think. The Vro-Hi always respected privacy and did not read any thoughts save those contained in speech addressed solely to them. But my induction was obvious."

"What were you thinking about in the last trance?" asked Vargor. His voice was sharp with strain. "Did you reach any plan?"

"No, your highness," vibrated the Dreamer. "As long as the factors involved remain constant, we cannot logically do otherwise than we are doing. When new data appears, I will reconsider immediate necessities. No, I was working further on the philosophical basis which the Second Empire must have."

"What Second Empire?" sneered Vargor bitterly.

"The one which will come—some day," answered Taury quietly.

The Dreamer's wise eyes rested on Saunders and Belgotai. "With your permission," he thought, "I would like to scan your complete memory patterns, conscious, subconscious, and cellular. We know so little of your age." As they hesitated: "I assure you, sirs, that a nonhuman being half a million years old can keep secrets, and certainly does not pass moral judgments. And the scanning will be necessary anyway if I am to teach you the present language."

Saunders braced himself. "Go ahead," he said distastefully.

For a moment he felt dizzy, a haze passed over his eyes and there was an eerie thrill along every nerve of him. Taury laid an arm about his waist, bracing him.

It passed. Saunders shook his head, puzzled. "Is that *all?*"

"Aye, sir. A Vro-Hi brain can scan an indefinite number of units simultaneously." With a faint hint of a chuckle: "But did you notice what tongue you just spoke in?"

"I—eh—huh?" Saunders looked wildly at Taury's smiling face. The hard, open-voweled syllables barked from his mouth: "I—by the gods—I can speak Stellarian now!"

"Aye," thought the Dreamer. "The language centers are peculiarly receptive, it is easy to impress a pattern on them. The method of instruction will not work so well for information involving other faculties, but you must admit it is a convenient and efficient way to learn speech."

"Blast off wit me, den," said Belgotai cheerfully. "Ih allays was a dumkoff at languages."

When the Dreamer was through, he thought: "You will not take it amiss if I tell all that what I saw in both your minds was good—brave and honest, under the little neuroses which all beings at your level of evolution cannot help accumulating. I will be pleased to remove those for you, if you wish."

"No, thanks," said Belgotai. "I like my little neuroses."

"I see that you are debating staying here," went on, the Dreamer. "You will be valuable, but you should be fully warned of the desperate position we actually are in. This is not a pleasant age in which to live."

"From what I've seen," answered Saunders slowly, "golden ages are only superficially better. They may be easier on the surface, but there's death in them. To travel hopefully, believe me, is better than to arrive."

"That has been true in all past ages, aye. It was the great mistake of the Vro Hi. We should have known better, with ten million years of civilization behind us." There was a deep and tragic note in the rolling thought-pulse. "But we thought that since we had achieved a static physical state in which the new frontiers and challenges lay within our own minds, all beings at all levels of evolution could and should have developed in them the same ideal.

"With our help, and with the use of scientific psychodynamics and the great cybernetic engines, the coordination of a billion planets became possible. It was perfection, in a way—but perfection is death to imperfect beings, and even the Vro-Hi had many shortcomings. I cannot explain all the philosophy to you; it involves concepts you could not fully grasp, but you have seen the workings of the great laws in the rise and fall of cultures. I have proved rigorously that permanence is a self-contradictory concept. There can be no goal to reach, not ever."

"Then the Second Empire will have no better hope than decay and chaos again?" Saunders grinned humorlessly. "Why the devil do you want one?"

Vargor's harsh laugh shattered the brooding silence. "What indeed does it matter?" he cried. "What use to plan the future of the universe, when we are outlaws on a forgotten planet? The Anvardi are coming!" He sobered, and there was a set to his jaw that Saunders liked. "They're coming, and there's little we can do to stop it," said Vargor. "But we'll give them a fight. We'll give them such a fight as the poor old Galaxy never saw before!"

CHAPTER FIVE
Attack of the Anvardi

"OH, NO—oh no—oh no—"

The murmur came unnoticed from Vargor's lips, a broken cry of pain as he stared at the image that flickered and wavered on the great interstellar communiscreen. And there was horror in the eyes of Taury, grimness to the set of Hunda's mighty jaws, a sadness of many hopeless centuries in the golden gaze of the Dreamer.

After weeks of preparation and waiting, Saunders realized matters were at last coming to a head.

"Aye, your majesty," said the man in the screen. He was haggard, exhausted, worn out by strain and struggle and defeat. "Aye, fifty-four shiploads of us, and the Anvardian fleet in pursuit."

"How far behind?" rapped Hunda.

"About half a light-year, sir, and coming up slowly. We'll be close to Sol before they can overhaul us."

"Can you fight them?" rapped Hunda.

"No, sir," said the man. "We're loaded with refugees, women and children and unarmed peasants, hardly a gun on a ship—Can't you help us?" It was a cry, torn by the ripping static that filled the interstellar void. "Can't you help us, your majesty? They'll sell us for slaves!"

"How did it happen?" asked Taury wearily.

"I don't know, your majesty. We heard you were at Sol through your agents, and secretly gathered ships. We don't want to be under the Anvardi, Empress; they tax the life from us and conscript our men and take our women and children... We only communicated by ultrawave; it can't be traced, and we only used the code your agents gave us. But as we passed Canopus, they called on us to surrender in the name of their king—and they have a whole war fleet after us!"

"How long before they get here?" asked Hunda.

"At this rate, sir, perhaps a week," answered the captain of the ship. Static snarled through his words.

"Well, keep on coming this way," said Taury wearily. "We'll send ships against them. You may get away during the battle. Don't go to Sol, of course, we'll have to evacuate that. Our men will try to contact you later."

"We aren't worth it, your majesty. Save all your ships."

"We're coming," said Taury flatly, and broke the circuit.

She turned to the others, and her red head was still lifted. "Most of our people can get away," she said. "They can flee into the Arlath cluster; the enemy won't be able to find them in that wilderness." She smiled, a tired little smile that tugged at one corner of her mouth. "We all know what to do, we've planned against this day. Munidor, Falz, Mico, start readying for evacuation. Hunda, you and I will have to plan our assault. We'll want to make it as effective as possible, but use a minimum of ships."

"Why sacrifice fighting strength uselessly?" asked Belgotai.

"It won't be useless. We'll delay the Anvardi, and give those refugees a chance to escape."

"If we had weapons," rumbled Hunda. His huge fists clenched. "By the gods, if we had decent weapons!"

The Dreamer stiffened. And before he could vibrate it, the same thought had leaped into Saunders' brain, and they stared at each other, man and Vro-Hian, with a sudden wild hope...

SPACE glittered and flared with a million stars, thronging against the tremendous dark, the Milky Way foamed around the sky in a rush of cold silver, and it was shattering to a human in its utter immensity. Saunders felt the loneliness of it as he had never felt it on the trip to Venus—for Sol was dwindling behind them, they were rushing out into the void between the stars.

There had only been time to install the new weapon on the dreadnought and time and facilities were so cruelly short there had been no chance even to test it in maneuvers. They might, perhaps, have leaped back into time again and again, gaining weeks, but the shops of Terra could only turn out so much material in the one week they did have.

So it was necessary to risk the whole fleet and the entire fighting strength of Solon this one desperate gamble. If the old *Vengeance* could do her part, the outnumbered Imperials would have their chance. But if they failed…

Saunders stood on the bridge, looking out at the stellar host, trying to discern the Anvardian fleet. The detectors were far over scale, the enemy was close, but you couldn't visually detect something that outran its own image.

Hunda was at the control central, bent over the cracked old dials and spinning the corroded signal wheels, trying to coax another centimeter per second from a ship more ancient than the Pyramids had been in Saunders' day. The Dreamer stood quietly in a corner, staring raptly out at the Galaxy. The others at the court were each in charge of a squadron" Saunders had talked to them over the inter-ship visiscreen— Vargor, white-lipped and tense, Belgotai blasphemously cheerful, the rest showing only cool reserve.

"In a few minutes," said Taury quietly. "In just a few minutes, Martin."

She paced back from the viewport, lithe and restless as a tigress. The cold white starlight glittered in her eyes. A red cloak swirled about the strong, deep curves of her body, a Sunburst helmet sat proudly on her bronze-bright hair.

Saunders thought how beautiful she was—by all the gods, how beautiful!

She smiled at him. "It is your doing, Martin," she said. "You came from the past just to bring us hope. It's enough to make one believe in destiny." She took his hand. "But of course it's not the hope you wanted. This won't get you back home."

"It doesn't matter," he said.

"It does, Martin. But—may I say it? I'm still glad of it. Not only for the sake of the Empire, but—"

A voice rattled over the bridge communicator: "Ultrawave to bridge. The enemy is sending us a message, your majesty. Shall I send it up to you?"

"Of course." Taury switched on the bridge screen.

A face leaped into it, strong and proud and ruthless, the Sunburst shining in the green hair. "Greeting, Taury of Sol," said the Anvardian. "I am Ruulthan, Emperor of the Galaxy."

"I know who you claim to be," said Taury thinly, "and I don't recognize your assumed title."

"Our detectors report your approach with a fleet approximately one-tenth the size of ours. You have one Supernova ship, of course, but so do we. Unless you wish to come to terms, it will mean annihilation."

"What are your terms?"

"Surrender, execution of the criminals who led the attacks on Anvardian planets, and your own pledge of allegiance to me as Galactic Emperor." The voice was clipped, steel-hard.

Taury turned away in disgust. Saunders told Ruulthan in explicit language what to do with his terms, and then cut off the screen.

Taury gestured to the newly installed time-drive controls. "Take them, Martin," she said. "They're yours, really." She put her hands in his and looked at him with serious gray eyes. "And if we should fail in this—goodbye, Martin."

"Goodbye," he said thickly.

HE WRENCHED himself over the panel and sat down before its few dials. *Here goes nothing!*

He waved one hand, and Hunda cut off the hyperdrive. At low intrinsic velocity, the *Vengeance* hung in space while the invisible ships of her fleet flashed past toward the oncoming Anvardi.

Slowly then, Saunders brought down the time-drive switch. And the ship roared with power, atomic energy flowed into the mighty circuits which they had built to carry her huge mass through time—the lights dimmed, the giant machine throbbed and pulsed, and a featureless grayness swirled beyond the ports.

He took her back three days. They lay in empty space, the Anvardi were still fantastic distances away. His eyes strayed to the brilliant yellow spark of Sol. Right there, this minute, he was sweating his heart out installing the time projector that had just carried him back…

But no, that was meaningless, simultaneity was arbitrary. And there was a job to do right now.

The chief astrogator's voice came with a torrent of figures. They had to find the exact position in which the Anvardian flagship would be in precisely seventy-two hours. Hunda rang the signals to the robots in the engine room, and slowly, ponderously, the *Vengeance* slid across five million miles of space.

"All set," said Hunda. "Let's go!"

Saunders smiled, a mirthless skinning of teeth, and threw his main switch in reverse. Three days forward in time…

To lie alongside the Anvardian dreadnought!

Frantically Hunda threw the hyperdrive back in, matching

translight velocities. They could see the ship now, it loomed like a metal mountain against the stars. And every gun in the *Vengeance* cut loose!

Vortex cannon—blasters—atomic shells and torpedoes—gravity snatchers—all the hell which had ever been brewed in the tortured centuries of history vomited against the screens of the Anvardian flagship.

Under that monstrous barrage, filling space with raving energy till it seemed its very structure must boil, the screens went down, a flare of light searing like another nova. And through the solid matter of her hull those weapons bored, cutting, blasting, disintegrating. Steel boiled into vapor, into atoms, into pure devouring energy that turned on the remaining solid material. Through and through the hull that fury raged, a waste of flame that left not even ash in its track.

And now the rest of the Imperial fleet drove against the Anvardi. Assaulted from outside, with a devouring monster in its very midst, the Anvardian fleet lost the offensive, recoiled and broke up into desperately fighting units. War snarled between the silent white stars.

Still the Anvardi fought, hurling themselves against the ranks of the Imperials, wrecking ships and slaughtering men even as they went down. They still had the numbers, if not the organization, and they had the same weapons and the same bitter courage as their foes.

The bridge of the *Vengeance* shook and roared with the shock of battle. The lights darkened, flickered back, dimmed again. The riven air was sharp with ozone, and the intolerable energies loosed made her interior a furnace. Reports clattered over the communicator: "—Number Three screen down—Compartment Number Five doesn't answer—Vortex turret Five Hundred Thirty Seven out of action—"

Still she fought, still she fought, hurling metal and energy in an unending storm, raging and rampaging among the ships of the Anvardi. Saunders found himself manning a gun, shooting out at vessels he couldn't see, getting his aim by sweat-blinded glances at the instruments—and the hours dragged away in flame and smoke and racking thunder..."

"They're fleeing!"

The exuberant shout rang through every remaining compartment of the huge old ship. *Victory, victory, victory*— She had not heard such cheering for five thousand weary years.

Saunders staggered drunkenly back onto the bridge. He could see the scattered units of the Anvardi now that he was behind them, exploding out into the Galaxy in wild search of refuge, hounded and harried by the vengeful Imperial fleet.

And now the Dreamer stood up, and suddenly he was not a stump-legged little monster but a living god whose awful thought leaped across space, faster than light, to bound and roar through the skulls of the barbarians. Saunders fell to the floor under the impact of that mighty shout, he lay numbly staring at the impassive stars while the great command rang in his shuddering brain:

"Soldiers of the Anvardi, your false emperor is dead and Taury the Red, Empress of the Galaxy, has the victory. You have seen her power. Do not resist it longer, for it is unstoppable.

"Lay down your arms. Surrender to the mercy of the Imperium. We pledge you amnesty and safe-conduct. And bear this word back to your planets:

"Taury the Red calls on all the chiefs of the Anvardian Confederacy to pledge fealty to her and aid her in restoring the Galactic Empire!"

CHAPTER SIX
Flight without End

THEY stood on a balcony of Brontothor and looked again at old Earth for the first time in almost a year and the last time, perhaps, in their lives.

It was strange to Saunders, this standing again on the planet which had borne him after those months in the many and alien worlds of a Galaxy far bigger than he could really imagine. There was an odd little tug at his heart, for all the bright hope of the future. He was saying goodbye to Eve's world.

But Eve was gone, she was part of a past forty-eight thousand years dead, and he had seen those years rise and die, his one year of personal time was filled and stretched by the vision of history until Eve was a remote, lovely dream. God keep her, wherever her soul had wandered in these millenia— God grant she had had a happy life—but as for him, he had his own life to live, and a mightier task at hand than he had ever conceived.

The last months rose in his mind, a bewilderment of memory; After the surrender of the Anvardian fleet, the Imperials had gone under their escort directly to Canopus and thence through the Anvardian empire. And chief after chief, now that Ruulthan was dead and Taury had shown she could win a greater mastery than his, pledged allegiance to her.

Hunda was still out there with Belgotai, fighting a stubborn Anvardian earl. The Dreamer was in the great Polarian System, toiling at readjustment. It would be necessary, of course, for the Imperial capital to move from isolated Sol to central Polaris, and Taury did not think she would ever have time or opportunity to visit Earth again.

And so she had crossed a thousand starry light-years to the little lonely sun that had been her home. She brought ships, machines, and troops. Sol would have a military base sufficient to protect it. Climate engineers would drive the glacial winter of Earth back to its poles and begin the resettlement of the other planets. There would be schools, factories, civilization; Sol would have cause to remember its Empress.

Saunders came along because he couldn't quite endure the thought of leaving Earth altogether without farewell. Vargor, grown ever more silent and moody, joined them, but otherwise the old comradeship of Brontothor was dissolving in the sudden fury of work and war and complexity which claimed them.

And so they stood again in the old ruined castle, Saunders and Taury, looking out at the night of Earth.

It was late; all others seemed to be asleep. Below the balcony, the black walls dropped dizzily to the gulf of night that was the main courtyard. Beyond it, a broken section of outer wall showed snow lying white and mystic under the moon. The stars were huge and frosty, flashing and glittering with cold crystal light above the looming pines, grandeur and arrogance and remoteness wheeling enormously across the silent sky. The moon rode high, its scarred old face the only familiarity from Saunders' age, its argent radiance flooding down on the snow to shatter in a million splinters.

It was quiet—*quiet*. Sound seemed to have frozen to death in the bitter windless cold. Saunders had stood alone, wrapped in furs with his breath shining ghostly from his nostrils, looking out on the silent winter world and thinking his own thoughts. He had heard a soft footfall and turned to see Taury approaching.

"I couldn't sleep," she said.

She came out onto the balcony to stand beside him. The moonlight was white on her face, shimmering faintly from her eyes and hair, she seemed a dim goddess of the night.

"What were you thinking, Martin?" she asked after a while.

"Oh—I don't know," he said. "Just dreaming a little, I suppose. It's a strange thought to me, to have left my own time forever and now to be leaving even my own world."

She nodded gravely. "I know. I feel the same way." Her low voice dropped to a whisper. "I didn't have to come back in person, you know. They need me more at Polaris. But I thought I deserved this last farewell to the days when we fought with our own hands, and fared between the stars, when we were a small band of sworn comrades whose dreams outstripped our strength. It was hard and bitter, yes, but I don't think we'll have time for laughter any more. When you work for a million stars, you don't have a chance to see one peasant's wrinkled face light with a deed of kindness you did, or hear him tell you what you did wrong— the world will all be strangers to us—"

For another moment, silence under the far cold stars, then, "Martin—I am so lonely now."

He took her in his arms. Her lips were cold against his, cold with the cruel silent chill of the night, but she answered him with a fierce yearning.

"I think I love you, Martin," she said after a very long time. Suddenly she laughed, a clear and lovely musk echoing from the frosty towers of Brontothor. "Oh, Martin, I shouldn't have been afraid. We'll never be lonely, not ever again—"

The moon had sunk far toward the dark horizon when he took her back to her rooms. He kissed her good night and went down the booming corridor toward his own chambers.

His head was awhirl—he was drunk with the sweetness

and wonder of it, he felt like singing and laughing aloud and embracing the whole starry universe. Taury, Taury, Taury!

"Martin."

He paused. There was a figure standing before his door, a tall slender form wrapped in a dark cloak. The dull light of a fluoroglobe threw the face into sliding shadow and tormented highlights. Vargor.

"What is it?" he asked.

The prince's hand came up, and Saunders saw the blunt muzzle of a stun pistol gaping at him. Vargor smiled, lop-sidedly and sorrowfully. "I'm sorry, Martin," he said.

Saunders stood paralyzed with unbelief. Vargor—why, Vargor had fought beside him; they'd saved each other's lives laughed and worked and lived together—Vargor!

The gun flashed. There was a crashing in Saunders' head and he tumbled into illimitable darkness.

HE AWOKE very slowly, every nerve tingling with the pain of returning sensation. Something was restraining him. As his vision cleared, he saw that he was lying bound and gagged on the floor of his time projector.

The time machine—he'd all but forgotten it, left it standing in a shed while he went out to the stars, he'd never thought to have another look at it. The time machine!

Vargor stood in the open door, a fluoroglobe in one hand lighting his haggard face. His hair fell in disarray past his tired, handsome features, and his eyes were as wild as the low words that spilled from his mouth.

"I'm sorry, Martin, really I am. I like you, and you've done the Empire such a service as it can never forget, and this is as low a trick as one man can ever play on another. But I have to. I'll be haunted by the thought of this night all my life, but I have to."

Saunders tried to move, snarling incoherently through his

gag. Vargor shook his head. "Oh, no, Martin, I can't risk letting you make an outcry. If I'm to do evil, I'll at least do a competent job of it.

"I love Taury, you see. I've loved her ever since I first met her, when I came from the stars with a fighting fleet to her father's court and saw her standing there with the frost crackling through her hair and those gray eyes shining at me. I love her so it's like a pain in me. I can't be away from her, I'd pull down the cosmos for her sake. And I thought she was slowly coming to love me.

"And tonight I saw you two on the balcony, and knew I'd lost. Only I can't give up! Our breed has fought the Galaxy for a dream, Martin—it's not in us ever to stop fighting while life is in us. Fighting by any means, for whatever is dear and precious—but fighting!"

Vargor made a gesture of deprecation. "I don't want power, Martin, believe me. The consort's job will be hard and unglamorous, galling to a man of spirit—but if that's the only way to have her, then so be it. And I do honestly believe, right or wrong, that I'm better for her and for the Empire than you. You don't really belong here, you know. You don't have the tradition, the feeling, the training—you don't even have the biological heritage of five thousand years. Taury may care for you now, but think twenty years ahead!"

Vargor smiled wryly. "I'm taking a chance, of course. If you do find a means of negative time travel and come back here, it will be disgrace and exile for me. It would be safer to kill you. But I'm not quite that much of a scoundrel. I'm giving you your chance. At worst, you should escape into the time when the Second Empire is in its glorious bloom, a happier age than this. And if you do find a means of coming back—well, remember what I said about your not belonging, and try to reason with clarity and kindness. Kindness to Taury, Martin."

He lifted the fluoroglobe, casting its light over the dim interior of the machine. "So it's goodbye, Martin, and I hope you won't hate me too much. It should take you several thousand years to work free and stop the machine. I've equipped it with weapons, supplies, everything I think you may need for any eventuality. But I'm sure you'll emerge in a greater and more peaceful culture, and he happier there."

His voice was strangely tender, all of a sudden. "Goodbye, Martin my comrade. And—good luck!"

He opened the main-drive switch and stepped out as the projector began to warm up. The door clanged shut behind him.

Saunders writhed on the floor, cursing with a brain that was a black cauldron of bitterness. The great drone of the projector rose, he was on his way—*Oh no—stop the machine, God, set me free before it's too late!*

The plastic cords cut his wrists. He was lashed to a stanchion, unable to reach the switch with any part of his body. His groping fingers slid across the surface of a knot, the nails clawing for a hold. The machine roared with full power, driving ahead through the vastness of time.

Vargor had bound him skillfully. It took him a long time to get free. Toward the end he went slowly not caring, knowing with a dull knowledge that he was already more thousands of irretrievable years into the future than his dials would register.

He climbed to his feet, plucked the gag from his mouth, and looked blankly out at the faceless gray. The century needle was hard against its stop. He estimated vaguely that he was some ten thousand years into the future already.

Ten thousand years!

He yanked down the switch with a raging burst of savagery.

It was dark outside. He stood stupidly for a moment

before he saw water seeping into the cabin around the door. Water—he was under water—short circuits! Frantically, he slammed the switch forward again.

He tasted the water on the floor. It was salt. Sometime in that ten thousand years, for reasons natural or artificial, the sea had come in and covered the site of Brontothor.

A thousand years later he was still below its surface. Two thousand, three thousand, ten thousand...

Taury, Taury! For twenty thousand years she had been dust on an alien planet. And Belgotai was gone with his wry smile, Hunda's staunchness, even the Dreamer must long ago have descended into darkness. The sea rolled over dead Brontothor, and he was alone.

He bowed his head on his arms and wept.

FOR three million years the ocean layover. Brontothor's land. And Saunders drove onward.

He stopped at intervals to see if the waters had gone. Each time the frame of the machine groaned with pressure and the sea poured in through the crack of the door. Otherwise he sat dully in the throbbing loneliness, estimating time covered by his own watch and the known rate of the projector, not caring any more about dates or places.

Several times he considered stopping the machine, letting the sea burst in and drown him. There would be peace in its depths, sleep and forgetting. But no, it wasn't in him to quit that easily. Death was his friend, death would always be there waiting for his call.

But Taury was dead.

Time grayed to its end. In the four millionth year, he stopped the machine and discovered that there was dry air around him.

He was in a city. But it was not such a city as he had ever seen or imagined, he couldn't follow the wild geometry of the titanic structures that loomed about him and they were never the same. The place throbbed and pulsed with incredible forces, it wavered and blurred in a strangely unreal light. Great devastating energies flashed and roared around him— lightning come to Earth. The air hissed and stung with their booming passage.

The thought was a shout filling his skull, blazing along his nerves, too mighty a thought for his stunned brain to do more than grope after meaning:

CREATURE FROM OUT OF TIME, LEAVE THIS PLACE AT ONCE OR THE FORCES WE USE WILL DESTROY YOU!

Through and through him that mental vision seared, down to the very molecules of his brain, his life lay open to Them in a white flame of incandescence.

Can you help me? he cried to the gods. *Can you send me back through time?*

MAN, THERE IS NO WAY TO TRAVEL FAR BACKWARD IN TIME, IT IS INHERENTLY IMPOS-SIBLE. YOU MUST GO ON TO THE VERY END OF THE UNIVERSE, AND BEYOND THE END, BE-CAUSE THAT WAY LIES—

He screamed with the pain of unendurably great thoughtand concept filling his human brain.

GO ON, MAN, GO ON! BUT YOU CANNOT SURVIVE IN THAT MACHINE AS IT IS. I WILL CHANGE IT FOR YOU…GO!

The time projector started again by itself. Saunders fell forward into a darkness that roared and flashed.

GRIMLY, desperately, like a man driven by demons, Saunders hurtled into the future.

There could be no gain saying the awful word that had been laid on him. The mere thought of the gods had engraven itself on the very tissue of his brain. Why he should go on to the end of time, he could not imagine, nor did he care. But go on he must!

The machine had been altered. It was airtight now, and experiment showed the window to now be utterly unbreakable. Something had been done to the projector so that it hurled him forward at an incredible rate, millions of years passed while a minute or two ticked away within the droning shell.

But what had the gods been?

He would never know. Beings from beyond the Galaxy, beyond the very universe—the ultimately evolved descendants of man—something at whose nature he could not even guess—there was no way of telling. This much was plain: whether it had become extinct or had changed into something else, the human race was gone. Earth would never feel human tread again.

I wonder what finally became of the Second Empire? I hope it had a long and good life. Or—could that have been its unimaginable end product?

The years reeled past, millions, billions mounting on each other while Earth spun around her star and the Galaxy aged. Saunders fled onward.

He stopped now and then, unable to resist a glimpse of the world and its tremendous history.

A hundred million years in the future, he looked out on great sheets of flying snow. The gods were gone. Had they too died, or abandoned Earth—perhaps for an altogether different plane of existence? He would never know.

There was a being coming through the storm. The wind flung the snow about him in whirling, hissing clouds. Frost was in his gray fur. He moved with a lithe, unhuman grace, carrying a curved staff at whose tip was a blaze like a tiny sun.

Saunders hailed him through the psychophone, letting his

amplified voice shout through the blizzard: "Who are you?
"What are you doing on Earth?"

The being carried a stone ax in one hand and wore a string
of crude beads about his neck. But he stared with bold
yellow eyes at the machine and the psychophone brought his
harsh scream: "You must be from the far past, one of the
earlier cycles."

"They told me to go on, back almost a hundred million
years ago. They told me to go to the end of time!"

The psychophone hooted with metallic laughter. "If *They*
told you so—then go!"

The being walked on into the storm.

Saunders flung himself ahead. There was no place on
Earth for him anymore, he had no choice but to go on.

A billion years in the future there was a city standing on a
plain where grass grew that was blue and glassy and tinkled
with a high crystalline chiming as the wind blew through it.
But the city had never been built by humans, and it warned
him away with a voice he could not disobey.

Then the sea came, and for a long time thereafter he was
trapped within a mountain, he had to drive onward till it had
eroded back to the ground.

The sun grew hotter and whiter as the hydrogen-helium
cycle increased its intensity. Earth spiraled slowly closer to it,
the friction of gas and dust clouds in space taking their
infinitesimal toll of its energy over billions of years.

How many intelligent races had risen on Earth and had
their day, and died, since the age when man first came out of
the jungle? *At least*, he thought tiredly, *we were the first.*

A hundred billion years in the future, the sun had used up
its last reserves of nuclear reactions. Saunders looked out on
a bare mountain scene, grim as the Moon—but the Moon
had long ago fallen back toward its parent world and
exploded into a meteoric rain. Earth faced its primary now;

its day was as long as its year. Saunders saw part of the sun's huge blood-red disc shining wanly.

So goodbye, Sol, he thought. *Goodbye, and thank you for many million years of warmth and light. Sleep well, old friend.*

Some billions of years beyond, there was nothing but the elemental dark. Entropy had reached a maximum, the energy sources were used up, the universe was dead.

The universe was dead!

He screamed with the graveyard terror of it and flung the machine onward. Had it not been for the gods' command, he might have let it hang there, might have opened the door to airlessness and absolute zero to die. But he had to go on. He had reached the end of all things, but he had to go on. *Beyond the end of time—*

Billions upon billions of years fled. Saunders lay in his machine, sunk into an apathetic coma. Once he roused himself to eat, feeling the sardonic humor of the situation—the last living creature, the last free energy in all the cindered cosmos, fixing a sandwich.

Many billions of years in the future, Saunders paused again. He looked out into blackness. But with a sudden shock he discerned a far faint glow, the vaguest imaginable blur of light out in the heavens.

Trembling, he jumped forward another billion years. The light was stronger now, a great sprawling radiance swirling inchoately in the sky.

The universe was reforming.

It made sense, thought Saunders, fighting for self-control. Space had expanded to some kind of limit, now it was collapsing in on itself to start the cycle anew—the cycle that had been repeated none knew how many times in the past. The universe was mortal, but it was a phoenix that would never really die.

But he was disturbingly mortal, and suddenly he was free

of his death wish. At the very least he wanted to see what the next time around looked like. But the universe would, according to the best theories of twentieth-century cosmology, collapse to what was virtually a pointsource, a featureless blaze of pure energy out of which the primal atoms would be reformed. If he wasn't to be devoured in that raging furnace, he'd better leap a long ways ahead. A hell of a long ways!

He grinned with sudden reckless determination and plunged the switch forward.

Worry came back. How did he know that a planet would be formed under him? He might come out in open space, or in the heart of a sun... Well, he'd have to risk that. The gods must have foreseen and allowed for it.

HE CAME out briefly—and flashed back into time-drive. The planet was still molten!

Some geological ages later, he looked out at a spuming gray rain, washing with senseless power from a hidden sky, covering naked rocks with a raging swirl of white water. He didn't go out; the atmosphere would be unbreathable until plants had liberated enough oxygen.

On and on! Sometimes he was under seas, sometimes on land. He saw strange jungles like overgrown ferns and mosses rise and wither in the cold of a glacial age and rise again in altered life-form.

A thought nagged at him, tugging at the back of his mind as he rode onward. It didn't hit him for several million years, then: *The moon! Oh, my God, the moon!*

His hands trembled too violently for him to stop the machine. Finally, with an effort, he controlled himself enough to pull the switch. He skipped on, looking for a night of full moon.

Luna. The same old face—*Luna!*

The shock was too great to register. Numbly, he resumed his journey. And the world began to look familiar, there were low forested hills and a river shining in the distance...

He didn't really believe it till he saw the village. It was the same—Hudson, New York.

He sat for a moment; letting his physicist's brain consider the tremendous fact. In Newtonian terms, it meant that every particle newly formed in the Beginning had exactly the same position and velocity as every corresponding particle formed in the previous cycle. In more acceptable Einsteinian language, the continuum was spherical in all four dimensions. In any case—if you traveled long enough, through space or time, you got back to your starting point.

He could go home!

He ran down the sunlit hill, heedless of his foreign garments, ran till the breath sobbed in raw lungs and his heart seemed about to burst from the ribs. Gasping, he entered the village; went into a bank, and looked at the tear-off calendar and the wall clock.

June 17, 1936, 1:30 P.M. From that, he could figure his time of arrival in 1973 to the minute.

As he walked slowly back to the time machine he noticed a strange, low hum, like an energy source, as though some power source was building up from somewhere inside the machine. With trembling legs he walked inside and did a few tests. Everything seemed to be in order. He paused for a moment then started the machine again. Grayness was outside for the last time.

1973.

Martin Saunders stepped out of the machine. Its moving in space, at Brontothor, had brought it outside MacPherson's house; it lay halfway up the hill at the top of which the rambling old building stood.

The strange low hum he had detected at his previous time

stop was still apparent, only stronger this time. He gazed back at the machine, a curious expression on his face. A moment later there came a flare of soundless energy. Saunders sprang back in alarm and saw the machine dissolve into molten metal—gas—a nothingness that shone briefly and was gone.

The gods must have put some annihilating device into it. Saunders was lucky not to have lost the machine during his previous time stop. The gods didn't want their fantastic devices from the future loose in the twentieth century.

But there was no danger of that, thought Saunders as he walked slowly up the hill through the rain-wet grass. He had seen too much of war and horror ever to give men knowledge they weren't ready for. He and Eve and MacPherson would have to suppress the story of his return around time—for that would offer a means of travel into the past, remove the barrier that would keep man from too much use of the machine for murder and oppression. The Second Empire and the Dreamer's philosophy lay a long time in the future.

He went on. The hill seemed strangely unreal, after all that he had seen from it, the whole enormous tomorrow of the cosmos. He would never quite fit into the little round of days that lay ahead.

Taury—her bright lovely face floated before him, he thought he heard her voice whisper in the cool wet wind that stroked his hair like her strong, gentle hands.

"Goodbye," he whispered into the reaching immensity of time. "Goodbye, my dearest."

He went slowly up the steps and in the front door. There would be Sam to mourn. And then there would be the carefully censored thesis to write, and a life spent in satisfying work with a girl who was sweet and kind and beautiful even if she wasn't Taury. It was enough for a mortal man.

He walked into the living room and smiled at Eve and MacPherson. "Hello," he said. "I guess I must be a little early."

THE END

If you've enjoyed this book, you will not want to miss these terrific titles…

ARMCHAIR SCI-FI & HORROR DOUBLE NOVELS, $12.95 each

D-1 **THE GALAXY RAIDERS** by William P. McGivern
SPACE STATION #1 by Frank Belknap Long

D-2 **THE PROGRAMMED PEOPLE** by Jack Sharkey
SLAVES OF THE CRYSTAL BRAIN by William Carter Sawtelle

D-3 **YOU'RE ALL ALONE** by Fritz Leiber
THE LIQUID MAN by Bernard C. Gilford

D-4 **CITADEL OF THE STAR LORDS** by Edmund Hamilton
VOYAGE TO ETERNITY by Milton Lesser

D-5 **IRON MEN OF VENUS** by Don Wilcox
THE MAN WITH ABSOLUTE MOTION by Noel Loomis

D-6 **WHO SOWS THE WIND…** by Rog Phillips
THE PUZZLE PLANET by Robert A. W. Lowndes

D-7 **PLANET OF DREAD** by Murray Leinster
TWICE UPON A TIME by Charles L. Fontenay

D-8 **THE TERROR OUT OF SPACE** by Dwight V. Swain
QUEST OF THE GOLDEN APE by Ivar Jorgensen and Adam Chase

D-9 **SECRET OF MARRACOTT DEEP** by Henry Slesar
PAWN OF THE BLACK FLEET by Mark Clifton.

D-10 **BEYOND THE RINGS OF SATURN** by Robert Moore Williams
A MAN OBSESSED by Alan E. Nourse

ARMCHAIR SCIENCE FICTION CLASSICS, $12.95 each

C-1 **THE GREEN MAN**
by Harold M. Sherman

C-2 **A TRACE OF MEMORY**
By Keith Laumer

ARMCHAIR MASTERS OF SCI-FI SERIES, $16.95 each

M-1 **MASTERS OF SCIENCE FICTION, Vol. One**
Bryce Walton—"Dark of the Moon" and other tales

M-2 **MASTERS OF SCIENCE FICTION, Vol. Two**
Jerome Bixby: "One Way Street" and other tales

If you've enjoyed this book, you will not want to miss these terrific titles...

ARMCHAIR SCI-FI & HORROR DOUBLE NOVELS, $12.95 each

D-21   **EMPIRE OF EVIL** by Robert Arnette
THE SIGN OF THE TIGER by Alan E. Nourse & J. A. Meyer

D-22   **OPERATION SQUARE PEG** by Frank Belknap Long
ENCHANTRESS OF VENUS by Leigh Brackett

D-23   **THE LIFE WATCH** by Lester del Rey
CREATURES OF THE ABYSS by Murray Leinster

D-24   **LEGION OF LAZARUS** by Edmond Hamilton
STAR HUNTER by Andre Norton

D-25   **EMPIRE OF WOMEN** by John Fletcher
ONE OF OUR CITIES IS MISSING by Irving Cox

D-26   **THE WRONG SIDE OF PARADISE** by Raymond F. Jones
THE INVOLUNTARY IMMORTALS by Rog Phillips

D-27   **EARTH QUARTER** by Damon Knight
ENVOY TO NEW WORLDS by Keith Laumer

D-28   **SLAVES TO THE METAL HORDE** by Milton Lesser
HUNTERS OUT OF TIME by Joseph E. Kelleam

D-29   **RX JUPITER SAVE US** by Ward Moore
BEWARE THE USURPERS by Geoff St. Reynard

D-30   **SECRET OF THE SERPENT** by Don Wilcox
CRUSADE ACROSS THE VOID by Dwight V. Swain

ARMCHAIR SCIENCE FICTION CLASSICS, $12.95 each

C-7   **THE SHAVER MYSTERY, Book One**
by Richard S. Shaver

C-8   **THE SHAVER MYSTERY, Book Two**
by Richard S. Shaver

C-9   **MURDER IN SPACE** by David V. Reed
by David V. Reed

ARMCHAIR MASTERS OF SCIENCE FICTION SERIES, $16.95 each

M-3   **MASTERS OF SCIENCE FICTION, Vol. Three**
Robert Sheckley, "The Perfect Woman" and other tales

M-4   **MASTERS OF SCIENCE FICTION, Vol. Four**
Mack Reynolds, "Stowaway" and other tales

Made in United States
North Haven, CT
22 July 2022

21684744R00131